MARY J. L.

P9-EDE-462

## MISTRESS OF MELLYN

Martha Leigh knew that becoming a governess was
the only course that a respectable Victorian girl could
take when she was alone in the world. A high-
spirited, attractive girl, she hated the idea. When
she first saw the cold, brooding house on the
Cornish cliffs and met her arrogant employer, Con
TreMellyn, and his resentful daughter, she realised
why three governesses before her had left. The
neighbours and servants were full of hints and half
confidences, and the house seemed to hold dark
secrets. It was only her growing love for the child
and an unwilling attraction to the father that made
her stay on and try to solve the mysteries which
shrouded their lives. She couldn't know that she
was putting her life in danger . . .

*Available in Fontana*
*by the same author*

BRIDE OF PENDORRIC
KIRKLAND REVELS
THE LEGEND OF THE SEVENTH VIRGIN
MENFREYA
KING OF THE CASTLE

VICTORIA HOLT

# *Mistress of Mellyn*

*Collins*
FONTANA BOOKS

*First published in Great Britain 1961*
*First issued in Fontana Books 1963*
*Twenty-first Impression June 1974*

"There are two courses open to a gentlewoman when she finds herself in penurious circumstances," my Aunt Adelaide had said. "One is to marry, and the other to find a post in keeping with her gentility."

As the train carried me through wooded hills and past green meadows, I was taking this second course; partly, I suppose, because I had never had an opportunity of trying the former.

I pictured myself as I must appear to my fellow travellers if they bothered to glance my way, which was not very likely: A young woman of medium height, already past her first youth, being twenty-four years old, in a brown merino dress with cream lace collar and little tufts of lace at the cuffs. (Cream being so much more serviceable than white, as Aunt Adelaide told me.) My black cape was unbuttoned at the throat because it was hot in the carriage, and my brown velvet bonnet, tied with brown velvet ribbons under my chin, was of the sort which was so becoming to feminine people like my sister Phillida but, I always felt, sat a little incongruously on heads like mine. My hair was thick with a coppery tinge, parted in the centre, brought down at the sides of my too-long face, and made into a cumbersome knot to project behind the bonnet. My eyes were large, in some lights the colour of amber, and were my best feature; but they were too bold—so said Aunt Adelaide; which meant that they had learned none of the feminine graces which were so becoming to a woman. My nose was too short, my mouth too wide. In fact, I thought, nothing seemed to fit; and I must resign myself to journeys such as this when I travel to and from the various posts which I shall occupy for the rest of my life, since it is necessary for me to earn a living, and I shall never achieve the first of those alternatives: a husband.

We had passed through the green meadows of Somerset and were now deep in the moorland and wooded hills of Devon. I had been told to take good note of that masterpiece of bridge-

building, Mr. Brunel's bridge, which spanned the Tamar at
Saltash and, after crossing which, I should have left England
behind me and have passed into the Duchy of Cornwall.

I was becoming rather ridiculously excited about crossing the
bridge. I was not a fanciful woman at this time—perhaps I
changed later, but then a stay in a house like Mount Mellyn
was enough to make the most practical of people fanciful—so
I could not understand why I should feel this extraordinary
excitement.

It was absurd, I told myself. Mount Mellyn may be a
magnificent mansion; Connan TreMellyn may be as romantic
as his name sounds; but that will be no concern of yours. You
will be confined to below stairs, or perhaps to the attics above
stairs, concerned only with the care of little Alvean.

What strange names these people had! I thought, staring out
of the window. There was sun on the moorland but the grey
tors in the distance looked oddly menacing. They were like
petrified people.

This family to which I was going was Cornish, and the
Cornish had a language of their own. Perhaps my own name,
Martha Leigh, would sound odd to them. Martha! It always
gave me a shock when I heard it. Aunt Adelaide always used
it, but at home when my father had been alive he and Phillida
never thought of calling me Martha. I was always Marty. I
could not help feeling that Marty was a more lovable person
than Martha could ever be, and I was sad and a little frightened
because I felt that the River Tamar would cut me off completely
from Marty for a long time. In my new post I should be Miss
Leigh, I supposed; perhaps Miss, or more undignified still—
Leigh.

One of Aunt Adelaide's numerous friends had heard of
" Connan TreMellyn's predicament." He needed the right
person to help him out of his difficulties. She must be patient
enough to care for his daughter, sufficiently educated to teach
her, and genteel enough for the child not to suffer through the
proximity of someone who was not quite of her own class.
Obviously what Connan TreMellyn needed was an impover-
ished gentlewoman. Aunt Adelaide decided that I fitted the
bill.

When our father, who had been vicar of a country parsonage, had died, Aunt Adelaide had swooped on us and taken us to London. There should be a season, she told us, for twenty-year-old Martha and eighteen-year-old Phillida. Phillida had married at the end of that season; but after four years of living with Aunt Adelaide, I had not. So there came a day when she pointed out the two courses to me.

I glanced out of the window. We were drawing into Plymouth. My fellow passengers had alighted and I sat back in my seat watching the activities on the platform.

As the guard was blowing his whistle and we were about to move on, the door of the carriage opened and a man came in. He looked at me with an apologetic smile as though he were hinting that he hoped I did not mind sharing the compartment with him, but I averted my eyes.

When we had left Plymouth and were approaching the bridge, he said : " You like our bridge, eh?"

I turned and looked at him.

I saw a man, a little under thirty, well dressed, but in the manner of the country gentleman. His tail coat was dark blue, his trousers grey; and his hat was what in London we called a " pot hat " because of its resemblance to that vessel. This hat he laid on the seat beside him. I thought him somewhat dissipated, with brown eyes that twinkled ironically as though he were fully aware of the warnings I must have received about the inadvisability of entering into conversation with strange men.

I answered : " Yes, indeed. I think it is a very fine piece of workmanship."

He smiled. We had crossed the bridge and entered Cornwall.

His brown eyes surveyed me and I was immediately conscious of my somewhat drab appearance. I thought : He is only interested in me because there is no one else to claim his attention. I remembered then that Phillida had once said that I put people off by presuming, when they showed interest, that I believed it was because no one else was available. " See

yourself as a makeshift," was Phillida's maxim, " and you'll
be one."

" Travelling far?" he asked.

" I believe I have now only a short distance to go. I leave
the train at Liskeard."

" Ah, Liskeard." He stretched his legs and turned his gaze
from me to the tips of his boots. " You have come from
London?" he went on.

" Yes," I answered.

" You'll miss the gaiety of the big city."

" I once lived in the country so I know what to expect."

" Are you staying in Liskeard?"

I was not sure that I liked this catechism, but I remembered
Phillida again : " You're far too gruff, Marty, with the
opposite sex. You scare them off."

I decided I could at least be civil, so I answered : " No, not
in Liskeard. I'm going to a little village on the coast called
Mellyn."

" I see." He was silent for a few moments and once more
turned his attention to the tips of his boots.

His next words startled me. " I suppose a sensible young
lady like you would not believe in second sight . . . and that
sort of thing?"

" Why . . ." I stammered. " What an extraordinary
question !"

" May I look at your palm?"

I hesitated and regarded him suspiciously. Could I offer my
hand to a stranger in this way? Aunt Adelaide would suspect
that some nefarious advances were about to be made. I thought
in this case she might be right. After all I was a woman, and
the only available one.

He smiled. " I assure you that my only desire is to look into
the future."

" But I don't believe in such things."

" Let me look anyway." He leaned forward and with a
swift movement secured my hand.

He held it lightly, scarcely touching it, contemplating it with
his head on one side.

" I see," he said, " that you have come to a turning point in your life . . . You are moving into a strange new world which is entirely different from anything you have known before. You will have to exercise caution . . . the utmost caution."

I smiled cynically. "You see me taking a journey. What would you say if I told you I was visiting relatives and could not possibly be moving into your strange new world?"

"I should say you were not a very truthful young lady." His smile was puckish. I could not help feeling a little liking for him. I thought he was a somewhat irresponsible person, but he was very lighthearted and, being in his company, to some extent made me share that lightheartedness. "No," he went on, "you are travelling to a new life, a new post. There's no mistake about that. Before, you lived a secluded life in the country, then you went to the town."

"I believe I implied that."

"You did not need to imply it. But it is not the past which concerns us on occasions like this, is it? It is the future."

"Well, what of the future?"

"You are going to a strange house, a house full of shadows. You will have to walk warily in that house, Miss er——"

He waited, but I did not supply what he was asking for, and he went on: "You have to earn your living. I see a child there and a man. . . . Perhaps it is the child's father. They are wrapped in shadows. There is someone else there . . . but perhaps she is already dead."

It was the deep sepulchral note in his voice rather than the words he said which momentarily unnerved me.

I snatched my hand away. "What nonsense!" I said.

He ignored me and half closed his eyes. Then he went on: "You will need to watch little Alice, and your duties will extend beyond the care of her. You must most certainly beware of Alice."

I felt a faint tingling which began at the base of my spine and seemed to creep up to my neck. This, I supposed, was what is known as making one's flesh creep.

Little Alice! But her name was not Alice. It was Alvean. It had unnerved me for the moment because it had sounded similar.

Then I felt irritated and a little angry. Did I look the

part then? Was it possible that I already carried the mark of the penurious gentlewoman forced to take the only course open to her? A governess!

Was he laughing at me? He lay back against the upholstery of the carriage, his eyes still closed. I looked out of the window as though he and his ridiculous fortune-telling were of not the slightest interest to me.

He opened his eyes then and took out his watch. He studied it gravely, for all the world as though this extraordinary conversation had not taken place between us.

"In four minutes' time," he said briskly, "we shall pull into Liskeard. Allow me to assist you with your bags."

He took them down from the rack. "Miss Martha Leigh," was clearly written on the labels, "Mount Mellyn, Mellyn, Cornwall."

He did not appear to glance at these labels and I felt that he had lost interest in me.

When we came into the station, he alighted and set my bags on the platform. Then he took off the hat which he had set upon his head when he picked up the bags, and with a deep bow he left me.

While I was murmuring my thanks I saw an elderly man coming towards me, calling: "Miss Leigh! Miss Leigh! Be you Miss Leigh then?" And for the moment I forgot about my travelling companion.

I was facing a merry little man with a brown, wrinkled skin and eyes of reddish brown; he wore a corduroy jacket and a sugar-loaf hat which he had pushed to the back of his head and seemed to have forgotten. Ginger hair sprouted from under this, and his brows and moustaches were of the same gingery colour.

"Well, Miss," he said, "so I picked you out then. Be these your bags? Give them to me. You and me and old Cherry Pie 'ull soon be home."

He took my bags and I walked behind him, but he soon fell into step beside me.

"Is the house far from here?" I asked.

" Old Cherry Pie'll carry us there all in good time," he answered, as he loaded my bags into the trap and I climbed in beside him.

He seemed to be a garrulous man and I could not resist the temptation of trying to discover, before I arrived, something about the people among whom I was going to live.

I said : " This house, Mount Mellyn, sounds as though it's on a hill."

" Well, 'tis built on a cliff top, facing the sea, and the gardens run down to the sea. Mount Mellyn and Mount Widden are like twins. Two houses, standing defiant like, daring the sea to come and take 'em. But they'm built on firm rock."

" So there are two houses," I said. " We have near neighbours."

" In a manner of speaking. Nansellocks, they who are at Mount Widden, have been there these last two hundred years. They be separated from us by more than a mile, and there's Mellyn Cove in between. The families have always been good neighbours until——"

He stopped and I prompted : " Until——?"

" You'll hear fast enough," he answered.

I thought it was beneath my dignity to probe into such matters so I changed the subject. " Do you keep many servants?" I asked.

" There be me and Mrs. Tapperty and my girls, Daisy and Kitty. We live in the rooms over the stables. In the house there's Mrs. Polgrey and Tom Polgrey and young Gilly. Not that you'd call her a servant. But they have her there and she passes for such."

" Gilly!" I said. " That's an unusual name."

" Gillyflower. Reckon Jennifer Polgrey was a bit daft to give her a name like that. No wonder the child's what she is."

" Jennifer? Is that Mrs. Polgrey?"

" Nay! Jennifer was Mrs. Polgrey's girl. Great dark eyes and the littlest waist you ever saw. Kept herself to herself until one day she goes lying in the hay—or maybe the gillyflowers— with someone. Then, before we know where we are, little

Gilly's arrived; as for Jennifer—her just walked into the sea one morning. We reckoned there wasn't much doubt who Gilly's father was."

I said nothing and, disappointed by my lack of interest, he went on : " She wasn't the first. We knowed her wouldn't be the last. Geoffry Nansellock left a trail of bastards wherever he went." He laughed and looked sideways at me. " No need for you to look so prim, Miss. He can't hurt you. Ghosts can't hurt a young lady, and that's all Master Geoffry Nansellock is now . . . nothing more than a ghost."

" So he's dead too. He didn't . . . walk into the sea after Jennifer?"

That made Tapperty chuckle. " Not him. He was killed in a train accident. You must have heard of that accident. It was just as the train was running out of Plymouth. It ran off the lines and over a bank. The slaughter was terrible. Mr. Geoff, he were on that train, and up to no good on it either. But that was the end of him."

" Well, I shall not meet him, but I shall meet Gillyflower, I suppose. And is that all the servants?"

" There are odd boys and girls—some for the gardens, some for the stables, some in the house. But it ain't what it was. Things have changed since the mistress died."

" Mr. TreMellyn is a very sad man, I suppose."

Tapperty lifted his shoulders.

" How long is it since she died?" I asked.

" It would be little more than a year, I reckon."

" And he has only just decided that he needs a governess for little Miss Alvean?"

" There have been three governesses so far. You be the fourth. They don't stay, none of them. Miss Bray and Miss Garrett, they said the place was too quiet for them. There was Miss Jansen—a real pretty creature. But she was sent away. She took what didn't belong to her. 'Twas a pity. We all liked her. She seemed to look on it as a privilege to live in Mount Mellyn. Old houses were her hobby, she used to tell us. Well, it seemed she had other hobbies besides, so out she went."

I turned my attention to the countryside. It was late August and, as we passed through lanes with banks on either side, I caught occasional glimpses of fields of corn among which poppies and pimpernels grew; now and then we passed a cottage of grey Cornish stone which looked grim, I thought, and lonely.

I had my first glimpse of the sea through a fold in the hills, and I felt my spirits lifted. It seemed that the nature of the landscape changed. Flowers seemed to grow more plentifully on the banks; I could smell the scent of pine trees; and fuchsias grew by the roadside, their blossoms bigger than any we had ever been able to cultivate in our vicarage garden.

We turned off the road from a steep hill and went down and down nearer the sea. I saw that we were on a cliff road. Before us stretched a scene of breath-taking beauty. The cliff rose steep and straight from the sea on that indented coast; grasses and flowers grew there, and I saw sea pinks and red and white valerian mingling with the heather—rich, deep, purple heather.

At length we came to the house. It was like a castle, I thought, standing there on the cliff plateau—built of granite like many houses I had seen in these parts, but grand and noble—a house which had stood for several hundred years, and would stand for several hundred more.

" All this land belongs to the Master," said Tapperty with pride. " And if you look across the cove, you'll see Mount Widden."

I did look and saw the house. Like Mount Mellyn it was built of grey stone. It was smaller in every way and of a later period. I did not give it much attention because now we were approaching Mount Mellyn, and that was obviously the house which was more interesting to me.

We had climbed to the plateau and a pair of intricately wrought-iron gates confronted us.

" Open up there!" shouted Tapperty.

There was a small lodge beside the gates and at the door sat a woman knitting.

"Now, Gilly girl," she said, "you go and open the gates and save me poor legs."

Then I saw the child who had been sitting at the old woman's feet. She rose obediently and came to the gate. She was an extraordinary looking girl with long straight hair almost white in colour and wide blue eyes.

"Thanks, Gilly girl," said Tapperty as Cherry Pie went happily through the gates. "This be Miss, who's come to live here and take care of Miss Alvean."

I looked into a pair of blank blue eyes which stared at me with an expression impossible to fathom. The old woman came up to the gate and Tapperty said : "This be Mrs. Soady."

"Good day to you," said Mrs. Soady. "I hope you'll be happy here along of us."

"Thank you," I answered, forcing my gaze away from the child to the woman. "I hope so."

"Well, I do hope so," added Mrs. Soady. Then she shook her head as though she feared her hopes were somewhat futile.

I turned to look at the child but she had disappeared. I wondered where she had gone, and the only place I could imagine was behind the bushes of hydrangeas which were bigger than any hydrangeas I had ever seen, and of deep blue, almost the colour of the sea on this day.

"The child didn't speak," I observed as we went on up the drive.

"No. Her don't talk much. Sing, her do. Wander about on her own. But talk . . . not much."

The drive was about half a mile in length and on either side of it the hydrangeas bloomed. Fuchsias mingled with them, and I caught glimpses of the sea between the pine trees. Then I saw the house. Before it was a wide lawn and on this two peacocks strutted before a peahen, their almost incredibly lovely tails fanned out behind them. Another sat perched on a stone wall; and there were two palm trees, tall and straight, one on either side of the porch.

The house was larger than I had thought when I had seen it from the cliff path. It was of three stories, but long and built in an L shape. The sun caught the glass of the mullioned windows and I immediately had the impression that I was being watched.

Tapperty took the gravel approach to the front porch and, when we reached it, the door opened and I saw a woman standing there. She wore a white cap on her grey hair; she was tall, with a hooked nose and, as she had an obviously dominating manner, I did not need to be told that she was Mrs. Polgrey.

" I trust you've had a good journey, Miss Leigh," she said.

" Very good, thank you," I told her.

" And worn out and needing a rest, I'll be bound. Come along in. You shall have a nice cup of tea in my room. Leave your bags. I'll have them taken up."

I felt relieved. This woman dispelled the eerie feeling which had begun, I realised, since my encounter with the man in the train. Joe Tapperty had done little to disperse it, with his tales of death and suicide. But Mrs. Polgrey was a woman who would stand no nonsense, I was sure of that. She seemed to emit common sense, and perhaps because I was fatigued by the long journey I was pleased about this.

I thanked her and said I would greatly enjoy the tea, and she led the way into the house.

We were in an enormous hall which in the past must have been used as a banqueting room. The floor was of flagged stone, and the timbered roof was so lofty that I felt it must extend to the top of the house. The beams were beautifully carved and the effect decorative. At one end of the hall was a dais and at the back of this a great open fireplace. On the dais stood a refectory table on which were vessels and plates of pewter.

" It's magnificent," I said involuntarily; and Mrs. Polgrey was pleased.

" I superintend all the polishing of the furniture myself," she told me. " You have to watch girls nowadays. Those Tapperty wenches are a pair of flibbertigibbets, I can tell 'ee. You'd need eyes that could see from here to Land's End to see all they'm up to. Beeswax and turpentine, that's the mixture, and nothing like it. All made by myself."

" It certainly does you credit," I complimented her.

I followed her to the end of the hall where there was a door. She opened this and a short flight of some half a dozen steps confronted us. To the left was a door which she indicated and after a moment's hesitation, opened.

" The chapel," she said, and I caught a glimpse of blue slate flagstones, an altar and a few pews. There was a smell of dampness about the place.

She shut the door quickly.

"We don't use it nowadays," she said. "We go to the Mellyn church. It's down in the village, the other side of the cove . . . just beyond Mount Widden."

We went up the stairs and into a room which I saw was a dining room. It was vast and the walls were hung with tapestry. The table was highly polished and there were several cabinets in the room within which I saw beautiful glass and china. The floor was covered with blue carpet and through the enormous windows I saw a walled courtyard.

"This is not *your* part of the house," Mrs. Polgrey told me, "but I thought I would take you round the front of the house to my room. It's as well you know the lay of the land, as they say."

I thanked her, understanding that this was a tactful way of telling me that as a governess I would not be expected to mingle with the family.

We passed through the dining room to yet another flight of stairs and mounting these we came to what seemed like a more intimate sitting room. The walls were covered with exquisite tapestry and the chair backs and seats were beautifully wrought in the same manner. I could see that the furniture was mostly antique and that it all gleamed with beeswax and turpentine and Mrs. Polgrey's loving care.

"This is the punch room," she said. "It has always been called so because it is here that the family retires to take punch. We follow the old custom still in this house."

At the end of this room was another flight of stairs; there was no door leading to them, merely a heavy brocade curtain which Mrs. Polgrey drew aside, and when we had mounted these stairs we were in a gallery, the walls of which were lined with portraits. I gave each of them a quick glance, wondering if Connan TreMellyn were among them; but I could see no one depicted in modern dress, so I presumed his portrait had not yet taken its place among those of his ancestors.

There were several doors leading from the gallery, but we went quickly along it, to one of those at the far end. As we passed through it I saw that we were in a different wing of the house, the servants' quarters I imagined, because the spaciousness was missing.

"This," said Mrs. Polgrey, "will be *your* part of the house. You will find a staircase at the end of this corridor which leads to the nurseries. Your room is up there. But first come to my sitting room and we'll have that tea. I told Daisy to see to it as soon as I heard Joe Tapperty was here. So there shouldn't be long to wait."

"I fear it will take some time to learn my way about the house," I said.

"You'll know it in next to no time. But when you go out you won't go the way I brought you up. You'll use one of the other doors; when you've unpacked and rested awhile, I'll show you."

"You're very kind."

"Well, I do want to make you happy here with us. Miss Alvean needs discipline, I always say. And what can I do about giving in to her, with all I have to do! A nice mess this place would be in if I let Miss Alvean take up *my* time. No, what she wants is a sensible governess, and 'twould seem they'm not all that easy to come by. Why, Miss, if you show us that you can look after the child, you'll be more than welcome here."

"I gather I have had several predecessors." She looked a trifle blank and I went on quickly. "There have been other governesses."

"Oh yes. Not much good, any of them. Miss Jansen was the best, but it seemed she had habits. You could have knocked me down with a feather. She quite took *me* in!" Mrs. Polgrey looked as though she thought that anyone who could do that must be smart. "Well, I suppose appearances are deceptive, as they say. Miss Celestine was real upset when it came out."

"Miss Celestine?"

"The young lady at Widden. Miss Celestine Nansellock. She's often here. A quiet young lady and she loves the place. If I as much as move a piece of furniture she knows it. That's why she and Miss Jansen seemed to get on. Both interested in old houses, you see. It was such a pity and such a shock.

You'll meet her sometime. As I say, scarcely a day passes when she's not here. There's some of us that think. . . . Oh, my dear life! 'twould seem as though I'm letting my tongue run away with me, and you longing for that cup of tea."

She threw open the door of the room and it was like stepping into another world. Gone was the atmosphere of brooding antiquity. This was a room which could not have fitted into any other time than the present, and I realised that it confirmed my impression of Mrs. Polgrey. There were antimacassars on the chair; there was a " what-not " in the corner of the room filled with china ornaments including a glass slipper, a gold pig and a cup with " A present from Weston " inscribed on it. It seemed almost impossible to move in a room so crammed with furniture. Even on the mantel-piece Dresden shepherdesses seemed to jostle with marble angels for a place. There was an ormolu clock which ticked sedately; there were chairs and little tables everywhere, it seemed. It showed Mrs. Polgrey to me as a woman of strong conventions, a woman who would have a great respect for the right thing—which would, of course, be the thing she believed in.

Still, I felt something comfortingly normal about this room as I did about the woman.

She looked at the main table and tutted in exasperation; then she went to the bell rope and pulled it. It was only a few minutes later when a black-haired girl with saucy eyes appeared carrying a tray on which was a silver teapot, a spirit lamp, cups and saucers, milk and sugar.

" And about time too," said Mrs. Polgrey. " Put it here, Daisy."

Daisy gave me a look which almost amounted to a wink. I did not wish to offend Mrs. Polgrey so I pretended not to notice.

Then Mrs. Polgrey said : " This is Daisy, Miss. You can tell her if you find anything is not to your liking."

" Thank you Mrs. Polgrey, and thank you, Daisy."

They both looked somewhat startled and Daisy dropped a little curtsy, of which she seemed half ashamed, and went out.

" Nowadays . . ." murmured Mrs. Polgrey, and lighted the spirit lamp.

I watched her unlock the cabinet and take out the tea canister which she set on the tray.

"Dinner," she went on, "is served at eight. Yours will be brought to your room. But I thought you would be needing a little reviver. So when you've had this and seen your room, I'll introduce you to Miss Alvean."

"What would she be doing at this time of day?"

Mrs. Polgrey frowned. "She'll be off somewhere by herself. She goes off by herself. Master don't like it. That's why 'e be anxious for her to have a governess, you see."

I began to see. I was sure now that Alvean was going to be a difficult child.

Mrs. Polgrey measured the tea into the pot as though it were gold dust, and poured the hot water on it.

"So much depends on whether she takes a fancy to you or not," went on Mrs. Polgrey. "She's unaccountable. There's some she'll take to and some she won't. Her was very fond of Miss Jansen." Mrs. Polgrey shook her head sadly. "A pity she had habits."

She stirred the tea in the pot, put on the tea cosy and asked me : "Cream? Sugar?"

"Yes, please," I said.

"I always do say," she remarked, as though she thought I needed some consolation, "there ain't nothing like a good cup of tea."

We ate tea biscuits with the tea, and these Mrs. Polgrey took from a tin which she kept in her cabinet. I gathered, as we sat together, that Connan TreMellyn, the Master, was away.

"He has an estate farther west," Mrs. Polgrey told me. "Penzance way." Her dialect was more noticeable when she was relaxed as she was now. "He do go to it now and then to see to it like. Left him by his wife, it were. Now *she* was one of the Pendletons. They'm from Penzance way."

"When does he return?" I asked.

She looked faintly shocked, and I knew that I had offended because she said in a somewhat haughty way : "He will come back in his own time."

I saw that if I was going to keep in her good books, I must

be strictly conventional; and presumably it was not good form for a governess to ask questions about the master of the house. It was all very well for Mrs. Polgrey to speak of him; she was a privileged person. I could see that I must hastily adjust myself to my own position.

Very soon after that she took me up to my room. It was large with big windows equipped with window seats from which there was a good view of the front lawn, the palm trees and the approach. My bed was a four-poster and seemed in keeping with the rest of the furniture; and although it was a big bed it looked dwarfed in a room of this size. There were rugs on the floor, the boards of which were so highly polished that the rugs looked somewhat dangerous. I could see that I might have little cause to bless Mrs. Polgrey's love of polishing everything within sight. There was a tallboy and a chest of drawers; and I noticed that there was a door in addition to the one by which I had entered.

Mrs. Polgrey followed my gaze. "The schoolroom," she said. "And beyond that is Miss Alvean's room."

"I see. So the schoolroom separates us."

Mrs. Polgrey nodded.

Looking round the room I saw that there was a screen in one corner and as I approached this I noticed that it shielded a hip bath.

"If you want hot water at any time," she said, "ring the bell and Daisy or Kitty will bring it to you."

"Thank you." I looked at the open fireplace and pictured a roaring fire there on winter days. "I can see I'm going to be very comfortable here."

"It's a pleasant room. You'll be the first governess to have it. The other governesses used to sleep in a room on the other side of Miss Alvean's room. It was Miss Celestine who thought this would be better. It's a more pleasant room, I must say."

"Then I owe thanks to Miss Celestine."

"A very pleasant lady. She thinks the world of Miss Alvean." Mrs. Polgrey shook her head significantly and I wondered whether she was thinking that it was only a year since the master's wife had died, and that perhaps one day he would marry again. Who more suitable to be his wife than his neighbour who was so fond of Miss Alvean? Perhaps they were only waiting for a reasonable lapse of time.

" Would you like to wash your hands and unpack? Dinner will be in two hours' time. But perhaps first you would like to take a look at the schoolroom."

" Thank you, Mrs. Polgrey," I said, " but I think I'll wash and unpack first."

" Very well. And perhaps you'd like a little rest. Travelling is so fatiguing, I do know. I'll send Daisy up with hot water. Meals could be taken in the schoolroom. Perhaps you'd prefer that?"

" With Miss Alvean?"

" She takes her meals nowadays with her father, except her milk and biscuits last thing. All the children have taken meals with the family from the time they were eight years old. Miss Alvean's birthday was in May."

" There are other children?"

" Oh, my dear life, no! I was talking of the children of the past. It's one of the family rules, you see."

" I see."

" Well, I'll be leaving you. If you cared for a stroll in the grounds before dinner, you could take it. Ring for Daisy or Kitty and whoever is free will show you the stairs you will use in future. It will take you down to the kitchen garden, but you can easily get from there to wherever you want to go. Don't 'ee forget though—dinner at eight."

" In the schoolroom."

" Or in your own room if you prefer it."

" But," I added, " in the governess's quarters."

She did not know what to make of this remark, and when Mrs. Polgrey did not understand, she ignored. In a few minutes I was alone.

As soon as she had gone the strangeness of the house seemed to envelop me. I was aware of silence—the eerie silence of an ancient house.

I went to the window and looked out. It seemed a long time ago that I had driven up to the house with Tapperty. I heard the august notes of a bird which might have been a linnet.

I looked at the watch pinned to my blouse and saw that it was just past six o'clock. Two hours to dinner. I wondered whether to ring for Daisy or Kitty and ask for hot water; but I found my eyes turning to the other door in my room, the one which led to the schoolroom.

The schoolroom was, after all, my domain, and I had a right to inspect it, so I opened the door. The room was larger than my bedroom but it had the same type of windows and they were all fitted with window seats on which were red plush fitted cushions. There was a table in the centre of the room. I went over to it and saw that there were scratches on it and splashes of ink, so I guessed that this was the table where generations of TreMellyns had learned their lessons. I tried to imagine Connan TreMellyn as a little boy, sitting at this table. I imagined him a studious boy, quite different from his erring daughter, the difficult child who was going to be my problem.

A few books lay on the table. I examined them. They were children's readers, containing the sort of stories and articles which looked as if they were of an uplifting nature. There was an exercise book on which was scrawled " Alvean TreMellyn. Arithemetic." I opened it and saw several sums, to most of which had been given the wrong answers. Idly turning the pages I came to a sketch of a girl, and immediately I recognised Gilly, the child whom I had seen at the lodge gates.

" Not bad," I muttered. " So our Alvean is an artist. That's something."

I closed the book. I had the strange feeling, which I had had as soon as I entered the house, that I was being watched.

" Alvean! " I called on impulse. " Are you there, Alvean? Alvean, where are you hiding?"

There was no answer and I flushed with embarrassment, feeling rather absurd in the silence.

Abruptly I turned and went back to my room. I rang the bell and when Daisy appeared I asked her for hot water.

By the time I had unpacked my bags and hung up my things it was nearly eight o'clock, and precisely as the stable clock was striking eight Kitty appeared with my tray. On it was a leg of roast chicken with vegetables and, under a pewter cover, an egg custard.

Daisy said: " Are you having it in here, Miss, or in the schoolroom?"

I decided against sitting in that room where I felt I was overlooked.

" Here, please, Daisy," I answered. Then, because Daisy looked the sort of person who wanted to talk, I added: " Where is Miss Alvean? It seems strange that I have not seen her yet."

" She's a bad 'un," cried Daisy. " Do 'ee know what would have happened to Kit and me if we'd got up to such tricks? A good tanning—that's what we'd have had—and in a place where 'tweren't comfortable to sit down on after. Her heard new Miss was coming, and so off her goes. Master be away and we don't know where her be until the house boy comes over from Mount Widden to tell we that she be over there—calling on Miss Celestine and Master Peter, if you do please."

" I see. A sort of protest at having a new governess."

Daisy came near and nudged me. " Miss Celestine do spoil the child. Dotes on her so's you'd think she was her own daughter. Listen! That do sound like the carriage." Daisy was at the window beckoning me. I felt I ought not to stand at the window with a servant spying on what was happening below, but the temptation to do so was too strong for me.

So I stood beside Daisy and saw them getting out of the carriage . . . a young woman, whom I judged to be of my own age or perhaps a year or so older, and a child. I scarcely looked at the woman; my attention was all on the child. This was Alvean on whom my success depended, so naturally enough in those first seconds I had eyes for no one but her.

From what I could see she looked ordinary enough. She was somewhat tall for her eight years; her light brown hair had been plaited, and I presumed it was very long, for it was wound round her head; this gave her an appearance of maturity and I imagined her to be terrifyingly precocious. She was wearing a dress of brown gingham with white stockings and black shoes with ankle straps. She looked like a miniature woman and, for some vague reason, my spirits fell.

Oddly enough she seemed to be conscious that she was being watched, and glanced upwards. Involuntarily I stepped back, but I was sure she had seen the movement. I felt at a disadvantage before we had met.

"Up to tricks," murmured Daisy at my side.

"Perhaps," I said as I walked into the centre of the room, "she is a little alarmed at the prospect of having a new governess."

Daisy let out a burst of explosive laughter. "What, her! Sorry, Miss, but that do make me laugh, that do."

I went to the table and, sitting down, began to eat my dinner. Daisy was about to go when there was a knock on the door and Kitty entered.

She grimaced at her sister and grinned rather familiarly at me. "Oh, Miss," she said, "Mrs. Polgrey says that when you'm finished will you go down to the punch room. Miss Nansellock be there and her would like to see you. Miss Alvean have come home. They'd like 'ee to come down as soon as you can. 'Tis time Miss Alvean were in her own room."

"I will come when I have finished my dinner," I said.

"Then would you pull the bell when you'm ready, Miss, and me or Daisy'll show you the way."

"Thank you." I sat down and, in a leisurely fashion, finished my meal.

I rose and went to the mirror which stood on my dressing table. I saw that I was unusually flushed and that this suited me; it made my eyes look decidedly the colour of amber. It was fifteen minutes since Daisy and Kitty had left me and I imagined that Mrs. Polgrey, Alvean and Miss Nansellock would be impatiently awaiting my coming. But I had no intention of becoming the poor little drudge that so many governesses were. If Alvean was what I believed her to be, she needed to be shown, right at the start, that I was in charge and must be treated with respect.

I rang the bell and Daisy appeared.

"They'm waiting for you in the punch room," she said. "It's well past Miss Alvean's supper time."

"Then it is a pity that she did not return before," I replied serenely.

When Daisy giggled, her plump breasts, which seemed to

be bursting out of her cotton bodice, shook. Daisy enjoyed laughing, I could see. I judged her to be as lighthearted as her sister.

She led the way to the punch room through which I had passed with Mrs. Polgrey on my way to my own quarters. She drew aside the curtains and with a dramatic gesture cried: " Here be Miss!"

Mrs. Polgrey was seated in one of the tapestry-backed chairs, and Celestine Nansellock was in another. Alvean was standing, her hands clasped behind her back. She looked, I thought, dangerously demure.

" Ah," said Mrs. Polgrey, rising, " here is Miss Leigh. Miss Nansellock have been waiting to see you." There was a faint reproach in her voice. I knew what it meant. I, a mere governess, had kept a *lady* waiting while I finished my dinner.

" How do you do?" I asked.

They looked surprised. I suppose I should have curtsied or made some gesture to show that I was conscious of my menial position. I was aware of the blue eyes of the child fixed upon me; indeed I was aware of little but Alvean in those first few seconds. Her eyes were startlingly blue. I thought, she will be a beauty when she grows up. And I wondered whether she was like her father or mother.

Celestine Nansellock was standing by Alvean, and she laid a hand on her shoulder.

" Miss Alvean came over to see us," she said. " We're great friends. I'm Miss Nansellock of Mount Widden. You may have seen the house."

" I did so on my journey from the station."

" I trust you will not be cross with Alvean."

I answered, looking straight into those defiant blue eyes: " I could hardly scold for what happened before my arrival, could I?"

" She looks on me . . . on us . . . as part of her own family," went on Celestine Nansellock. " We've always lived so close to each other."

" I am sure it is a great comfort to her," I replied; and for the first time I gave my attention solely to Celestine Nansellock. She was taller than I, but by no standards a beauty. Her hair was of a nondescript brown and her eyes were hazel. There was little colour in her face and an air of intense quietness about her. I decided she had little personality, but perhaps she was overshadowed by the defiance of Alvean and the conventional dignity of Mrs. Polgrey.

" I do hope," she said, " that if you need my advice about anything, Miss Leigh, you won't hesitate to call on me. You see, I am quite a near neighbour, and I think I am looked on here as one of the family."

" You are very kind."

Her mild eyes looked into mine. " We want you to be happy here, Miss Leigh. We all want that."

" Thank you. I suppose," I went on, " the first thing to do is to get Alvean to bed. It must be past her bedtime."

Celestine smiled. " You are right. Indeed it is. She usually has her milk and biscuits in the schoolroom at half past seven. It is now well past eight. But to-night I will look after her. I suggest that you return to your room, Miss Leigh. You must be weary after your journey."

Before I could speak Alvean cried out : " No, Celestine. I want *her* to. She's my governess. She should, shouldn't she?"

A hurt look immediately appeared in Celestine's face, and Alvean could not repress the triumph in hers. I felt I understood. The child wanted to feel her own power; she wanted to prevent Celestine from superintending her retirement simply because Celestine wished so much to do it.

" Oh, very well," said Celestine. " Then there's no further need for me to stay."

She stood looking at Alvean as though she wanted her to beg her to stay, but Alvean's curious gaze was all for me.

" Good night," she said flippantly. And to me : " Come on. I'm hungry."

" You've forgotten to thank Miss Nansellock for bringing you back," I told her.

" I didn't forget," she retorted. " I never forget anything."

" Then your memory is a great deal better than your manners," I said.

They were astonished—all of them. Perhaps I was a little astonished myself. But I knew that if I were going to assume control of this child I should have to be firm.

Her face flushed and her eyes grew hard. She was about to retort, but, not knowing how to do so, she ran out of the room.

"There!" said Mrs. Polgrey. "Why, Miss Nansellock, it was good of you——"

"Nonsense, Mrs. Polgrey," said Celestine. "Of course I brought her back."

"She will thank you later," I assured her.

"Miss Leigh," said Celestine earnestly, "it will be necessary for you to go carefully with that child. She has lost her mother . . . quite recently." Celestine's lips trembled. She smiled at me. "It is such a short time ago and the tragedy seems near. She was a dear friend of mine."

"I understand," I replied. "I shall not be harsh with the child, but I can see she needs discipline."

"Be careful, Miss Leigh." Celestine had taken a step closer and laid a hand on my arm. "Children are delicate creatures."

"I shall do my best for Alvean," I answered.

"I wish you good luck." She smiled and then turned to Mrs. Polgrey. "I'll be going back now. I want to get back before dark."

Mrs. Polgrey rang the bell and Daisy appeared.

"Take Miss to her room, Daisy," she commanded. "And has Miss Alvean got her milk and biscuits?"

"Yes, M'am," was the answer.

I said good night to Celestine Nansellock, who inclined her head. Then I left with Daisy.

I went into the schoolroom where Alvean sat at a table drinking milk and eating biscuits. She deliberately ignored me as I went to the table and sat beside her.

"Alvean," I said, "if we're going to get along together, we'd better come to an understanding. Don't you think that would be advisable?"

"Why should I care?" she replied curtly.

"But of course you'll care. We shall all be happier if we do."

Alvean shrugged her shoulders. "If we don't," she told me brusquely, "you'll have to go. I'll have another governess. It's of no account to me."

She looked at me triumphantly and I knew that she was telling me I was merely a paid servant and that it was for her to call the tune. I felt myself shiver involuntarily. For the first time I understood the feelings of those who depended on the goodwill of others for their bread and butter.

Her eyes were malicious and I wanted to slap her.

"It should be of the greatest account," I answered, "because it is far more pleasant to live in harmony than in discord with those about us."

"What does it matter, if they're *not* about us . . . if we can have them sent away?"

"Kindness matters more than anything in the world."

She smiled into her milk and finished it.

"Now," I said, "to bed."

I rose with her and she said : "I go to bed by myself. I am not a baby, you know."

"Perhaps I thought you were younger than you are because you have so much to learn."

She considered that. Then she gave that shrug of her shoulders which I was to discover was characteristic.

"Good night," she said, dismissing me.

"I'll come and say good night when you are in bed."

"There's no need."

"Nevertheless, I'll come."

She opened the door which led to her room from the schoolroom. I turned and went into mine.

I felt very depressed because I was realising the size of the problem before me. I had no experience of handling children, and in the past when I thought of them I had visualised docile and affectionate little creatures whom it would be a joy to care for. Here I was with a difficult child on my hands. And what would happen to me if it were decided that I was unfit to undertake her care? What did happen to penurious gentlewomen who failed to please their employers?

I could go to Phillida. I could be one of those old aunts who were at the beck and call of all and lived out their miserable lives dependent on others. I was not the sort of person to take dependence lightly. I should have to find other posts.

I accepted the fact that I was a little frightened. Not until I had come face to face with Alvean had I realised that I might not succeed with this job. I tried not to look down the years ahead when I might slip from one post to another, never giving satisfaction. What happened to women like myself, women who, without those attractions which were so important, were forced to battle against the world for a chance to live?

I felt that I could have thrown myself on my bed and wept, wept with anger against the cruelty of life, which had robbed me of two loving parents and sent me out ill-equipped into the world.

I imagined myself appearing at Alvean's bedside, my face stained with tears. What triumph for her! That was no way to begin the battle which I was sure must rage between us.

I walked up and down my room, trying to control my emotions. I went to the window and looked out across the lawns to the hilly country beyond. I could not see the sea because the house was so built that the back faced the coast and I was at the front. Instead I looked beyond the plateau on which the house stood, to the hills.

Such beauty! Such peace without, I thought. Such conflict within. When I leaned out of the window I could see Mount Widden across the cove. Two houses standing there over many years; generations of Nansellocks, generations of TreMellyns had lived here and their lives had intermingled so that it could well be that the story of one house was the story of the other.

I turned from the window and went through the schoolroom to Alvean's room.

" Alvean," I whispered. There was no answer. But she lay there in the bed, her eyes tightly shut, too tightly.

I bent over her.

" Good night, Alvean. We're going to be friends, you know," I murmured.

There was no answer. She was pretending to be asleep.

Exhausted as I was, my rest was broken that night. I would
fall into sleep and then awake startled. I repeated this several
times until I was fully awake.

I lay in bed and looked about my room in which the
furniture showed up in intermittent moonlight like dim
figures. I had a feeling that I was not alone; that there were
whispering voices about me. I had an impression that there
had been tragedy in this house which still hung over it.

I wondered if it was due to the death of Alvean's mother.
She had been dead only a year; I wondered in what circumstances she had died.

I thought of Alvean who showed a somewhat aggressive face
to the world. There must be some reason for this. I was sure
that no child would be eager to proclaim herself the enemy of
strangers without some cause.

I determined to discover the reason for Alvean's demeanour.
I determined to make her a happy, normal child.

It was light before sleep came; the coming of day comforted
me because I was afraid of the darkness in this house. It was
childish, but it was true.

I had breakfast in the schoolroom with Alvean, who told me,
with pride, that when her father was at home she had breakfast
with him.

Later we settled to work, and I discovered that she was an
intelligent child; she had read more than most children of her
age and her eyes would light up with interest in her lessons
almost in spite of her determination to preserve a lack of
harmony between us. My spirits began to rise and I felt that
I would in time make a success of this job.

Luncheon consisted of boiled fish and rice pudding, and
afterwards when Alvean volunteered to take me for a walk,
I felt I was getting on better with her.

There were woods on the estate, and she said she wished to
show them to me. I was delighted that she should do so and
gladly I followed her through the trees.

"Look," she cried, picking a crimson flower and holding it
out to me. "Do you know what this is?"

" It's betony, I believe."

She nodded. " You should pick some and keep it in your room, Miss. It keeps evil away."

I laughed. " That's an old superstition. Why should I want to keep evil away?"

" Everybody should. They grow this in graveyards. It's because people are buried there. It's grown there because people are afraid of the dead."

" It's foolish to be afraid. Dead people can hurt no one."

She was placing the flower in the buttonhole of my coat. I was rather touched. Her face looked gentle as she fixed it and I had a notion that she felt a sudden protective feeling towards me.

" Thank you, Alvean," I said gently.

She looked at me and all the softness vanished from her face. It was defiant and full of mischief.

" You can't catch me," she cried; and off she ran.

I did not attempt to do so. I called : " Alvean, come here." But she disappeared through the trees and I heard her mocking laugher in the distance.

I decided to return to the house, but the wood was thick, and I was not sure of my direction. I walked back a little way but it seemed to me that it was not the direction from which we had come. A panic seized me, but I told myself this was absurd. It was a sunny afternoon and I could not be half an hour's walk from the house. Moreover, I did not believe that the wood could be very extensive.

I was not going to give Alvean the satisfaction of having brought me to the wood to lose me. So I walked purposefully through the trees; but as I walked they grew thicker and I knew that we had not come this way. My anger against Alvean was rising when I heard the crackle of leaves as though I were being followed. I was sure the child was somewhere near, mocking me.

Then I heard singing; it was a strange voice, slightly off key, and the fact that the song was one of those which were being sung in drawing rooms all over the country did nothing to reassure me.

" *Alice, where art thou?*
*One year back this even*
*And thou wert by my side,*
*Vowing to love me,*
*Alice, what e'er may betide——*"

" Who is there?" I called.

There was no answer, but in the distance I caught a glimpse of a child with lint-white hair, and I knew that it was only little Gilly who had stared at me from the hydrangea bushes by the lodge gates.

I walked swiftly on and after a while the trees grew less dense and through them I saw the road. I came out into this and realised that I was on the slope which led up to the plateau and the lodge gates.

Mrs. Soady was sitting at the door of the lodge as she had been when I arrived, her knitting in her hands.

" Why, Miss," she called. " So you've been out walking then?"

" I went for a walk with Miss Alvean. We lost each other in the woods."

" Ah yes. So her run away, did her." Mrs. Soady shook her head, as she came to the gate trailing her ball of wool behind her.

" I expect she'll find her way home," I said.

" My dear life, yes. There ain't an inch of them woods Miss Alvean don't know. Oh, I see you've got yourself a piece of betony. Like as not 'tis as well."

" Miss Alvean picked it and insisted on putting it in my buttonhole."

" There now ! You be friends already."

" I heard the little girl, Gilly, singing in the woods," I said.

" I don't doubt 'ee. Her's always singing in the woods."

" I called to her but she didn't come."

" Timid as a doe, she be."

" Well, I think I'll be getting along. Goodbye, Mrs. Soady."

" Good day to 'ee, Miss."

I went up the drive, past the hydrangeas and the fuchsias. I realised I was straining my ears for the sound of singing, but there was no sound but that of an occasional small animal in the undergrowth.

I was hot and tired when I reached the house. I went straight up to my room and rang for water and, when I had washed and brushed my hair, went into the schoolroom where tea was waiting for me.

Alvean was at the table; she looked demure and made no reference to our afternoon's adventure; nor did I.

After tea I said to her : " I don't know what rules your other governesses made, but I propose we do our lessons in the morning, have a break between luncheon and tea, and then start again from five o'clock until six, when we will read together."

Alvean did not answer; she was studying me intently.

Then suddenly she said : " Miss, do you like my name? Have you ever known anyone else called Alvean?"

I said I liked the name and had never heard it before.

" It's Cornish. Do you know what it means?"

" I have no idea."

" Then I will tell you. My father can speak and write Cornish." She looked wistful when she spoke of her father, and I thought : He at least is one person she admires and for whose approval she is eager. She went on : " In Cornish, Alvean means Little Alice."

" Oh!" I said, and my voice shook a little.

She came to me and placed her hands on my knees; she looked up into my face and said solemnly : " You see, Miss, my mother was Alice. She isn't here any more. But I was called after her. That's why I am little Alice."

I stood up because I could no longer bear the scrutiny of the child. I went to the window.

" Look," I said, " two of the peacocks are on the lawn."

She was standing at my elbow. " They've come to be fed. Greedy things! Daisy will soon be coming with their peas. They know it."

I was not seeing the peacocks on the lawn. I was remembering the mocking eyes of the man on the train, the man who had warned me that I should have to beware of Alice.

B

Three days after my arrival at Mount Mellyn, the Master of the house returned.

I had slipped into a routine as far as my duties were concerned. Alvean and I did lessons each morning after breakfast, and apart from an ever present desire to disconcert me by asking questions which, I knew, she hoped I should not be able to answer, I found her a good pupil. It was not that she meant to please me; it was merely that her desire for knowledge was so acute that she could not deny it. I believe that there was some plot in her head that if she could learn all I knew she could then confront her father with a question : Since there is no more Miss can teach me, is there any point in her remaining here?

I often thought of tales I had heard of governesses whose declining years were made happy by those whom they had taught as children. No such happy fate would be mine—at least as far as Alvean was concerned.

I had been shocked when I first heard the name of Alice mentioned, and after the daylight had passed I would consequently feel that the house was full of eerie shadows. That was pure fancy of course. It had been a bad beginning, meeting that man in the train and his talk of second sight.

I did wonder, when I was alone in my room and the house was quiet, of what Alice had died. She must have been quite a young woman. It was, I told myself, because she was so recently dead—for after all a year was not a very long time—that her presence seemed to haunt the place.

I would wake in the night to hear what I thought were voices, and they seemed to be moaning : " Alice. Alice. Where is Alice?"

I went to my window and listened, and the whispering voices seemed to be carried on the air.

Daisy who, like her sister, was by no means a fanciful person, explained away my fancies the very next morning when she brought my hot water.

"Did 'ee hear the sea last night, Miss, in old Mellyn Cove? Sis . . . sis . . . sis . . . woa . . . woa . . . woa . . . all night long. Just like two old biddies having a good gossip down there."

"Why, yes, I heard it."

" 'Tis like that on certain nights when the sea be high and the wind in a certain direction."

I laughed at myself. There was an explanation to everything.

I had grown to know the people of the household. Mrs. Tapperty called me in one day for a glass of her parsnip wine. She hoped I was comfortable at the house; then she told me of the trial Tapperty was to her because he couldn't keep his eyes nor his hands from the maidens—and the younger the better. She feared Kitty and Daisy took after their father. It was a pity for their mother was, according to herself, a Godfearing body who would be seen in Mellyn Church every Sunday, night and morning. Now the girls were grown up she had not only to wonder whether Joe Tapperty was after Mrs. Tully from the cottages, but what Daisy was doing in the stables with Billy Trehay or Kitty with that house boy from Mount Widden. It was a hard life for a Godfearing woman who only wanted to do right and see right done.

I went to see Mrs. Soady at the lodge gates and heard about her three sons and their children. "Never did I see such people for putting their toes through their stockings. It's one body's work to keep them in stockings."

I was very eager to learn about the house in which I lived, and the intricacies of heel-turning did not greatly excite me; therefore I did not often call on Mrs. Soady.

I tried on occasions to catch Gilly and talk to her; but although I saw her now and then, I did not succeed. I called her, but that only made her run away more swiftly. I could never hear her soft crooning voice without being deeply disturbed.

I felt that something should be done for her. I was angry with these country folk who, because she was unlike they were, believed her to be mad. I wanted to talk to Gilly if that were possible. I wanted to find out what went on behind that blank blue stare.

I knew she was interested in me, and I believed that in some way she had sensed my interest in her. But she was afraid of me. Something must have happened to frighten her at some time, because she was so unnaturally timid. If I could only discover what, if I could teach her that in me at least she had nothing to fear, I believed I could help her to become a normal child.

During those days I believe I thought more of Gilly than I did of Alvean. The latter seemed to me to be merely a naughty spoilt child; there were thousands such. I felt that the gentle creature called Gillyflower was unique.

It was impossible to talk to Mrs. Polgrey about her grand-daughter, for she was such a conventional woman. In her mind a person was either mad or sane, and the degree of sanity depended on the conformity with Mrs. Polgrey's own character. As Gilly was as different from her grandmother as anyone could be, Gilly was therefore irremediably crazy.

So although I did broach the subject with Mrs. Polgrey she was grimly uncommunicative and told me by her looks alone to remember that I was here to take charge of Miss Alvean, and that Gilly was no concern of mine.

This was the state of affairs when Connan TreMellyn returned to Mount Mellyn.

As soon as I set eyes on Connan TreMellyn he aroused deep feelings within me. I was aware of his presence, indeed, before I saw him.

It was afternoon when he arrived. Alvean had gone off by herself and I had sent for hot water to wash before I went for a stroll. Kitty brought it and I noticed the difference in her from the moment she entered the room. Her black eyes gleamed and her mouth seemed a little slack.

" Master be home," she said.

I tried not to show that I was faintly disturbed; and at that moment Daisy put her head round the door. The sisters looked very much alike just then. There was about them both a certain expectancy which sickened me. I thought I understood the expression in the faces of these lusty girls. I suspected that neither of them was virgin. There was suggestion in their very gestures and I had seen them in scuffling intimacy with Billy Trehay in the stables and with the boys who came in from the village to work about the place. They changed subtly when they were in the presence of the opposite sex and I understood what that meant. Their excitement over the return of the Master, of whom I gathered everyone was in awe, led me to one conclusion, and I felt faintly disgusted, not only with them but with myself for entertaining such thoughts.

Is he *that* sort of man then? I was asking myself.

"He came in half an hour ago," said Kitty.

They were studying me speculatively and once more I thought I read their thoughts. They were telling themselves that there would be little competition from me.

My disgust increased and I turned away.

I said coolly: "Well, I'll wash my hands and you can take the water away. I am going for a walk."

I put on my hat and, even as I went out quickly by way of the back stairs, I sensed the change. Mr. Polgrey was busy in the gardens, and the two boys who came in from the village were working as though their lives depended on it. Tapperty was cleaning out the stables; he was so intent on his work that he did not notice me.

There was no doubt that the whole household was in awe of the Master.

As I wandered through the woods I told myself that if he did not like me I could leave at any time. I supposed I could stay with Phillida while I looked round. At least I had some relations to whom I could go. I was not entirely alone in the world.

I called on Alvean, but my voice was lost in the thickness of the trees and there was no response. Then I called: "Gilly! Are you there, Gillyflower? Do come and talk to me if you are. I won't hurt you."

There was no answer.

At half past three I went back to the house and, as I was mounting the back stairs to my quarters, Daisy came running after me.

"Master have been asking for you, Miss. He do wish to see you. He be waiting in the punch room."

I inclined my head and said: "I will take off my things and then go to the punch room."

"He have seen you come in, Miss, and have said for you to go right away."

"I will take off my hat first," I answered. My heart was beating fast and my colour was heightened. I did not know why I felt antagonistic. I believed that I should soon be packing my bags and going back to Phillida; and I decided that if it had to be done it should be done with the utmost dignity.

In my room I took off my hat and smoothed my hair. My eyes were certainly amber to-day. They were resentful, which seemed ridiculous before I had met the man. I told myself as I went down to the punch room that I had built up a picture of him because of certain looks I had seen in the faces of those two flighty girls. I had already assured myself that poor Alice had died of a broken heart because she had found herself married to a philanderer.

I knocked at the door.

"Come in." His voice was strong—arrogant, I called it even before I set eyes on him.

He was standing with his back to the fireplace and I was immediately conscious of his great height; he was well over six feet tall, and the fact that he was so thin—one could almost say gaunt—accentuated this. His hair was black but his eyes were light. His hands were thrust into the pockets of his riding breeches and he wore a dark blue coat with a white cravat. There was an air of careless elegance about him as though he cared nothing for his clothes but could not help looking well in them.

He gave an impression of both strength and cruelty. There was sensuality in that face, I decided—that came through; but there was much else which was hidden. Even in that moment when I first saw him I knew that there were two men in that body—two distinct personalities—the Connan TreMellyn who faced the world, and the one who remained hidden.

"So, Miss Leigh, at last we meet."

He did not advance to greet me, and his manner seemed insolent as though he were reminding me that I was only a governess.

" It does not seem a long time," I answered, " for I have only been in your house a few days."

" Well, let us not dwell on the time it has taken us to get together. Now you are here, let that suffice."

His light eyes surveyed me mockingly, so that I felt awkward and unattractive, and that I stood before a connoisseur of women when even to the uninitiated I was not a very desirable specimen.

" Miss Polgrey gives me good reports of you."

" That is kind of her."

" Why should it be kind of her to tell me the truth? I expect that from my employees."

" I meant that she has been kind to me and that has helped to make this good report possible."

" I see that you are a woman who does not use the ordinary clichés of conversation but means what she says."

" I hope so."

" Good. I have a feeling that we shall get on well together."

His eyes were taking in each detail of my appearance, I knew. He probably was aware that I had been given a London season and what Aunt Adelaide would call " every opportunity,' and had failed to acquire a husband. As a connoisseur of women he would know why.

I thought, at least I shall be safe from the attentions which I feel sure he tries to bestow on all attractive women with whom he comes into contact.

" Tell me," he said, " how do you find my daughter? Backward for her age?"

" By no means. She is extremely intelligent, but I find her in need of discipline."

" I am sure you will be able to supply that lack."

" I intend to try."

" Of course. That is why you are here."

" Please tell me how far I may carry that discipline."

" You are thinking of corporal punishment?"

" Nothing was farther from my thoughts. I mean, have I

your permission to apply my own code? To restrict her liberty, shall we say, if I feel she needs such punishment."

"Short of murder, Miss Leigh, you have my permission to do what you will. If your methods do not meet with my approval, you will hear."

"Very well, I understand."

"If you wish to make any alterations in the . . . curriculum, I think is the word . . . you must do so."

"Thank you."

"I believe in experiments. If your methods have not made an improvement in say . . . six months . . . well, then we could review the situation, could we not?"

His eyes were insolent. I thought : He intends to get rid of me soon. He was hoping I was a silly, pretty creature not averse to carrying on an intrigue with him while pretending to look after his daughter. Very well, the best thing I can do is to get out of this house.

"I suppose," he went on, "we should make excuses for Alvean's lack of good manners. She lost her mother a year ago."

I looked into his face for a trace of sorrow. I could find none.

"I had heard that," I answered.

"Of course you had heard. I'll swear there were many ready to tell you. It was doubtless a great shock to the child."

"It must have been a great shock," I agreed.

"It was sudden." He was silent for a few seconds and then he continued : "Poor child, she has no mother. And her father . . .?" He lifted his shoulders and did not complete his sentence.

"Even so," I said, "there are many more unfortunate than she is. All she needs is a firm hand."

He leaned forward suddenly and surveyed me ironically.

"I am sure," he said, "that you possess that necessary firm hand."

I was conscious in that brief moment of the magnetism of the man. The clear-cut features, the cool, light eyes, the mockery behind them—all these I felt were but a mask hiding something which he was determined to keep hidden.

At that moment there was a knock on the door and Celestine Nansellock came in.

" I heard you were here, Connan," she said, and I thought she seemed nervous. So he had that effect even on those of his own station.

" How news travels!" he murmured. " My dear Celestine, it was good of you to come over. I was just making the acquaintance of our new governess. She tells me that Alvean is intelligent and needs discipline."

" Of course she is intelligent!" Celestine spoke indignantly. " I hope Miss Leigh is not planning to be too harsh with her. Alvean is a *good* child."

Connan TreMellyn threw an amused glance in my direction. " I don't think Miss Leigh entirely agrees with that," he said. " You see our little goose as a beautiful swan, Celeste my dear."

" Perhaps I am over fond——"

" Would you like me to leave now?" I suggested, for I had a great desire to get away from them.

" But I am interrupting," cried Celestine.

" No," I assured her. " We had finished our talk, I believe."

Connan TreMellyn looked in some amusement from her to me. It occurred to me that he probably found us equally unattractive. I was sure that neither of us was the least like the woman he would admire.

" Let us say it is to be continued," he said lightly. " I fancy, Miss Leigh, that you and I will have a great deal more to discuss, regarding my daughter."

I bowed my head and left them together.

In the schoolroom tea was laid, ready for me. I felt too excited to eat, and when Alvean did not appear I guessed she was with her father.

At five o'clock she still had not put in an appearance, so I summoned Daisy and sent her to find the child and to remind her that from five to six we had work to do.

I waited. I was not surprised because I had expected Alvean to rebel. Her father had arrived and she preferred to be with him rather than come to me for an hour of our reading.

I wondered what would happen when the child refused to

come to the schoolroom. Could I go down to the punch room or the drawing room or wherever they were and demand that she return with me? Celestine was with them and she would take her stand on Alvean's side against me.

I heard footsteps on the stairs. The door of Alvean's room which led into the schoolroom was opened, and there stood Connan TreMellyn holding Alvean my the arm.

Alvean's expression astonished me. She looked so unhappy that I found myself feeling sorry for her. Her father was smiling and I thought he looked like a satyr, as though the situation which caused pain to Alvean and embarrassment to me amused him—and perhaps for these reasons. In the background was Celestine.

"Here she is," announced Connan TreMellyn. "Duty is duty, my daughter," he said to Alvean. "And when your governess summons you to your lessons, you must obey."

Alvean muttered and I could see that she was hard put to it to restrain her sobs: "But it is your first day, Papa."

"But Miss Leigh says there are lessons to be done, and she is in command."

"Thank you, Mr. TreMellyn," I said. "Come and sit down, Alvean."

Alvean's expression changed as she looked at me. All the wistfulness was replaced by anger and a fierce hatred.

"Connan," Celestine said quietly, "it *is* your first day back, you know, and Alvean so looked forward to your coming."

He smiled but I thought how grim his mouth was.

"Discipline," he murmured. "That, Celeste, is of the utmost importance. Come, we will leave Alvean with her governess."

He inclined his head in my direction, while Alvean threw a pleading glance at him which he quite obviously ignored.

The door shut leaving me alone with my pupil.

That incident had taught me a great deal. Alvean adored her father and he was indifferent to her. My anger against him increased as my pity for the child grew. Small wonder that she was a difficult child. What could one expect when she was such an unhappy one? I saw her . . . ignored by the father whom she loved, spoiled by Celestine Nansellock. Between them they were doing their best to ruin the girl.

I would have liked Connan TreMellyn better, I told myself, if he had decided to forget discipline on his first day back, and devote a little time to his daughter's company.

Alvean was rebellious all that evening, but I insisted on her going to bed at her usual time. She told me she hated me, though there was no need for her to have mentioned a fact which was apparent.

I felt so disturbed when she was in her bed that I slipped out of the house and went into the woods, where I sat on a fallen tree trunk, brooding.

It had been a hot day and there was a deep stillness in the woods.

I wondered whether I was going to keep this job. It was not easy to say at this stage, and I was not sure whether I wanted to go or stay.

There were so many things to keep me. There was, for one thing, my interest in Gillyflower; there was my desire to wipe the rebellion from Alvean's heart. But I felt less eagerness for these tasks now that I had seen the Master.

I was a little afraid of the man although I could not say why. I was certain that he would leave *me* alone, but there was something magnetic about him, some quality which made it difficult for me to put him out of my mind. I thought more of dead Alice than I had before, because I could not stop myself wondering what sort of person she could have been.

I amused him in some way. Perhaps because I was so unattractive in his eyes; perhaps because he knew that I belonged to that army of women who are obliged to earn their living and are so dependent on the whim of people like himself. Was there a streak of sadism in his nature? I believed so. Perhaps poor Alice had found it intolerable. Perhaps she, like poor Gillyflower's mother, had walked into the sea.

As I sat there I heard the sound of footsteps coming through the wood and I hesitated, wondering whether to wait there or go back to the house.

A man was coming towards me, and there was something familiar about him which made my heart beat faster.

He started when he saw me; then he began to smile and I recognised him as the man I had met on the train.

"So we meet," he said. "I knew our reunion would not be long delayed. Why, you look as though you have seen a ghost. Has your stay at Mount Mellyn made you look for ghosts? I've heard some say that there *is* a ghostly atmosphere about the place."

"Who are you?" I asked.

"My name is Peter Nansellock. I have to confess to a little deception."

"You're Miss Celestine's brother?"

He nodded. "I knew who you were when we met in the train. I deliberately bearded you in your carriage. I saw you sitting there, looking the part, and I guessed. Your name on the labels of your baggage confirmed my guess for I knew that they were expecting Miss Martha Leigh at Mount Mellyn."

"I am comforted to learn that my looks conform with the part I have been called upon to play in life."

"You really are a most untruthful young lady. I remember I had reason to reprimand you for the same sort of thing at our first meeting. You are in fact quite discomfited to learn that you were taken for a governess."

I felt myself grow pink with indignation. "Because I am a governess that is no reason why I should be forced to accept insults from strangers."

I rose from the tree trunk, but he laid a hand on my arm and said pleadingly : "Please let us talk awhile. There is much I have to say to you. There are things you should know."

My curiosity overcame my dignity and I sat down.

"That's better, Miss Leigh. You see I remember your name."

"Most courteous of you! And how extraordinary that you should first notice a mere governess's name and then keep it in your memory."

"You are like a hedgehog," he retorted. "One only has to mention the word 'governess' and up come your spines. You will have to learn resignation. Aren't we taught that we must be content in that station of life to which we have been called?"

" Since I resemble a hedgehog, at least I am not spineless."

He laughed and then was immediately sober. " I do not possess second sight, Miss Leigh," he said quietly. " I know nothing of palmistry. I deceived you, Miss Leigh."

" Do you think I was deceived for a moment?"

" For many moments. Until this one, in fact, you have thought of me with wonder."

" Indeed, I have not thought of you at all."

" More untruths! I wonder if a young lady with such little regard for veracity is worthy to teach our little Alvean."

" Since you are a friend of the family your best policy would be to warn them at once."

" But if Connan dismissed his daughter's governess, how sad that would be! I should wander through these woods without hope of meeting her."

" I see you are a frivolous person."

" It's true." He looked grave. " My brother was frivolous. My sister is the only commendable member of the family."

" I have already met her."

" Naturally. She is a constant visitor to Mount Mellyn. She dotes on Alvean."

" Well, she is a very near neighbour."

" And we, Miss Leigh, shall in future be very near neighbours. How does that strike you?"

" Without any great force."

" Miss Leigh, you are cruel as well as untruthful. I hoped you would be grateful for my interest. I was going to say, if ever things should become intolerable at Mount Mellyn you need only walk over to Mount Widden. There you would find me most willing to help. I feel sure that among my wide circle of acquaintances I could find someone who is in urgent need of a governess."

" Why should I find life intolerable at Mount Mellyn?"

" It's a tomb of a place, Connan is overbearing, Alvean is a menace to anyone's peace, and the atmosphere since Alice's death is not congenial."

I turned to him abruptly and said : " You told me to beware of Alice. What did you mean by that?"

" So you remember?"

" It seemed a strange thing to say."

" Alice is dead," he said, " but somehow she remains. That's what I always feel at Mount Mellyn. Nothing was the same after the day she . . . went."

" How did she die?"

" You have not heard the story yet?"

" No."

" I should have thought Mrs. Polgrey or one of those girls would have told you. But they haven't, eh? They're probably somewhat in awe of the governess."

" I should like to hear the story."

" It's a very simple one. The sort of thing which must happen in many a home. A wife finds life with her husband intolerable. She walks out . . . with another man. It's ordinary enough, you see. Only Alice's story had a different ending."

He looked at the tips of his boots as he had when we were travelling in the train to Liskeard together. " The man in the case was my brother," he went on.

" Geoffry Nansellock !" I cried.

" So you have heard of him !"

I thought of Gillyflower, whose birth had so distressed her mother that she had walked into the sea.

" Yes," I said, " I've heard of Geoffry Nansellock. He was evidently a philanderer."

" It sounds a harsh word to apply to poor old Geoff. He had charm . . . all the charm of the family, some say." He smiled at me. " Others may think he did not get it all. He was not a bad sort. I was fond of old Geoff. His great weakness was women. He loved women; he found them irresistible. And women love men who love them. How can they help it? I mean, it is such a compliment, is it not? One by one they fell victim to his charm."

" He did not hesitate to include other men's wives among his victims."

" Spoken like a true governess ! Alas, my dear Miss Leigh, it appeared he did not . . . since Alice was among them. It is true that all was not well at Mount Mellyn. Do you think Connan would be an easy man to live with?"

" It is surely not becoming for a governess to discuss her employer in such a manner."

" What a contrary young lady you are, Miss Leigh. You make the most of your situation. You use the governess when you wish to, and then expect others to ignore her when you do not wish her to be recognised. I believe that anyone who is obliged to live in a house should know something of its secrets."

" What secrets?"

He bent a little closer to me. " Alice was afraid of Connan. Before she married him she had known my brother. She and Geoffry were on the train . . . running away together."

" I see." I drew myself away from him because I felt it was undignified to be talking of past scandals in this way, particularly as these scandals had nothing whatever to do with me.

" They identified Geoffry although he was badly smashed up. There was a woman close to him. She was so badly burned that it was impossible to recognise her as Alice. But a locket she was wearing was recognised as one she was known to possess. That was how she was identified . . . and of course there was the fact that Alice had disappeared."

" How dreadful to die in such a way!"

" The prim governess is shocked because poor Alice died in the act of forming a guilty partnership with my charming but erring brother."

" Was she so unhappy at Mount Mellyn?"

" You have met Connan. Remember he knew that she had once been in love with Geoffry, and Geoffry was still in the offing. I can imagine life was hell for Alice."

" Well, it was very tragic," I said briskly. " But it is over Why did you say, ' Beware of Alice,' as though she were still there?"

" Are you fey, Miss Leigh? No, of course you are not. You are a governess with more than your fair share of common-sense. You would not be influenced by fantastic tales."

" What fantastic tales?"

He grinned at me, coming even closer, and I realised that in a very short time it would be dark. I was anxious to get back to the house, and my expression became a little impatient.

"They recognised her locket, not her. There are some who think that it was not Alice who was killed on the train with Geoffry."

"Then if it was not, where is she?"

"That is what some people ask themselves. That is why there are long shadows at Mount Mellyn."

I stood up. "I must get back. It will soon be dark."

He was standing beside me—a little taller than I—and our eyes met.

"I thought you should know these things," he said almost gently. "It seems only fair that you should know."

I began walking back in the direction from which I had come.

"My duties are with the child," I answered somewhat brusquely. "I am not here for any other purpose."

"But how can even a governess, overburdened with common sense though she may be, know to what purposes fate will put her?"

"I think I know what is expected of me." I was alarmed because he walked beside me; I wanted to escape from him that I might be alone with my thoughts. I felt this man impaired my precious dignity to which I was clinging with that determination only possible to those who are in constant fear of losing what little they possess. He had mocked me in the train. I felt he was waiting for an opportunity to do so again.

"I am sure you do."

"There is no need for you to escort me back to the house."

"I am forced to contradict you. There is every reason."

"Do you think I am incapable of looking after myself?"

"I think none more capable of doing that than yourself. But as it happens I was on my way to call, and this is the most direct way to the house."

I was silent until we came to Mount Mellyn.

Connan TreMellyn was coming from the stable.

"Hallo there, Con!" cried Peter Nansellock.

Connan TreMellyn looked at us in mild surprise, which I supposed was due to the fact that we were together.

I hurried round to the back of the house.

It was not easy to sleep that night. The events of the day crowded into my mind and I saw pictures of myself and Connan TreMellyn, pictures of Alvean, of Celestine, and of myself in the woods with Peter Nansellock.

The wind was in a certain direction that night, and I could hear the waves thundering into Mellyn Cove.

In my present mood it certainly seemed that there were whispering voices down there, and that the words they said to each other were: " Alice! Alice! Where is Alice? Alice, where are you?"

III

In the morning the fancies of the previous night seemed foolish. I asked myself why so many people—including myself—wanted to make a mystery of what had happened in this house. It was an ordinary enough story.

I know what it is, I told myself. When people consider an ancient house like this, they make themselves believe it could tell some fantastic stories if it could only speak. They think of the generations who have lived and suffered within these walls, and they grow fanciful. So that when the mistress of the house is tragically killed they imagine her ghost still walks and that, although she is dead, she is still here. Well, I am a sensible woman, I hope. Alice was killed on a train, and that was the end of Alice.

I laughed at my folly in allowing myself to be caught up in such notions. Had not Daisy or Kitty explained that the whispering voices, which I heard in the night, were merely the sound of waves thundering in the cove below?

From now on I was entertaining no more such fantastic thoughts.

My room was filled with sunshine and I felt differently from the way I had felt on any other morning. I was exhilarated. I knew why. It was due to that man, Connan TreMellyn. Not that I liked him—quite in reverse; but it was as though he had issued a challenge. I was going to make a success of this job. I was going to make of Alvean not only a model pupil but a charming, unaffected, uninhibited little girl.

I felt so pleased that I began to hum softly under my breath. *Come into the Garden, Maud.* . . . That was a song Father used to like to play while Phillida sang, for in addition to her other qualities Phillida possessed a charming voice. Then I passed to *Sweet and Low*, and I for a moment forgot the house I was in and saw Father at the piano, his glasses slipping down his nose, his slippered feet making the most of the pedals.

I was almost astonished to find that I had unconsciously slipped into the song I had heard Gilly singing in the woods: *Alice, where art thou——*

Oh no, not that, I said sharply to myself.

I heard the sound of horses' hoofs and I went to the window to look out. No one was visible. The lawns looked fresh and lovely with the early morning dew on them. What a beautiful sight, I thought; the palm trees gave the scene a tropical look and it was one of those mornings when there was every promise of a beautiful day.

" One of the last we can expect this summer, I daresay," I said aloud; and I threw open my window and leaned out, my thick coppery plaits, the ends tied with pieces of blue ribbon for bedtime, swinging out with me.

I went back to *Sweet and Low* and was humming this when Connan TreMellyn emerged from the stables. He saw me before I was able to draw back, and I felt myself grow scarlet with embarrassment to be seen with my hair down and in my nightgown thus.

He called jauntily : " Good morning, Miss Leigh."

In that moment I said to myself : So it was his horse I heard. And has he been riding in the early morning, or out all night? I imagined his visiting one of the gay ladies of the neighbourhood if such existed. That was my opinion of him. I was angry that he should be the one to show no embarrassment whatsoever while I was blushing—certainly in every part that was visible.

" Good morning," I said, and my voice sounded curt.

He was coming swiftly across the lawn, hoping, I was sure, to embarrass me further by a closer look at me in my night attire.

" A beautiful morning," he cried.

" Extremely so," I answered.

I withdrew into my room as I heard him shout: " Hallo, Alvean! So you're up too."

I was standing well back from the window now and I heard Alvean cry: " Hallo, Papa!" and her voice was soft and gentle with that wistful note which I had detected when she spoke of him on the previous day. I knew that she was delighted to have seen him, that she had been awake in her room when she had heard his voice, and had dashed to her window, and that it would make her extremely happy if he stopped awhile and chatted with her.

He did no such thing. He went into the house. Standing before my mirror, I looked at myself. Most unbecoming, I thought. And quite undignified. Myself in a pink flannelette nightdress buttoned high at the throat, with my hair down and my face even now the colour of flannelette!

I put on my dressing gown and on impulse crossed the schoolroom to Alvean's room. I opened the door and went in. She was sitting astride a chair and talking to herself.

" There's nothing to be afraid of really. All you have to do is hold tight and not be afraid . . . and you won't fall off."

She was so intent on what she was doing that she had not heard the door open, and I stood for a few seconds watching her, for she had her back to the schoolroom door.

I learnt a great deal in that moment. He was a great horseman, this father of hers; he wanted his daughter to be a good horsewoman, but Alvean, who desperately wanted to win his approval, was afraid of horses.

I started forward, my first impulse to talk to her, to tell her that I would teach her to ride. It was one thing I could do really well because we had always had horses in the country, and at five Phillida and I were competing in local shows.

But I hesitated because I was beginning to understand Alvean. She was an unhappy child. Tragedy had hit her in more ways than one. She had lost her mother, and that was the biggest tragedy which could befall any child; but when her father did not seem anything but indifferent to her, and she adored him, that was a double tragedy.

I quietly shut the door and went back to my room. I looked at the sunshine on the carpet and my elation returned. I *was* going to make a success of this job. I was going to fight Connan TreMellyn, if he wanted it that way. I was going to make him proud of his daughter; I was going to force him to give her that attention which was her right and which none but a brute would deny her.

Lessons were trying that morning. Alvean was late for them, having breakfasted with her father in accordance with the custom of the family. I pictured them at the big table in the room which I had discovered was used as a dining room when there were no guests. They called it the small dining room, but it was only small by Mount Mellyn standards.

He would be reading the paper, or looking through his letters, I imagined; Alvean would be at the other end of the table hoping for a word, which of course he would be too selfish to bestow.

I had to send for her to come to lessons; and that she deeply resented.

I tried to make lessons as interesting as I could, and I must have succeeded, for in spite of her resentment towards me she could not hide her interest in the history and geography lessons which I set for that morning.

She took luncheon with her father while I ate alone in the schoolroom, and after that I decided to approach Connan TreMellyn.

While I was wondering where I could find him I saw him leave the house and go across to the stables. I immediately followed him and, when I arrived at the stables, I heard him giving orders to Billy Trehay to saddle Royal Russet for him.

He looked surprised to see me; and then he smiled and I was sure that he was remembering the last time he had seen me—in dishabille.

" Why," he said, " it is Miss Leigh."

" I had hoped to have a few words with you," I said primly. " Perhaps this is an inconvenient time."

" That depends," he said, " on how many words you wish us to exchange." He took out his watch and looked at it. " I can give you five minutes, Miss Leigh."

I was aware of Billy Trehay, and if Connan TreMellyn was going to snub me I was eager that no servant should overhear.

Connan TreMellyn said : " Let us walk across the lawn. Ready in five minutes, Billy?"

" Very good, Master," answered Billy.

With that Connan TreMellyn began to walk away from the stables, and I fell into step beside him.

" In my youth," I said, " I was constantly in the saddle. I believe Alvean wishes to learn to ride. I am asking your permission to teach her."

" You have my permission to try, Miss Leigh," he said.

" You sound as though you doubt my ability to succeed."

" I fear I do."

" I don't understand why you should doubt my ability to teach when you have not tested my skill."

" Oh, Miss Leigh," he said almost mockingly, " you wrong me. It is not your ability to teach that I doubt; it is Alvean's to learn."

" You mean others have failed to teach her?"

" I have failed."

" But surely——"

He lifted a hand. " It is strange," he said, " to find such fear in a child. Most children take to it like breathing."

His tone was clipped, his expression hard; I wanted to shout at him : What sort of father are you! I pictured the lessons, the lack of understanding, the expectation of miracles. No wonder the child had been scared.

He went on : " There are some people who can never learn to ride."

Before I could stop myself I had burst out : " There are some people who cannot teach."

He stopped to stare at me in astonishment, and I knew that nobody in this house had ever dared to talk to him in such a way.

I thought : This is it. I shall now be told that my services are no longer required, and at the end of the month I may pack my bags and depart.

There was a violent temper there, and I could see that he was fighting to control it. He still looked at me and I could not read the expression in those light eyes. I believed it was contemptuous. Then he glanced back at the stables.

" You must excuse me, Miss Leigh," he said; and he left me.

I went straight back to Alvean. I found her in the schoolroom. There was the sullen defiant look in her eyes, and I believed she had seen me talking to her father.

I came straight to the point. " Your father has said I may give you riding lessons, Alvean. Would you like that?"

I saw the muscles of her face tighten, and my heart sank. Would it be possible to teach a child who was as scared as that?

I went on quickly, before she had time to answer : " When we were your age my sister and I were keen riders. She was two years younger than I and we used to compete together in the local shows. The exciting days in our lives were those when there was a horse show in our village."

" They have them here," she said.

" It's great fun. And once you've really mastered the trick you feel quite at home in the saddle."

She was silent for a moment, then she said : " I can't do it. I don't like horsese."

" You don't like horses!" My voice was shocked. " Why, they're the gentlest creatures in the world."

" They're not. They don't like me. I rode Grey Mare and she ran fast and wouldn't stop, and if Tapperty hadn't caught her rein she would have killed me."

" Grey Mare wasn't the mount for you. You should have a pony to start with."

" Then I had Buttercup. She was as bad in a different way. She wouldn't go when I tried to make her. She took a mouthful of the bushes on the bank and I tugged and tugged and she wouldn't move for me. When Billy Trehay said ' Come on, Buttercup,' she just let go and started walking away as though it were all my fault."

I laughed and she threw me a look of hatred. I hastened to assure her that was the way horses behaved until they understood you. When they did understand you they loved you as though you were their very dear friend.

I saw the wistful look in her eyes then and I exulted because I knew that the reason for aggressiveness was to be found in her intense loneliness and desire for affection.

I said : " Look here, Alvean, come out with me now. Let's see what we can do together."

She shook her head and looked at me suspiciously. I knew she felt that I might be trying to punish her for her ungraciousness towards me by making her look foolish. I wanted to put my arm about her, but I knew that was no way to approach Alvean.

" There's one thing to learn before you can begin to ride," I said as though I had not noticed her gesture, " and that is to love your horse. Then you won't be afraid. As soon as you're not afraid, your horse will begin to love you. He'll know you're his master, and he wants a master; but it must be a tender, loving master."

She was giving me her attention now.

" When a horse runs away as Grey Mare did, that means that she is frightened. She's as frightened as you are, and her way of showing it is to run. Now when you're frightened you should never let her know it. You just whisper to her, ' it's all right, Grey Mare . . . I'm here.' As for Buttercup—she's a mischievous old nag. She's lazy and she knows that you can't handle her, so she won't do as she's told. But once you let her know you're the master she'll obey. Look how she did with Billy Trehay!"

" I didn't know Grey Mare was frightened of me," she said.

" Your father wants you to ride," I told her.

It was the wrong thing to have said; it reminded her of past fears, past humiliations; I saw the stubborn fear return to her eyes, and felt a new burst of resentment towards that arrogant man who could be so careless of the feelings of a child.

" Wouldn't it be fun," I said, " to surprise him. I mean . . . suppose you learned and you could jump and gallop, and he didn't know about it . . . until he saw you do it."

It hurt me to see the joy in her face and I wondered how any man could be so callous as to deny a child the affection she asked.

" Alvean," I said. " Let's try."

" Yes," she said, " let's try. I'll go and change into my things."

I gave a little cry of disappointment, remembering that I had no riding habit with me. During my years with Aunt Adelaide I had had little opportunity for wearing it. Aunt Adelaide was no horsewoman herself and consequently was never invited to the country to hunt. Thus I had no opportunity for riding. To ride in Rotten Row would have been far beyond my means. When I had last looked at my riding clothes I had seen that the moth had got at them. I had felt resigned. I believed that I should never need them again.

Alvean was looking at me and I told her : " I have no riding clothes."

Her face fell and then lit up. " Come with me," she said. She was almost conspiratorial and I enjoyed this new relationship between us which I felt to be a great advance towards friendship.

We went along the gallery until we were in that part of the house which Mrs. Polgrey had told me was not for me. Alvean paused before a door and I had the impression that she was steeling herself to go in. She at length threw open the door and stood aside for me to enter, and I could not help feeling that she wanted me to go in first.

It was a small room which I judged to be a dressing room. In it was a long mirror, a tallboy, a chest of drawers and an oak chest. Like most of the rooms in the house this room had two doors. These rooms in the gallery appeared to lead from one to another, and this other door was slightly opened and, as Alvean went to it and looked round the room beyond, I followed her.

It was a bedroom in there. A large room beautifully furnished, the floor carpeted in blue, the curtains of blue velvet; the bed was a four-poster and, although I knew it to be large, it was dwarfed by the size of the room.

Alvean seemed distressed to see my interest in the bedroom. She went to the communicating door and shut it.

"There are lots of clothes here," she said. "In the chests and the tallboy. There's bound to be riding clothes. There'll be something you can have."

She had thrown up the lid of the chest and it was something new for me to see her so excited. I was delighted to have discovered a way to her affections that I allowed myself to be carried along.

In the chest were dresses, petticoats, hats and boots.

Alvean said quickly: "There are a lot of clothes in the attics. Great trunks of them. They were grandmamma's and great grandmamma's. When there were parties they used to dress up in them and play charades——"

I held up a lady's black beaver hat—obviously meant to be worn for riding. I put it on my head and Alvean laughed with a little catch in her voice. That laughter moved me more than anything had done since I had entered this house. It was the laughter of a child who is unaccustomed to laughter and laughs in a manner which is almost guilty. I determined to have her laughing often and without the slightest feeling of guilt.

She suddenly controlled herself as though she remembered where she was.

"You look so funny in it, Miss," she said.

I got up and stood before the long mirror. I certainly looked unlike myself. My eyes were brilliant, my hair looked quite copper against the black. I decided that I looked slightly less unattractive than usual, and that was what Alvean meant by "funny."

"Not in the least like a governess," she explained. She was

pulling out a dress, and I saw that it was a riding habit made of black woollen cloth and trimmed with braid and ball fringe. It had a blue collar and blue cuffs and it was elegantly cut.

I held it up against myself. " I think," I said, " that this would fit."

" Try it on," said Alvean. Then . . . " No, not here. You take it to your room and put it on." She suddenly seemed obsessed by the desire to get out of this room. She picked up the hat and ran to the door. I thought that she was eager for us to get started on our lesson, and there was not a great deal of time if we were to be back for tea at four.

I picked up the dress, took the hat from her and went back to my room. She hurried through to hers, and I immediately put on the riding habit.

It was not a perfect fit, but I had never been used to expensive clothes and was prepared to forget it was a little tight at the waist, and that the sleeves were on the short side, for a new woman looked back at me from my mirror, and when I set the beaver hat on my head I was delighted with myself.

I ran along to Alvean's room; she was in her habit, and when she saw me her eyes lit up and she seemed to look at me with greater interest than ever before.

We went down to the stables and I told Billy Trehay to saddle Buttercup for Alvean and another horse for myself as we were going to have a riding lesson.

He looked at me with some astonishment, but I told him that we had little time and were impatient to begin.

When we were ready I put Buttercup on a leading rein and took her with Alvean on her back into the paddock.

For nearly an hour we were there and when we left it I knew that Alvean and I had entered into a new relationship. She had not accepted me completely—that would have been asking too much—but I did believe that from that afternoon she knew that I was not an enemy.

I concentrated on giving her confidence. I made her grow accustomed to sitting her horse, to talking to her horse. I made her lean back full length on Buttercup's back and look up at the sky; then I made her shut her eyes. I gave her lessons in mounting and dismounting. Buttercup did no more than walk round that field, but I do believe that at the end of the hour I had done a great deal towards making Alvean lose her fear; and that was what I had determined should be the first lesson.

I was astonished to find that it was half past three, and I think Alvean was too.

"We must return to the house at once," I said, "if we are to change in time for tea."

As we came out of the field a figure rose from the grass and I saw to my surprise that it was Peter Nansellock.

He clapped his hands as we came along.

"Here endeth the first lesson," he cried, "and an excellent one. I did not know," he went on, turning to me, "that equestrian skill was included in your many accomplishments."

"Were you watching us, Uncle Peter?" demanded Alvean.

"For the last half hour. My admiration for you both is beyond expression."

Alvean smiled slowly. "Did you really admire us?"

"Much as I could be tempted to compliment two beautiful ladies," he said placing his hand on his heart and bowing elegantly, "I could never tell a lie."

"Until this moment," I said tartly.

Alvean's face fell and I added : "There is nothing very admirable in learning to ride. Thousands are doing it every day."

"But the art was never so gracefully taught, never so patiently learned."

"Your uncle is a joker, Alvean," I put in.

"Yes," said Alvean almost sadly, "I know."

"And," I added, "it is time that we returned for tea."

"I wonder if I might be invited to schoolroom tea?"

"You are calling to see Mr. TreMellyn?" I asked.

"I am calling to take tea with you two ladies."

Alvean laughed suddenly; I could see that she was not unaffected by what I supposed was the charm of this man.

"Mr. Tremellyn left Mount Mellyn early this afternoon," I said. "I have no idea whether or not he has returned."

"And while the cat's away . . ." he murmured, and his eyes swept over my costume in a manner which I could only describe as insolent.

I said coolly : " Come along, Alvean, we must go at once if we are to be in time for tea."

I let the horse break into a trot, and holding Buttercup's leading rein, started towards the house.

Peter Nansellock walked behind us, and when we reached the stables I saw him making for the house.

Alvean and I dismounted, handed our horses to two of the stable boys, and hurried up to our rooms.

I got out of the riding habit and into my dress and, glancing at myself, I thought how drab I looked in my grey cotton. I made a gesture of impatience at my folly and picked up the riding habit to hang in my cupboard, deciding that I would take the first opportunity of asking Mrs. Polgrey if it was in order for me to use it. I was afraid I had acted on impulse by doing so this afternoon, but I had been stung into prompt action, I realised, by the attitude of Connan TreMellyn.

As I lifted the habit I saw the name on the waist band. It gave me a little start, as I suppose everything in that connection would do for some time. " Alice TreMellyn " was embossed in neat and tiny letters on the black satin facings.

Then I understood. That room had been her dressing room; the bedroom I had glimpsed, her bedroom. I wondered that Alvean had taken me there and given me her mother's clothes.

My heart felt as though it were leaping into my throat. This, I said to myself, is absurd. Where else could we have found a modern riding habit? Not in those chests in the attics she had spoken of; the clothes in those were used for charades.

I was being ridiculous. Why should I not wear Alice's riding habit? She had no need for it now. And was I not accustomed to wearing cast-off clothes?

Boldly I picked up the riding dress and hung it in my cupboard.

I was impelled to go to my window and looked along the line of windows, trying to place that one which would have been that of her bedroom. I thought I placed it.

In spite of myself I shivered. Then I shook myself. She would be glad I used her habit, I told myself. Of course she would be glad. Am I not trying to help her daughter?

I realised that I was reassuring myself—which was ridiculous.

What had happened to my commonsense? Whatever I told myself I could not hide the fact that I wished the dress had belonged to anyone but Alice.

When I had changed there was a knock on my door and I was relieved to see Mrs. Polgrey standing there.

" Do come in," I said. " You are just the lady I wished to see."

She came into my room, and I was very fond of her in that moment. There was an air of normality about her such as must inevitably put fancy to flight.

" I have been giving Miss Alvean a riding lesson," I said quickly, for I was anxious to have this matter of the dress settled before she could tell me why she had come. " And as I had no riding habit with me she found one for me. I believe it to have been her mother's." I went to my wardrobe and produced it.

Mrs. Polgrey nodded.

" I wore it this once. Perhaps it was wrong of me."

" Did you have the Master's permission to give her this riding lesson?"

" Oh yes, indeed. I made sure of that."

" Then there is nothing to worry about. He would have no objection to your wearing the dress. I can see no reason why you should not keep it in your room, providing of course you only wear it when giving Miss Alvean her riding lesson."

" Thank you," I said. " You have set my mind at rest."

Mrs. Polgrey bowed her head in approval. I could see that she was rather pleased that I had brought my little problem to her.

" Mr. Peter Nansellock is downstairs," she said.

" Yes, we saw him as we came in."

" The Master is not at home. And Mr. Peter has asked that you entertain him for tea—you and Miss Alvean."

" Oh, but should we. . . . I mean should I?"

" Well, yes, Miss, I think it would be in order. I think that is what the Master would wish, particularly as Mr. Peter suggests it. Miss Jansen, during the time she was here, often helped to entertain. Why, there was an occasion I remember, when she was invited to the dinner table."

"Oh!" I said, hoping I sounded duly impressed.

"You see, Miss, having no mistress in the house, makes it a little difficult at times; and when a gentleman expressly asks for your company—well, I really don't see what harm there could be in it. I have told Mr. Nansellock that tea will be served in the punch room and that I am sure you will be ready to join him and Miss Alvean. You have no objection?"

"No, no. I have no objection."

Mrs. Polgrey smiled graciously. "Then will you come down?"

"Yes, I will."

She sailed out as majestically as she had arrived; and I found myself smiling not without a little complacence. It was turning out to be a most enjoyable day.

When I reached the punch room, Alvean was not there, but Peter Nansellock was sprawling in one of the tapestry-covered chairs.

He leaped to his feet on my entrance.

"But this is delightful."

"Mrs. Polgrey has told me that I am to do the honours in the absence of Mr. TreMellyn."

"How like you, to remind me that you are merely the governess!"

"I felt," I replied, "that it was necessary to do so, since you may have forgotten."

"You are such a charming hostess! And indeed I never saw you look less like a governess than when you were giving Alvean her lesson."

"It was my riding habit. Borrowed plumes. A pheasant would look like a peacock, if it could acquire the tail."

"My dear Miss Pheasant, I do not agree. 'Manners makyth the man'—or woman—not fine feathers. But let me ask you this before our little Alvean appears. What do you think of this place? You are going to stay with us?"

"It is really more a question of how this place likes me, and whether the powers that be decide to keep me."

"Ah—the powers that be in this case are a little unaccountable, are they not? What do you think of old Connan?"

"The adjective you use is inaccurate, and it is not my place to give an opinion."

He laughed aloud showing white and perfect teeth. "Dear Governess," he said, "you'll be the death of me."

"I'm sorry to hear it."

"Though," he went on, "I have often thought that to die of laughing must be a very pleasant way to do so."

This banter was interrupted by the appearance of Alvean.

"Ah, the little lady herself!" cried Peter. "Dear Alvean, how good it is of you and Miss Leigh to allow me to take tea with you."

"I wonder why you want to," replied Alvean. "You never have before . . . except when Miss Jansen was here."

"Hush, hush! You betray me," he murmured.

Mrs. Polgrey came in with Kitty. The latter set the tray on a table, while Mrs. Polgrey lighted the spirit lamp. I saw that a canister of tea was on the tray. Kitty laid a cloth on a small table and brought in cakes and cucumber sandwiches.

"Miss, would you care to make the tea yourself?" asked Mrs. Polgrey. I said I would do so with pleasure, and Mrs. Polgrey signed to Kitty, who was staring at Peter Nansellock with an expression close to idolatry.

Kitty seemed reluctant to leave the room and I felt it was unkind to have dismissed her. I believed that Mrs. Polgrey was also to some extent under the spell of the man. It must be, I told myself, because he is such a contrast to the master. Peter managed to flatter with a look, and I had noticed that he was ready to lavish this flattery on all females; Kitty, Mrs. Polgrey and Alvean, no less than on myself.

So much for its worth! I told myself and I felt a little piqued, for the man had that comforting quality of making any woman in his company feel that she was an attractive one.

I made tea and Alvean handed him bread and butter.

"What luxury!" he cried. "I feel like a sultan with two beautiful ladies to wait on me."

"You're telling lies again," cried Alvean. "We're neither of us ladies, because I'm not grown up and Miss is a governess."

"What sacrilege!" he murmured, and his warm eyes were or me, almost caressingly. I felt uncomfortably embarrassed under his scrutiny.

I changed the conversation briskly. "I think Alvean will make a good horsewoman in time," I said. "What was your opinion?"

I saw how eagerly the girl waited on his words.

"She'll be the champion of Cornwall; you see!"

She could not hide her pleasure.

"And," he lifted a finger and wagged it at her—"don't forget whom you have to thank for it."

The glance Alvean threw at me was almost shy, and I felt suddenly happy, and glad that I was here. My resentment against life had never been so far away; I had ceased to envy my charming sister. At that moment there was only one person I wanted to be: That person was Martha Leigh, sitting in the punch room taking tea with Peter Nansellock and Alvean TreMellyn.

Alvean said: "It's to be a secret for a while."

"Yes, we're going to surprise her father."

"I'll be as silent as the grave."

"Why do people say 'silent as the grave'?" asked Alvean.

"Because," put in Peter, "dead men don't talk."

"Sometimes they have ghosts perhaps," said Alvean looking over her shoulder.

"What Mr. Nansellock meant," I said quickly, "was that he will keep our little secret. Alvean, I believe Mr. Nansellock would like some more cucumber sandwiches."

She leapt up to offer them to him; it was very pleasant to have her so docile and friendly.

"You have not paid a visit to Mount Widden yet, Miss Leigh," he said.

"It had not occurred to me to do so."

"That is a little unneighbourly. Oh, I know what you're going to say. You did not come here to pay calls; you came to be a governess."

" It is true," I retorted.

" The house is not as ancient nor as large as this one. It has no history, but it's a pleasant place and I'm sure my sister would be delighted if you and Alvean paid us a visit one day. Why not come over and take tea with us?"

" I am not sure . . ." I began.

" That it lies within your duties? I'll tell you how we'll arrange it. You shall bring Miss Alvean to take tea at Mount Widden. Bringing her to us and taking her home again, I am sure, would come well within the duties of the most meticulous governess."

" When shall we come?" asked Alvean.

" This is an open invitation."

I smiled. I knew what that meant. He was again talking for the sake of talking; he had no intention of asking me to tea. I pictured him, coming over to the house, attempting a flirtation with Miss Jansen who, by all accounts, was an attractive young woman. I knew his sort, I told myself.

The door opened suddenly and, to my embarrassment— which I hoped I managed to hide—Connan TreMellyn came in.

I felt as though I had been caught playing the part of mistress of the house in his absence.

I rose to my feet, and he gave me a quick smile. " Miss Leigh," he said, " is there a cup of tea for me?"

" Alvean," I said, " ring for another cup, please."

She got up to do so immediately but she had changed. Now she was alert, eager to do the right thing and please her father. It made her somewhat clumsy, and as she rose from her chair she knocked over her cup of tea. She flushed scarlet with mortification.

I said : " Never mind. Ring the bell. Kitty will clear it up when she comes."

I knew that Connan TreMellyn was watching with some amusement. If I had known he would return I should have been very reluctant to entertain Peter Nansellock to tea in the punch room, which I was sure my employer felt was definitely not my part of the house.

Peter said : " It was most kind of Miss Leigh to act as hostess. I begged her to do so, and she graciously consented."

"It was certainly kind," said Connan TreMellyn lightly.

Kitty came and I indicated the mess of tea and broken china on the carpet. "And please bring another cup for Mr. TreMellyn," I added.

Kitty was smirking a little as she went out. The situation evidently amused her. As for myself, I felt it ill became me. I was not the type to make charming play with the teacups and, now that the Master of the house had appeared, I felt awkward, even as I knew Alvean had. *I* must be careful to avoid disaster.

"Had a busy day, Connan?" asked Peter.

Connan TreMellyn then began to talk of complicated estate business, which I felt might have been to remind me that my duties consisted of dispensing tea and nothing else. I was not to imagine that I was in truth a hostess. I was there as an upper servant, nothing more.

I felt angry with him for coming in and spoiling my little triumph. I wondered how he would react when I presented him with the good little horsewoman I was determined Alvean was to become. He would probably make some slighting remark and show us such indifference that we should feel our trouble was wasted.

You poor child, I thought, you are trying to win the affections of a man who doesn't know the meaning of affection. Poor Alvean! Poor Alice!

Then it seemed to me that Alice had intruded into the punch room. In that moment I pictured her more clearly than I had ever done before. She was a woman of about my height, a little more slender at the waist—but then I had never gone in wholeheartedly for tight lacing—a trifle shorter. I could fit this figure into a black riding habit with blue collar and cuffs and black beaver hat. All that was vague and shadowy was the face.

The cup and saucer was brought to me and I poured out his tea. He was watching me, expecting me to rise and take it to him.

"Alvean," I said, "please pass this to your father."

And she was very eager to do so.

He said a brief "thanks," and Peter took advantage of the pause to draw me into the conversation.

" Miss Leigh and I met on the train on the day she arrived."

" Really?"

"Indeed, yes. Although of course she was not aware of my identity. How could she be? She had never heard then of the famous Nansellocks. She did not even know of the existence of Mount Widden. I knew her of course. By some strange irony of chance I shared her compartment."

" That," said Connan, " is very interesting." And he looked as though nothing could be less so.

" So," went on Peter, " it was a great surprise to her when she found that we were near neighbours."

" I trust," said Connan, " that it was not an unpleasant one."

" By no means," I said.

" Thank you, Miss Leigh, for those kind words," said Peter.

I looked at my watch, and said : " I am going to ask you to excuse Alvean and me. It is nearly five o'clock and we have our studies between five and six."

" And we must," said Connan, " on no account interfere with those."

" But surely," cried Peter, " on such an occasion there could be a little relaxation of the rules."

Alvean was looking eager. She was unhappy in her father's presence but she could not bear to leave it.

" I think it would be most unwise," I said, rising. " Come along, Alvean."

She threw me a look of dislike and I believed that I had forfeited the advance I had made that afternoon.

" Please, Papa . . ." she began.

He looked at her sternly. " My dear child, you heard what your governess said."

Alvean blushed and looked uncomfortable, but I was already saying " Good afternoon " to Peter Nansellock and making my way to the door.

In the schoolroom Alvean glared at me.

" Why do you have to spoil everything?" she demanded.

" Spoil?" I repeated. " Everything?"

"We could have done our reading any time . . . any time——"

"But we do our reading between five and six, not any time," I retorted, and my voice sounded the colder because I was afraid of the emotion which was rising in me. I wanted to explain to her : You love your father. You long for his approval. But, my dear child, you do not know the way to make it yours. Let me help you. But of course I said no such thing. I had never been demonstrative and could not begin to be so now.

"Come," I went on, "we have only an hour, so let us not waste a minute of that time."

She sat at the table sullenly glaring at the book which we were reading. It was Mr. Dickens's *Pickwick Papers* which I had thought would bring light relief into my pupil's rather serious existence.

She had lost her habitual enthusiasm; she was not even attending, for she looked up suddenly and said : "I believe you hate him. I believe you cannot bear to be in his company."

I replied : "I do not know to whom you refer, Alvean."

"You do," she accused. "You know I mean my father."

"What nonsense," I murmured; but I was afraid my colour would deepen. "Come," I said, "we are wasting time."

And so I concentrated on the book and told myself that we could not read together the nightly adventure concerning the elderly lady in curlpapers. That would be most unsuitable for a child of Alvean's age.


That night when Alvean had retired to her room I went for a stroll in the woods. I was beginning to look upon these woods as a place of refuge, a place in which to be quiet and think about my life while I wondered what shape it would take.

The day had been eventful, a pleasant day until Connan TreMellyn had come into it and disturbed the peace. I wondered if his business ever took him away for long periods —really long periods, not merely a matter of a few days. If this were so, I thought, I might have a chance of making Alvean into a happier little girl.

Forget the man, I admonished myself. Avoid him when possible. You can do no more than that.

It was all very well but, even when he was not present, he intruded into my thoughts.

I stayed in the woods until it was almost dusk. Then I made for the house, and I had not been in my room more than a few minutes when Kitty knocked.

" I thought I 'eard 'ee come in, Miss," she said. " Master be asking for 'ee. He be in his library."

" Then you had better take me there," I said, " for it is a room I have never visited."

I should have liked to comb my hair and tidy myself a little, but I had a notion that Kitty was constantly looking for one aspect of the relationship between any man or woman and I was not going to have her thinking that I was preening myself before appearing before the master.

She led me to a wing of the house which I had as yet not visited, and the vastness of Mount Mellyn was brought home to me afresh. These, I gathered, were the apartments which were set aside for his especial use, for they seemed more luxurious than any other part of the house which I had so far seen.

Kitty opened a door, and with that vacuous smile on her face announced : " Miss be here, Master."

" Thank you, Kitty," he said. And then, " Oh, come along in, Miss Leigh."

He was sitting at a table on which were leather-bound books and papers. The only light came from a rose quartz lamp on the table.

He said : " Do sit down, Miss Leigh."

I thought, He has discovered that I wore Alice's riding habit. He is shocked. He is going to tell me that my services are no longer required.

I held my head high, even haughtily, waiting.

" I was interested to learn this afternoon," he began, " that you had already made the acquaintance of Mr. Nansellock."

" Really?" The surprise in my voice was not assumed.

" Of course," he went on, " it was inevitable that you would meet him sooner or later. He and his sister are constant visitors at the house, but——"

"But you feel that it is unnecessary that he should make the acquaintance of your daughter's governess," I said quickly.

"That necessity, Miss Leigh," he replied reprovingly, "is surely for you or him to decide."

I felt embarrassed and I stumbled on : "I imagine that you feel that, as a governess, it is unbecoming of me to be . . . on terms of apparently equal footing with a friend of your family."

"I beg you, Miss Leigh, do not put words into my mouth which I had no intention of uttering. What friends you make, I do assure you, must be entirely your own concern. But your aunt, in a manner of speaking, put you under my care when she put you under my roof, and I have asked you to come here that I may offer you a word of advice on a subject which, I fear, you may think a little indelicate."

I was flushing scarlet and my embarrassment was not helped by the fact that this, I was sure, secretly amused him.

"Mr. Nansellock has a reputation for being . . . how shall I put it . . . susceptible to young ladies."

"Oh!" I cried, unable to suppress the exclamation, so great was my discomfort.

"Miss Leigh." He smiled, and for a moment his face looked almost tender. "This is in the nature of a warning."

"Mr. TreMellyn," I cried, recovering myself with an effort, "I do not think I am in need of such a warning."

"He is very handsome," he went on, and the mocking note had come back to his voice. "He has a reputation for being a charming fellow. There was a young lady here before you, a Miss Jansen. He often called to see her. Miss Leigh, I do beg of you not to misunderstand me. And there is another thing I would also ask : Please do not take all that Mr. Nansellock says too seriously."

I heard myself say in a high-pitched voice unlike my habitual tone : "It is extremely kind of you, Mr. TreMellyn, to concern yourself with my welfare."

"But of course I concern myself with your welfare. You are here to look after my daughter. Therefore it is of the utmost importance to me."

He rose and I did the same. I saw that this was dismissal.

He came swiftly to my side and placed his hand on my shoulder.

" Forgive me," he said. " I am a blunt man, lacking in those graces which are so evident in Mr. Nansellock. I merely wish to offer you a friendly warning."

For a few seconds I looked into those cool light eyes and I thought I had a fleeting glimpse of the man behind the mask. I was sobered suddenly and, in a moment of bewildering emotion, I was deeply conscious of my loneliness, of the tragedy of those who are alone in the world with no one who really cares for them. Perhaps it was self-pity. I do not know. My feelings in that moment were so mixed that I cannot even at this day define them.

" Thank you," I said; and I escaped from the library back to my room.

Each day Alvean and I went to the field and had an hour's riding. As I watched the little girl on Buttercup I knew that her father must have been extremely impatient with her, for the child, though not a born rider perhaps, would soon be giving a good account of herself.

I had discovered that every November a horse show was held in Mellyn village, and I had told Alvean that she should certainly enter for one of the events.

It was enjoyable planning this, because Connan TreMellyn would be one of the judges and we both imagined his astonishment when a certain rider, who came romping home with first prize, was his daughter who he had sworn would never learn to ride.

The triumph in that dream was something Alvean and I could both share. Hers was of course the more admirable emotion. She wanted to succeed for the sake of the love she bore her father; for myself I wanted to imply : See, you arrogant man, I have succeeded where you failed !

So every afternoon, I would put on Alice's riding habit (I had ceased to care to whom it had previously belonged, for it had become mine now) and we would go to the field and there I would put Alvean through her paces.

On the day we tried her first gallop we were elated.

Afterwards she returned to the stables with me and I watched her run on ahead after we had left the horses there. Every now and then she would jump into the air—a gesture, I thought, of complete joyousness. I knew she was seeing herself at the show anticipating that glorious moment when her father stared at her in astonishment and cried : " You . . . Alvean ! My dear child, I am proud of you."

I was smiling to myself as I crossed the lawn in her wake. When I entered the house she was nowhere to be seen, and I pictured her taking the stairs several at a time.

This was more like the normal, happy child I intended her to become.

I mounted the first flight of stairs and came to a dark landing, when there was a step on the next flight, and I heard a quick gasp and voice which said : " Alice ! "

For a second my whole body seemed to freeze. Then I saw that Celestine Nansellock was standing on the stairs ; she was gripping the banisters and was so white that I thought she was going to faint.

I understood. It was she who had spoken. She had seen me in Alice's riding habit and she believed in that second that I *was* Alice . . . or her ghost.

" Miss Nansellock," I said quickly to reassure her, " Alvean and I have been having a riding lesson."

She swayed a little ; her face had turned a greyish colour.

" I'm sorry I startled you," I went on.

She murmured : " For the moment I thought——"

" I think you should sit down, Miss Nansellock. You've had a shock." I bounded up the stairs and took her arm. " Would you care to come into my bedroom and sit down awhile?"

She nodded, and I noted that she was trembling.

" I am so sorry to have upset you," I said as I threw open the door of my room. We went in, and I put her gently into a chair.

" Shall I ring for brandy?" I asked.

She shook her head. " I'm all right now. You did startle me, Miss Leigh. I see now it is the clothes."

" It is a little dark on that landing," I said.

She repeated : " For the moment, I thought. . . ." Then

she looked at me again, fearfully, perhaps hopefully. I believed she was thinking that I was an apparition which had assumed the face of Martha Leigh, the governess, and would change at any moment.

I hastened to reassure her. " It's only these clothes," I said.

" Mrs. TreMellyn had a habit exactly like that. I remember the collar and cuffs so well. We went riding together . . . only a day or so before . . . You see, we were great friends, always together, and then. . . ." She turned away and wiped her eyes.

" You thought I was Mrs. TreMellyn returned from the dead." I said. " I understand."

" It was so foolish of me. It seems so odd that you should have a riding habit . . . so exactly like hers."

" This was hers," I said.

She was startled. She put out a hand and touched the skirt. She held it between thumb and forefinger and her eyes had a hazy look as though she were staring into the past.

I went on quickly : " I have to give Alvean riding lessons, and I lacked the suitable clothes. The child took me to what I now know to have been her mother's apartments, and found this for me. I asked Mrs. Polgrey if it were in order for me to wear it and she assured me that it was."

" I see," said Celestine. " That explains everything. Please don't mention my folly, Miss Leigh. I'm glad no one else saw it."

" But anyone might have been startled, particularly as——"

" As what?"

" As there seems to be this feeling about Alice . . . about Mrs. TreMellyn."

" What feeling?"

" Perhaps there isn't a feeling. Perhaps it is my imagination only, but I did imagine that there was a belief in the house that she was not . . . at rest."

" What an extraordinary thing to say ! Why should she not be at rest? Who told you this?"

" I . . . I'm not sure," I floundered. " Perhaps it is merely my imagination. Perhaps no one suggested anything, and the idea just came to me. I'm sorry that I upset you."

"You must not be sorry, Miss Leigh. You have been kind to me. I feel better now. She stood up. "Don't tell anyone I was so silly. So you are giving Alvean riding lessons. I am glad. Tell me, are you getting along with her better now? I fancied, when you arrived, that there was a little antagonism . . . on her part."

"She is the kind of child who would automatically be antagonistic to authority. Yes, I think we are becoming friends. These riding lessons have helped considerably. By the way, they are secret from her father."

Celestine Nansellock looked a little shocked, and I hurried on : "Oh, it is only her good progress which is a secret. He knows about the lessons. Naturally I asked his permission first. But he does not realise how well she is coming along. It is to be a surprise."

"I see," said Celestine. "Miss Leigh, I do hope she is not over-strained by these lessons."

"Strained? But why? She is a normal healthy child."

"She is highly strung. I wonder whether she has the temperament to make a rider."

"She is so young that we have a chance of forming her character, which will have it's effect on her temperament. She is enjoying her lessons and is very eager to surprise her father."

"So she is becoming your friend, Miss Leigh. I am glad of that. Now I must go. Thank you again for your kindness. And do remember . . . not a word to anyone."

"Certainly not, if it is your wish."

She smiled and went out.

I went to the mirror and looked at myself—I'm afraid this was becoming a habit since I had come here—and murmured : "That might be Alice . . . apart from the face." Then I half closed my eyes and let the face become blurred while I imagined a different face there.

Oh yes, it must have been a shock for Celestine.

And I was not to say anything. I was very willing to agree to this. I wondered what Connan TreMellyn would say if he knew that I was going about in his wife's clothes and frightened practical people like Celestine Nansellock when they saw me in dim places.

I felt he would not wish me to continue to look so like Alice. So, since I needed Alice's clothes for my riding lessons with Alvean, and since I was determined they should continue, that I might have the pleasure of saying, I told you so! to Alvean's father, I was as anxious as Celestine Nansellock that nothing should be said about our encounter on the landing.

A week passed and I felt I was slipping into a routine. Lessons in the schoolroom and the riding field progressed favourably. Peter Nansellock came over to the house on two occasions, but I managed to elude him. I was deeply conscious of Connan TreMellyn's warning and I knew it to be reasonable. I faced the fact that I was stimulated by Peter Nansellock and that I could very easily find myself in a state of mind when I was looking forward to his visits. I had no intention of placing myself in that position for I did not need Connan TreMellyn to tell me that Peter Nansellock was a philanderer.

I thought now and then of his brother Geoffry, and I concluded that Peter must be very like him; and when I thought of Geoffry I thought also of Mrs. Polgrey's daughter of whom she had never spoken; Jennifer with the " littlest waist you ever saw," and a way of keeping herself to herself until she had lain in the hay or the gillyflowers with the fascinating Geoffry—the outcome of which had been that one day she walked into the sea.

I shivered to contemplate the terrible pitfalls which lay in wait for unwary women. There were unattractive ones like myself who depended on the whims of others for a living; but there were those even more unfortunate creatures, those who attracted the roving eyes of philanderers and found one day that the only bearable prospect life had to offer was its end.

My interest in Alvean's riding lessons and her father's personality had made me forget little Gillyflower temporarily. The child was so quiet that she was easily forgotten. Occasionally I heard her thin reedy voice, in that peculiar off-key singing out of doors or in the house. The Polgreys' room was immediately below my own, and Gillyflower's was next to theirs, so that when she sang in her own room her voice would float up to me.

I used to say to myself when I heard it : If she can learn
songs she can learn other things.

I must have been given to day-dreams, for side by side with
that picture of Connan TreMellyn, handing his daughter the
first prize for horse-jumping at the November horse show and
giving me an apologetic and immensely admiring and apprecia-
tive glance at the same time, there was another picture. This
was of Gilly sitting at the schoolroom table side by side with
Alvean, while I listened to whispering in the background :
" This could never have happened but for Miss Martha Leigh.
You see she is a wonder with the children. Look what she has
done for Alvean . . . and now for Gilly."

But at this time Alvean was still a stubborn child and Gillyflower elusive and, as the Tapperty girls said : " With a tile
loose in the upper story."

Then into those more or less peaceful days came two events
to disturb me.

The first was of small moment, but it haunted me and I
could not get it out of my mind.

I was going through one of Alvean's exercise books, marking
her sums, while she was sitting at the table writing an essay;
and as I turned the pages of the exercise book a piece of paper
fell out.

It was covered with drawings. I had already discovered that
Alvean had a distinct talent for drawing, and one day, when the
opportunity offered itself, I intended to approach Connan
TreMellyn about this, for I felt she should be encouraged. I
myself could teach her only the rudiments of the art, but I
believed she was worthy of a qualified drawing teacher.

The drawings were of faces. I recognised one of myself. It
was not bad. Did I really look as prim as that? Not always, I
hoped. But perhaps that was how he saw me. There was
her father . . . several of him. He was quite recognisable too.
I turned the page and this was covered with girls' faces. I was
not sure who they were meant to be. Herself? No . . . that
was Gilly, surely. And yet it had a look of herself.

I stared at the page. I was so intent that I did not realise she
had leaned across the table until she snatched it away.

" That's mine," she said.

" And that," I retaliated, " is extremely bad manners."

" You have no right to pry."

" My dear child, that paper was in your arthmetic book."

" Then it had no right to be there."

" You must take your revenge on the paper," I said lightly. And then more seriously : " I do beg of you not to snatch things in that ill-mannered way."

" I'm sorry," she murmured still defiantly.

I turned back to the sums, to most of which she had given inaccurate answers. Arithmetic was not one of her best subjects. Perhaps that was why she spent so much of her time drawing faces instead of getting on with her work. Why had she been so annoyed? Why had she drawn those faces which were part Gilly's, part her own?"

I said : " Alvean, you will have to work harder at your sums."

She grunted sullenly.

" You don't seem to have mastered the rules of practice nor even simple multiplication. Now if your arithmetic were half as good as your drawing I should be very pleased."

Still she did not answer.

" Why did you not wish me to see the faces you had drawn? I thought some of them quite good."

Still no answer.

" Particularly," I went on, " that one of your father."

Even at such a time the mention of his name could bring that tender, wistful curve to her lips.

" And those girl's faces. Do tell me who they were supposed to be—you or Gilly?"

The smile froze on her lips. Then she said almost breathlessly : " Who did you take them for, Miss?"

" Whom," I corrected gently.

" *Whom* did you take them for then?"

" Well, let me look at them again."

She hesitated, then she brought out the paper, and handed it to me ; her eyes were eager.

I studied the faces. I said : " This one could be either you or Gilly."

" You think we're alike then?"

" N . . . no. I hadn't thought so until this moment."

" And now you do," she said.

" You are of an age, and there often seems to be a resemblance between young people."

" I'm not like her!" she cried passionately. " I'm not like that . . . idiot."

" Alvean, you must not use such a word. Don't you realise that it is extremely unkind?"

" It's true. But I'm not like her. I won't have you say it. If you say it again I'll ask my father to send you away. He will . . . if I ask him. I only have to ask and you'll go."

She was shouting, trying to convince herself of two things, I realised. One that there was not the slightest resemblance between herself and Gilly, and the other that she only had to ask her father for something, and her wishes would be granted.

Why? I asked myself. What was the reason for this vehemence?

There was a shut-in expression on her face.

I said, calmly looking at the watch pinned to my grey cotton bodice : " You have exactly ten minutes in which to finish your essay."

I drew the arithmetic book towards me and pretended to give it my attention.

The second incident was even more upsetting.

It had been a moderately peaceful day, which meant that lessons had gone well. I had taken my late evening stroll in the woods and when I returned I saw two carriages drawn up in front of the house. One I recognised as from Mount Widden so I guessed that either Peter or Celestine was visiting. The other carriage I did not know, but I noticed a crest on it, and it was a very fine carriage. I wondered to whom it belonged before I told myself that it was no concern of mine.

I went swiftly up the back stairs to my apartment.

It was a warm night and as I sat at my window I heard music coming from another of the open windows. I realised that Connan TreMellyn was entertaining guests.

I pictured them in one of the rooms which I had not even seen. Why should you, I asked myself. You are only a governess. Connan TreMellyn, his gaunt body clothed elegantly, would be presiding at the card table or perhaps sitting with his guests listening to music.

I recognised the music as from Mendelssohn's *Midsummer Night's Dream* and I felt a sudden longing to be down there among them; but I was astonished that this desire should be greater than any I had ever had to be present at Aunt Adelaide's *soirées* or the dinner parties Phillida gave. I was overcome with curiosity and could not resist the temptation to ring the bell and summon Kitty or Daisy who always knew what was going on and were only too happy to impart that knowledge to anyone who was interested to hear it.

It was Daisy who came. She looked excited.

I said : " I want some hot water, Daisy. Could you please bring it for me?"

" Why yes, Miss," she said.

" There are guests here to-night, I understand."

" Oh yes, Miss. Though it's nothing to the parties we used to have. I reckon now the year's up, the Master will be entertaining more. That's what Mrs. Polgrey says."

" It must have been very quiet during the last year."

" But only right and proper . . . after a death in the family."

" Of course. Who are the guests to-night?"

" Oh, there's Miss Celestine and Mr. Peter of course."

" I saw their carriage." My voice sounded eager and I was ashamed. I was no better than any gossiping servant.

" Yes, and I'll tell you who else is here."

" Who?"

" Sir Thomas and Lady Treslyn."

She looked conspiratorial as though there was something very important about these two.

" Oh?" I said encouragingly.

" Though," went on Daisy, " Mrs. Polgrey says that Sir Thomas bain't fit to go gallivanting at parties, and should be abed."

" Why, is he ill?"

" Well, he'll never see seventy again and he's got one of those bad hearts. Mrs. Polgrey says you can go off sudden with a heart like that, and don't need no pushing neither. Not that——"

She stopped and twinkled at me. I longed to ask her to continue, but I felt it was beneath my dignity to do so. Disappointingly she seemed to pull herself up sharply.

"*She's* another kettle of fish."

"Who?"

"Why, Lady Treslyn of course. You ought to see her. She's got a gown cut right down to here and the loveliest flowers on her shoulder. She's a real beauty, and you can see she's only waiting——"

"I gather she is not of the same age as her husband."

Daisy giggled. "They say there's nearly forty years' difference in their ages, and she'd like to pretend it was fifty."

"You don't seem to like her."

"Me? Well, if I don't, some do!" That sent Daisy into hysterical laughter again, and as I looked at her ungainly form in her tight clothes and listened to her wheezy laughter, I was ashamed of myself for sharing the gossip of a servant, so I said : "I *would* like that hot water, Daisy."

Daisy subsided and went off to get it, leaving me with a clearer picture of what was happening in that drawing room.

I was still thinking of them when I had washed my hands and unpinned my hair preparatory to retiring for the night.

The musicians had been playing a Chopin waltz and it had seemed to spirit me away from my governess's bedroom and tantalise me with pleasures outside my reach—a dainty beauty, a place of salons such as that somewhere in this house, wit, charm, the power to make the chosen man love me.

I was startled by such thoughts. What had they to do with a governess such as myself.

I went to the window. The weather had been fine and warm for so long that I did not believe it could continue. The autumn mists would soon be with us and I heard that they and the gales which blew from the south-west were, as Tapperty would say, "something special in these parts."

I could smell the sea and hear the gentle rhythm of the waves. The "voices" were starting up in Mellyn Cove.

And then suddenly I saw a light in a dark part of the house and I felt the goose-pimples rise on my flesh. I knew that window belonged to the room to which Alvean had taken me to choose my riding habit. It was Alice's dressing room.

The blind had been down. I had not noticed that before. Indeed I was sure it had not been like that earlier in the evening because, since I had known that that was Alice's room, I had made a habit—which I regretted and of which I had tried to cure myself—of glancing at the window whenever I looked out of my own.

The blind was of thin material, for behind it I distinctly saw the light. It was a faint light but there was no mistaking it. It moved before my astonished eyes.

I stood at my window staring out and, as I did so, I saw a shadow on the blind. It was that of a woman.

I heard a voice close to me saying: " It is Alice!" and I realised that I had spoken aloud.

I'm dreaming, I told myself. I'm imagining this.

Then again I saw the figure silhouetted against the blind.

My hands which gripped the window sill were trembling as I watched that flickering light. I had an impulse to summon Daisy or Kitty, or go to Mrs. Polgrey.

I restrained myself, imagining how foolish it should look. So I remained staring at the window.

And after a while all was darkness.

I stood at my window for a long time watching, but I saw nothing more.

They were playing another Chopin waltz in the drawing room, and I stood until I was cold even on that warm September night.

Then I went to bed but I could not sleep for a long time.

And at last, when I did sleep, I dreamed that a woman came into my room; she was wearing a riding habit with blue collar and cuffs, trimmed with braid and ball fringe. She said to me : " I was not on that train, Miss Leigh. You wonder where I was. It is for you to find me."

Through my dreams I heard the whispering of the waves in the caves below; and the first thing I did on rising next

morning—which I did as soon as dawn appeared in the sky—
was to go to my window and look across at the room which—
little more than a year ago—had belonged to Alice.

The blinds were drawn up. I could clearly see the rich
blue velvet curtains.

# IV

It was about a week later when I first saw Linda Treslyn.

It was a few minutes past six o'clock. Alvean and I had put
away our books and had gone down to the stables to look at
Buttercup who we thought had strained a tendon that
afternoon.

The farrier had seen her and given her a poultice. Alvean
was really upset, and this pleased me because I was always
delighted to discover her softer feelings.

" Don't 'ee fret, Miss Alvean," Joe Tapperty told her.
" Buttercup 'll be right as two dogs on a bright and frosty
morning afore the week's out; you see! Jim Bond, he be the
best horse-doctor between here and Land's End, I do tell 'ee."

She was cheered and I told her that she should take Black
Prince in Buttercup's place to-morrow.

She was excited about this for she knew Black Prince would
test her mettle, and I was glad to see that her pleasure was only
faintly tinged with apprehension.

As we came out of the stables I looked at my watch.

" Would you care for half an hour's stroll through the
gardens?" I asked. " We have half an hour to spare."

To my surprise she said she would, and we set off.

The plateau on which Mount Mellyn stood was a piece of
land a mile or so wide. The slope to the sea was steep but there
were several zigzag paths which made the going easier. The
gardeners spent a great deal of time on this garden which was
indeed beautiful with the flowering shrubs which grew so
profusely in this part. At various points arbours had been set
up, constructed of trellis work around which roses climbed.

They were beautiful even as late as this and their perfume hung on the air.

One could sit in these arbours and gaze out to sea; and from these gardens the south side of the house was a vision of grandeur, rising nobly, a pile of grey granite there on the top of the cliff like a mighty fortress. It was inevitable that the house should have a defiant air, as though it represented a challenge, not only to the sea but to the world.

We made our way down those sweet-smelling paths and were level with the arbour before we noticed that two people were there.

Alvean gave a little gasp and, following her gaze, I saw them. They were sitting side by side and close. She was very dark and one of the most beautiful women I had ever seen; her features were strongly marked and she wore a gauzy scarf over her hair, and in this gauze sequins glistened. I thought that she looked like someone out of *A Midsummer Night's Dream*— Titania perhaps, although I had always imagined her fair. She had that quality of beauty which attracts the eyes as a needle is attracted by a magnet. You have to look whether you want to or not; you have to admire. Her dress was pale mauve of some clinging material such as chiffon and it was caught at the throat with a big diamond brooch.

Connan spoke first. " Why," he said, " it is my daughter with her governess. So, Miss Leigh, you and Alvean are taking the air."

" It is such a pleasant evening," I said, and I made to take Alvean's hand, but she eluded me in her most ungracious manner.

" May I sit with you and Lady Treslyn, Papa?" she asked.

" You are taking a walk with Miss Leigh," he said. " Do you not think that you should continue to do so?"

" Yes," I answered for her. " Come along, Alvean."

Connan had turned to his companion. " We are very fortunate to have found Miss Leigh. She is . . . admirable!"

" The perfect governess this time, I hope for your sake, Connan," said Lady Treslyn.

I felt awkward, as though I were in the position of a horse standing there while they discussed my points. I was sure he was aware of my discomfiture and rather amused by it. There were times when I believed he was a very unpleasant person.

I said, and my voice sounded very chilly: "I think it is time we turned back. We were merely taking an airing before Alvean retires for the night. Come, Alvean," I added. And I seized her arm so firmly that I drew her away.

"But," protested Alvean, "I want to stay. I want to talk to you, Papa."

"But you can see I am engaged. Some other time, my child."

"No," she said. "It is important . . . now."

"It cannot be all that important. Let us discuss it to-morrow."

"No . . . no . . . Now!" Alvean's voice had a hysterical note in it; I had never before known her defy him so utterly.

Lady Treslyn murmured: "I see Alvean is a very determined person."

Connan TreMellyn said coolly: "Miss Leigh will deal with this matter."

"Of course. The perfect governess. . . ." There was a note of mockery in Lady Treslyn's voice, and it goaded me to such an extent that I seized Alvean's arm roughly and almost dragged her back the way we had come.

She was half sobbing, but she did not speak until we were in the house.

Then she said: "I hate her. You know, don't you, Miss Leigh, that she wants to be my new mamma."

I said nothing then. I thought it dangerous to do so because I always felt that it was so easy to be overheard. It was only when we reached her room and I had followed her in and shut the door that I said: "That was an extraordinary remark to make. How could she wish to be your mamma when she has a husband of her own?"

"He will soon die."

"How can you know that?"

"Everybody says they are only waiting."

I was shocked that she should have heard such gossip and I thought: I will speak to Mrs. Polgrey about this. They must be careful what they say in front of Alvean. Is it those girls, Daisy and Kitty . . . or perhaps Joe Tapperty or his wife?

" She's always here," went on Alvean. " I won't let her take my mother's place. I won't let anybody."

" You are becoming quite hysterical about improbabilities, and I must insist that you never allow me to hear you say such things again. It is degrading to your papa."

That made her thoughtful. How she loves him! I thought. Poor little Alvean, poor lonely child!

A little while before, I had been sorry for myself as I stood in that beautiful garden and was forced to be quizzed by the beautiful woman in the arbour. I had said to myself : " It is not fair. Why should one person have so much, and others nothing? Should I be beautiful in chiffon and diamonds? Perhaps not as Lady Treslyn was, but I am sure they would be more becoming than cotton and merino and a turquoise brooch which had belonged to my grandmother."

Now I forgot to be sorry for myself, and my pity was all for Alvean.

I had seen Alvean to bed and had returned to my room, conscious of a certain depression. I kept thinking of Connan TreMellyn out there in the arbour with Lady Treslyn, asking myself if he were still there and what they talked about. Each other! I supposed. Of course Alvean and I had interrupted a flirtation. I felt shocked that he should indulge in such an undignified intrigue, for it seemed wholly undignified to me, since the lady had a husband to whom she owed her allegiance.

I went to the window and I was glad that it did not give me a view of the south gardens and the sea. I leaned my elbows on the sill and looked out at the scented evening. It was not quite dark yet but the sun had disappeared and the twilight was on us. My eyes turned to the window where I had seen the shadow on the blind.

The blinds were drawn up and I could see the blue curtains clearly. I stared at them, fixedly. I don't know what I expected. Was it to see a face appear at the window, a beckoning hand? There were times when I could laugh at myself for my fancies, but the twilight hour was not one of them.

Then I saw the curtains move, and I knew that someone was in that room.

I was in an extraordinary mood that evening. It had something to do with meeting Connan TreMellyn and Lady Treslyn together in the arbour, but I had not sufficiently analysed my feelings at this date to understand it. I felt our recent encounter to have been humiliating but I was ready to risk another which might be more so. Alice's room was not in my part of the house but I was completely at liberty to walk in the gardens if I wished to. If I were caught I should look rather foolish. But I was reckless. I did not care. Thoughts of Alice obsessed me. There were times when I felt such a burning desire to discover what mystery lay behind her death that I was prepared to go to any lengths.

So I slipped out of my room. I left my wing of the house and went along the gallery to Alice's dressing room. I knocked lightly on the door and, with my heart beating like a sledge hammer, I swiftly opened it.

For a second I saw no one. Then I detected a movement by the curtains. Someone was hiding behind them.

"Who is it?" I asked, and my voice successfully hid the trepidation I was feeling.

There was no answer, but whoever was behind those curtains was very eager not to be discovered.

I strode across the room, drew aside the curtains and saw Gilly cowering there.

The lids of her blank blue eyes fluttered in a terrified way. I put out a hand to seize her and she shrank from me towards the window.

"It's all right, Gilly," I said gently. "I won't hurt you."

She continued to stare at me, and I went on: "Tell me, what are you doing here?"

Still she said nothing. She had begun to stare about the room as though she were asking someone for help and for a moment I had the uncanny feeling that she *saw* something—or someone—I could not see.

" Gilly," I said, " you know you should not be in this room, do you not?" She drew away from me, and I repeated what I had said.

Then she nodded and immediately afterwards shook her head.

" I am going to take you back to my room, Gilly. Then we'll have a little talk."

I put my arm about her; she was trembling. I drew her to the door but she came very reluctantly, and at the threshold of the room she looked back over her shoulder; then she cried out suddenly : " Madam . . . come back, Madam. Come . . . *now*!"

I led her firmly from the room and shut the door behind us, then almost had to drag her along to my bedroom.

Once there I firmly shut my door and stood with my back against it. Her lips were trembling.

" Gilly," I said, " I do want you to understand that I won't hurt you. I want to be your friend." The blank look persisted and taking a shot in the dark I went on : " I want to be your friend as Mrs. TreMellyn was."

That startled her and the blank look disappeared for a moment. I had stumbled on another discovery. Alice had been kind to this poor child.

" You went there to look for Mrs. TreMellyn, did you not?"

She nodded.

She looked so pathetic that I was moved to a demonstration of feeling unusual with me. I knelt down and put my arms about her; now our faces were level.

" You can't find her, Gilly. She is dead. It is no use looking for her in this house."

Gilly nodded and I was not sure what she implied—whether she agreed with me that it was no use, or whether she believed that she could find Mrs. TreMellyn in the house.

" So," I went on, " we must try to forget her, mustn't we Gilly?"

The pale lids fell over the eyes to hide them from me.

" We'll be friends," I said. " I want us to be. If we were friends, you wouldn't be lonely, would you?"

She shook her head, and I fancied that the eyes which surveyed me had lost something of their blankness; she was not trembling now, and I was sure that she was no longer afraid of me.

Then suddenly she slipped out of my grasp and ran to the door. I did not pursue her and, as she opened the door and turned to look back at me, there was a faint smile on her lips. Then she was gone.

I believed that I had established a little friendliness between us. I believed that she had lost her fear of me.

Then I thought of Alice, who had been kind to this child. I was beginning to build up the picture of Alice more clearly in my mind.

I went to the window and looked across the L-shaped building to the window of the room, and I thought of that night when I had seen the shadow on the blind.

My discovery of Gilly did not explain that. It was no child I had seen silhouetted there. It had been a woman.

Gilly might hide herself in Alice's room, but the shadow I had seen on the blind that night did not belong to her.

It was the next day when I went to Mrs. Polgrey's room for a cup of tea. She was delighted to invite me. " Mrs. Polgrey," I had said, " I have a matter which I feel to be of some importance, and I should very much like to discuss this with you.

She was bridled with pride. I could see that the governess who sought her advice must be, in her eyes, the ideal governess.

" I shall be delighted to give you an hour of my company and a cup of my best Earl Grey," she told me.

Over the teacups she surveyed me with an expression bordering on the affectionate.

" Now, Miss Leigh, pray tell me what it is you would ask of me."

" I am a little disturbed," I told her, stirring my tea thoughtfully. " It is due to a remark of Alvean's. I am sure that she listens to gossip, and I think it most undesirable in a child of her age."

" Or in any of us as I am sure a young lady of your good

sense would feel," replied Mrs. Polgrey with what I could not help feeling was a certain amount of hypocrisy.

I told her how we had walked in the cliff gardens and met the master with Lady Treslyn. " And then," I went on, " Alvean made this offensive remark. She said that Lady Treslyn hoped to become her mamma."

Mrs. Polgrey shook her head. She said : " What about a spoonful of whisky in your tea, Miss? There's nothing like it for keeping up the spirits."

I had no desire for the whisky but I could see that Mrs. Polgrey had, and she would have been disappointed if I had refused to join her in her tea tippling, so I said : " A small teaspoonful, please, Mrs. Polgrey."

She unlocked the cupboard, took out the bottle and measured out the whisky even more meticulously than she measured her tea. I found myself wondering what other stores she kept in that cupboard of hers.

Now we were like a pair of conspirators and Mrs. Polgrey was clearly enjoying herself.

" I fear you will find it somewhat shocking, Miss," she began.

" I am prepared," I assured her.

" Well, Sir Thomas Treslyn is a very old man and only a few years ago he married this young lady, a play-actress, some say, from London. Sir Thomas went there on a visit and returned with her. He set the neighbourhood agog, I can tell you, Miss."

" I can well believe that."

" There's some that say she's one of the handsomest women in the country."

" I can believe that too."

" Handsome is as handsome does."

" But it remains handsome outwardly," I added.

" And men can be foolish. The Master has his weakness," admitted Mrs. Polgrey.

" If there is gossip I am most anxious that it shall not reach Alvean's ears."

" Of course you are, Miss. But gossip there is, and that child's got ears like a hare's."

" Do you think Daisy and Kitty chatter?"

Mrs. Polgrey came closer and I smelt the whisky on her breath. I was startled, wondering whether she could smell it on mine. " Everybody chatters, Miss."

" I see."

" There's some as say that they'm not the sort to wait for blessing of clergy."

" Well, perhaps they are not."

I felt wretched. I hate this, I told myself. It's so sordid. So horrible for a sensitive girl like Alvean.

" The Master is impulsive by nature and in his way he is fond of the women."

" So you think——"

She nodded gravely. " When Sir Thomas dies there'll be a new mistress in this house. All they have to wait for now is for him to go. Mrs. TreMellyn, her . . . her's already gone."

I did not want to ask the question which came to my lips but it seemed as though there were some force within me which would not let me avoid it. " And was it so . . . when Mrs. TreMellyn was alive?"

Mrs. Polgrey nodded slowly. " He visited her often. It started almost as soon as she came. Sometimes he rides out at night and we don't see him till morning. Well, he'm Master and 'tis for him to make his own rules. 'Tis for us to cook and dust and housekeep, or teach the child '. . . whatsoever we'm here for. And there's an end of it."

" So you think that Alvean is only repeating what everyone knows? When Sir Thomas dies Lady Treslyn *will* be her new mamma."

" There's some on us that thinks it's more than likely, and some that wouldn't be sorry to see it. Her ladyship's not the kind to interfere much with our side of the house; and 'tis better to have these things regularised, so I do say." She went on piously : " I'd sonner see the Master of the house I serve living in wedlock than in sin, I do assure you. And so would we all."

" Could we warn the girls not to chatter, before Alvean, of these matters?"

" As well try to keep a cuckoo from singing in the spring. I could wollop them two till I dropped with exhaustion and still they'd gossip. They can't help it. It be in their blood. And there's nothing much to choose between one girl and the other. Nowadays——"

I nodded sympathetically. I was thinking of Alice, who had watched the relationship between her husband and Lady Treslyn. No wonder she had been prepared to run away with Geoffry Nansellock.

Poor Alice! I thought. What you must have suffered, married to such a man.

Mrs. Polgrey was in such an expansive mood that I felt I might extend the conversation to other matters in which I happened to be interested.

I said: " Have you ever thought of teaching Gilly her letters?"

" Gilly! Why that would be a senseless thing to do. You must know, Miss, that Gilly is not quite as she should be." Mrs. Polgrey tapped her forehead.

" She sings a great deal. She must have learned the songs. If she could learn songs, could she not learn other things?"

" She's a queer little thing. Reckon it was the way she come. I don't often talk about such things, but I'll swear you've been hearing about my Jennifer." Mrs. Polgrey's voice changed a little, became touched with sentiment. I wondered if it had anything to do with the whisky and how many spoonfuls she had taken that day. " Sometimes I think that Gillyflower is a cursed child. Us didn't want her; why, she was only a little thing in a cradle . . . two months old . . . when Jennifer went. The tide brought her body in two days after. 'Twas found there in Mellyn Cove."

" I'm sorry," I said gently.

Mrs. Polgrey shook herself free of sentiment. " Her'd gone, but there was still Gilly. And right from the first her didn't seem quite like other children."

" Perhaps she sensed the tragedy," I ventured.

Mrs. Polgrey looked at me with hauteur. " We did all we could for her—me and Mr. Polgrey. He thought the world of her."

" When did you notice that she was not like other children?"

" Come to think of it it would be when she was about four years old."

" That would be how many years ago?"

" About four."

" She must be the same age as Alvean. She looks so much younger."

" Born a few months after Miss Alvean. They'd play together now and then . . . being in the house, you do see, and being of an age. There was an accident when she was, let me see . . . she'd be approaching her fourth birthday."

" What sort of accident?"

" She was playing in the drive there, not far from the lodge gates. The Mistress were riding along the drive to the house. She was a great horsewoman, the Mistress. Gilly, her darted out from the bushes and caught a blow from the horse. She fell on her head. It was a mercy she weren't killed."

" Poor Gilly," I said.

" The Mistress were distressed. Blamed herself although 'twas no blame to her. Gilly should have known better. She'd been told to watch the roads often enough. Darted out after a butterfly, like as not. Gilly has always been taken with birds and flowers and insects and such like. The Mistress made much of her after that. Gilly used to follow her about and fret when she was away."

" I see," I said.

Mrs. Polgrey poured herself another cup of tea and asked me if I would have another. I declined. I saw her tilt the teaspoonful of whisky into the cup. " Gilly," she went on, " were born in sin. Her had no right to come into the world. It looks like God be taking vengeance on her, for it do say that the sins of the fathers be visited on the children."

I felt a sudden wave of anger sweep over me. I was in revolt against such distortions. I felt I wanted to slap the face of the woman who could sit there calmly drinking her whisky and accepting the plight of her little granddaughter as God's will.

I marvelled too at the ignorance of these people, who did not connect Gilly's strangeness with the accident she had had but believed it was due punishment for her parents' sins meted out to her by a vengeful God.

But I said nothing, because I believed that I was battling against strange forces in this house and, if I were going to succeed, I needed all the allies I could command.

I wanted to understand Gilly. I wanted to soothe Alvean. I was discovering a fondness for children in myself which I had not known I possessed before I came into this house. Indeed since I had come here I had begun to discover quite a lot about myself.

There was one other reason why I wanted to concentrate on the affairs of these two children; doing so prevented my thinking of Connan TreMellyn and Lady Treslyn. Thoughts of them made me feel quite angry; at this time I called my anger " disgust."

So I sat in Mrs. Polgrey's room, listening to her talk, and I did not tell her what was in my mind.

There was excitement throughout the house because there was to be a ball—the first since Alice's death—and for a week there was little talk of anything else. I found it difficult to keep Alvean's attention on her lessons; Kitty and Daisy were almost hysterical with delight, and I was constantly coming upon them clasped in each other's arms in attempts to waltz.

The gardeners were busy. They were going to bring in flowers from the greenhouses to decorate the ballroom and were eager that the blooms should do them credit; and invitations were being sent out all over the countryside.

" I fail to see," I said to Alvean, " why you should feel this excitement. Neither you nor I will take part in the ball."

Alvean said dreamily : " When my mother was alive there were lots of balls. She loved them. She danced beautifully. She used to come in and show me how she looked. She was beautiful. Then she would take me into the solarium and I would sit in a recess behind the curtains and look down on the hall through the peep."

" The peep?" I asked.

" Ah, you don't know." She regarded me triumphantly. I suppose it was rather pleasing to her to discover that her governess, who was constantly shocked by her ignorance, should herself be discovered in that state.

"There is a great deal about this house that I do not know," I said sharply. "I have not seen a third of it."

"You haven't seen the solarium," she agreed. "There are several peeps in this house. Oh, Miss, you don't know what peeps are, but a lot of big houses have them. There's even one in Mount Widden. My mother told me that it is where the ladies used to sit when the men were feasting and it was considered no place for them among the men. They could look down and watch, but they must not *be* there. There's one in the chapel . . . a sort of one. We call it the lepers' squint there. They couldn't come in because they were lepers, so they could only look through the squint. But I shall go to the solarium and look down on the hall through the peep up there. Why Miss, you ought to come with me. Please do."

"We'll see," I said.

On the day of the ball Alvean and I took our riding lesson as usual, only instead of riding Buttercup Alvean was mounted on Black Prince.

When I had first seen the child on that horse I had felt a faint twinge of uneasiness, but I stifled this, for I told myself but if she were going to become a rider she must get beyond the Buttercup stage. Once she had ridden Prince she would gain more confidence, and very likely never wish to go back to Buttercup.

We had done rather well for the first few lessons. Prince behaved admirably and Alvean's confidence was growing. We had no doubt, either of us, that she would be able to enter for at least one of the events at the November horse show.

But this day we were not so fortunate. I suspect that Alvean's thoughts were on the ball rather than on her riding. She was still diffident with me, except perhaps during our riding lessons, when oddly enough we were the best of friends; but as soon as we had divested ourselves of our riding kit we seemed automatically to slip back to the old relationship. I had tried to change this, without success.

We were about half-way through the lesson when Prince broke into a gallop. I had not allowed her to gallop unless she was on the leading rein; and in any case there was little room for that sort of thing in the field; and I wanted to be absolutely sure of Alvean's confidence before I allowed her more licence.

All would have been well if Alvean had kept her head and remembered what I had taught her, but as Prince started to gallop she gave a little cry of fear and her terror seemed immediately to communicate itself to the frightened animal.

Prince was off; the thud of his hoofs on the turf struck terror into me. I saw Alvean, forgetting what I had taught her, swaying to one side.

It was all over in a flash because as soon as it happened I was on the spot. I was after her immediately. I had to grasp Prince's bridle before he reached the hedge for I believed that he might attempt to jump and that would mean a nasty fall for my pupil. Fear gave me new strength and I had his rein in my hands and had pulled him up just as he was coming up to the hedge. I brought him to a standstill while a white-faced trembling Alvean slid unharmed to the ground.

" It's all right," I said. " Your mind was wandering. You haven't reached that stage when you can afford to forget for a moment what you're doing."

I knew that was the only way to deal with her. Shaken as she was, I made her remount Prince; I knew that she had become terrified of horses through some such incident as this. I had overcome that fear and I was not going to allow it to return.

She obeyed me, although reluctantly. But by the time our lesson was finished she was well over her fright, and I knew that she would want to ride next day. So I was more satisfied that day that I would eventually make a rider of Alvean than I had been before.

It was when we were leaving the field that she suddenly burst out laughing.

" What is it?" I asked, turning my head, for I was riding ahead of her.

" Oh, Miss," she cried. " You've split!"

" What *do* you mean?"

" Your dress has split under the armhole. Oh. . . it's getting worse and worse."

I put my hand behind my back and realised what had

happened. The riding habit had always been a little too tight for me and during my efforts to save Alvean from a nasty fall the sleeve seam had been unable to stand the extra strain.

I must have shown my dismay, for Alvean said: "Never mind, Miss. I'll find you another. There *are* more, I know."

Alvean was secretly amused as we went back to the house. Odd that I had never seen her in such good spirits. It was however somewhat disconcerting to discover that the sight of my discomfiture could give her so much pleasure that she could forget the danger through which she had so recently passed.

The guests had begun to arrive. I had been unable to resist taking peeps at them from my window. The approach was filled with carriages, and the dresses I had glimpsed made me gasp with envy.

The ball was being held in the great hall which I had seen earlier that day. Before that I had not been in it since my arrival, for I always used the back staircase. It was Kitty who had urged me to take a peep. "It looks so lovely, Miss. Mr. Polgrey's going round like a dog with two tails. He'll murder one of us if anything happens to his plants."

I thought I had rarely seen a setting so beautiful. The beams had been decorated with leaves. "An old Cornish custom," Kitty told me, "specially at Maytime. But what's it matter, Miss, if this be September. Reckon there'll be other balls now the period of mourning be up. Well, so it should be. Can't go on mourning for ever, can 'ee. You might say this is a sort of Maytime, don't 'ee see? 'Tis the end of one old year and the beginning of another like."

I said, as I looked at the pots of hothouse blooms which had been brought in from the greenhouses and the great wax candles in their sconces, that the hall did Mr. Polgrey and his gardeners great credit. I pictured how it would look when those candles were lighted and the guests danced in their colourful gowns, their pearls and their diamonds.

I wanted to be one of the guests. How I wanted it! Kitty had begun to dance in the hall, smiling and bowing to an imaginary partner. I smiled. She looked so abandoned, so full of joy.

Then I thought that I ought not to be here like this. It was quite unbecoming. I was as bad as Kitty.

I turned away and there was a foolish lump in my throat.

Alvean and I had supper together that evening. She obviously could not dine with her father in the small dining room, as he would be busy with his guests.

" Miss," she said, " I've put a new riding habit for you in your cupboard."

" Thank you," I said; " that was thoughtful of you."

" Well, you couldn't go riding in that!" cried Alvean, pointing derisively at my lavender gown.

So it was only that I might not miss a riding lesson for want of the clothes, that she had taken such trouble on my behalf! I should have known that.

I asked myself in that moment whether I was not being rather foolish. Did I expect more than people were prepared to give? I was nothing to Alvean except when I could help her to attain what she wanted. It was as well to remember that.

I looked down distastefully at my lavender cotton gown. It was the favourite of the two which had been specially made for me by Aunt Adelaide's dressmaker when I had obtained this post. One was of grey—a most unbecoming colour to me —but I fancied I looked a little less prim, a little less of a governess in the lavender. But how becoming it seemed, with its bodice buttoned high at the neck and the cream lace collar and the cream lace cuffs to match. I realised I was comparing it with the dresses of Connan TreMellyn's guests.

Alvean said : " Hurry and finish, Miss. Don't forget we're going to the solarium."

" I suppose you have your father's permission . . ." I began.

" Miss, I always peep from the solarium. Everybody knows I do. My mother used to look up and wave to me." Her face puckered a little. " To-night," she went on, as though she were speaking to herself, " I'm going to imagine that she's down there after all . . . dancing there. Miss, do you think people come back after they're dead?"

" What an extraordinary question! Of course not."

" You don't believe in ghosts then. Some people do. They

D

say they've seen them. Do you think they lie when they say
they see ghosts, Miss?"

" I think that people who say such things are the victims of
their own imaginations."

" Still," she went on dreamily, " I shall imagine she is there
. . . dancing there. Perhaps if I imagine hard enough I shall
see her. Perhaps I shall be the victim of my imagination."

I said nothing because I felt uneasy.

" If she *were* coming back," she mused, " she would come to
the ball, because dancing was one of the things she liked doing
best." She seemed to remember me suddenly. " Miss," she
went on, " if you'd rather not come to the solarium with me, I
don't mind going alone."

" I'll come," I said.

" Let's go now."

" We will first finish our meal," I told her.

The vastness of the house continued to astonish me, as I
followed Alvean along the gallery, up stone staircases through
several bedrooms, to what she told me was the solarium. The
roof was of glass and I understood why it had received its
name. I thought it must be unbearably warm in the heat of the
summer.

The walls were covered with exquisite tapestries depicting
the story of the Great Rebellion and the Restoration. There
was the execution of the first Charles, and the second shown in
the oak tree, his dark face peering down at the Roundhead
soldiers; there were pictures of his arrival in England, of his
coronation and a visit to his shipyards.

" Never mind those now," said Alvean. " My mother used
to love being here. She said you could see what was going on.
There are two peeps up here. Oh, Miss, don't you want to
see them?"

I was looking at the escritoire, at the sofa and the gilt-backed
chairs; and I saw her sitting here, talking to her daughter here
—dead Alice who seemed to become more and more alive as
the days passed.

There were windows at each end of this long room, high
windows curtained with heavy brocade. The same brocade
curtains hung before what I presumed to be doors of which

there appeared to be four in this room—the one by which we
had entered, another at the extreme end of the room and one
other on either side. But I was wrong about the last two.

Alvean had disappeared behind one of these curtains and
called to be in a muffled voice, and when I went to her I found
we were in an alcove. In the wall was a star-shaped opening,
quite large but decorated so that one would not have noticed it
unless one had been looking for it.

I gazed through it and saw that I was looking down into the
chapel. I could see clearly all but one side of the chapel—the
small altar with the triptych and the pews.

" They used to sit up here and watch the service if they were
too ill to go down, my mother told me. They had a priest in
the house in the old days. My mother didn't tell me that. She
didn't know about the history of the house. Miss Jansen told
me. She knew a lot about the house. She loved to come up
here and look through the peep. She used to like the chapel
too."

" You were sorry when she went, Alvean, I believe."

" Yes, I was. The other peep's on the other side. Through
that you can see into the hall."

She went to the other side of the room and drew back the
hangings there. In the wall was a similar star-shaped opening.

I looked down on the hall and caught my breath for it was a
magnificent sight. Musicians were on the dais and the guests
who had not yet begun to dance, stood about talking.

There were a great many people down there and the sound
of the chatter rose clearly up to us. Alvean was breathless
beside me, her eyes searching . . . in a manner which made
me shiver slightly. Did she really believe that Alice would
come from the tomb because she loved to dance?

I felt an impulse to put my arm about her and draw her to
me. Poor motherless child, I thought. Poor bewildered little
creature!

But of course I overcame that impulse. Alvean had no desire
for my sympathy, I well knew.

I saw Connan TreMellyn in conversation with Celestine
Nansellock, and Peter was there too. If Peter was one of the
most handsome men I had ever seen, Connan, I told myself,

was the most elegant. There were few in that brilliant assembly whose faces were known to me, but I did see Lady Treslyn there. Even among the magnificently brilliant gathering she stood out. She was wearing a gown which seemed to be composed of yards and yards of chiffon, which was the colour of flame, and I guessed that she was one of the few who would have dared to wear such a colour. Yet had she wanted to attract attention to herself she could not have chosen anything more calculated to bring this result. Her dark hair looked almost black against the flame; her magnificent bust and shoulders were the whitest I had ever seen. She wore a band of diamonds in her hair, which was like a tiara, and diamonds sparkled about her person.

Alvean's attention was caught by her even as mine was and her brows were drawn together in a frown.

"*She* is there then," she murmured.

I said: "Is her husband present?"

"Yes, the little old man over there talking to Colonel Penlands."

"And which is Colonel Penlands?" She pointed the colonel out to me, and I saw with him a bent old man, white-haired and wrinkled. It seemed incredible that he should be the husband of that flamboyant creature.

"Look!" whispered Alvean. "My father is going to open the ball. He used to do it with Aunt Celestine, and at the same time my mother used to do it with Uncle Geoffry. I wonder who he will do it with this time."

"With whom he will do it," I murmured absentmindedly, but my attention, like Alvean's was entirely on the scene below.

"The musicians are going to start now," she said. "They always start with the same tune. Do you know what it is? It's the *Furry* Dance. Some of our ancestors came from Helston way and it was played then and it always has been since. You watch! Papa and Mamma used to dance the first bar or so with their partners, and all the others fell in behind."

The musicians had begun, and I saw Connan take Celestine by the hand and lead her into the centre of the hall; Peter Nansellock followed, and he had chosen Lady Treslyn to be his partner.

I watched the four of them dance the first steps of the traditional dance, and I thought, Poor Celestine! Even gowned as she was in blue satin she looked ill at ease in that quartette. She lacked the elegance and nonchalance of Connan, the beauty of Lady Treslyn and the dash of her brother.

I thought it was a pity that he had to choose Celestine to open the ball, but that was tradition. The house was filled with tradition. Such and such was done because it always had been done, and often for no other reason. Well, that was the way in great houses.

Neither Alvean nor I seemed to tire of watching the dancers. An hour passed and we were still there. I fancied that Connan glanced up once or twice. Did he know of his daughter's habit of watching? I thought that it must be Alvean's bedtime, but that perhaps on such an occasion a little leniency would be permissible.

I was fascinated by the way she watched the dancers tirelessly, fervently, as though she were certain that if she looked long enough she would see that face there which she longed to see.

It was now dark, but the moon had risen. I turned my eyes from the dance floor to look through the glass roof at that great gibbous moon which seemed to be smiling down on us. No candles for you, it seemed to say; you are banished from the gaiety and the glitter, but I will give you my soft and tender light instead.

The room, touched by moonlight, had a supernatural character all its own. I felt in such a room anything might happen.

I turned my attention back to the dancers. They were waltzing down there and I felt myself swaying to the rhythm. No one had been more astonished than myself when I had proved to be a good dancer. It had brought me partners at the dances to which Aunt Adelaide had taken me in those days when she had thought it possible to find a husband for me; alas for Aunt Adelaide, those invitations to the dances had not been extended to other pursuits.

And as I listened entranced I felt a hand touch mine and I was so startled that I gave an audible gasp.

I looked down. Standing beside me was a small figure, and I was relieved to see that it was only Gillyflower.

" You have come to see the dancers?" I said.

She nodded.

She was not quite so tall as Alvean and could not reach the star-shaped peep, so I lifted her in my arms and held her up. I could not see very clearly in the moonlight but I was sure the blankness had left her eyes.

I said to Alvean : " Bring a stool and Gillyflower can stand on it; then she will be able to see quite easily."

Alvean said : " Let her get it herself."

Gilly nodded and I put her on the floor; she ran to the stool and brought it with her. I thought, since she understands, why can she not talk with the rest of us?

Alvean did not seem to want to look now that Gilly had come. She moved away from the peep and as the musicians below began the opening bars of that waltz which always enchanted me—I refer to Mr. Strauss's *Blue Danube Waltz*—Alvean began to dance across the floor of the solarium.

The music seemed to have affected my feet. I don't know what came over me that night. It was as though some spirit of daring had entered into my body, but I could not resist the strains of the *Blue Danube Waltz.* I danced towards Alvean. I waltzed as I used to in those ballrooms to which I went accompanied by Aunt Adelaide, but I was sure that I never danced as I did that night in the solarium.

Alvean cried out with pleasure; I heard Gilly laugh too.

Alvean cried : " Go on, Miss. Don't stop, Miss. You do it well."

So I went on dancing with an imaginary partner, dancing down the moonlit solarium with the lopsided moon smiling in at me. And when I reached the end of the room a figure moved towards me and I was no longer dancing alone.

" You're exquisite," said a voice, and there was Peter Nansellock in his elegant evening dress, and he was holding me as it was the custom to hold a partner in the waltz.

My feet faltered. He said : "No . . . no. Listen, the children are protesting. You must dance with me, Miss Leigh, as you were meant to dance with me."

We went on dancing. It was as though my feet, having begun would not stop.

But I said: "This is most unorthodox."

"It is most delightful," he answered

"You should be with the guests."

"It is more fun to be with you."

"You forget——"

"That you are a governess? I could, if you would allow me to."

"There is no earthly reason why you should forget."

"Only that I think you would be happier if we could all forget it. How exquisitely you dance!"

"It is my only drawing room accomplishment."

"I am sure it is one of many that you are forced to squander on this empty room."

"Mr. Nansellock, do you not think this little jest has been played out?"

"It is no jest."

"I shall now rejoin the children." We had come close to them and I saw little Gilly's face enrapt, and I saw the admiration in Alvean's. If I stopped dancing I should revert to my old position; while I went on dancing I was an exalted being.

I thought how ridiculous were the thoughts I was entertaining; but to-night I wanted to be ridiculous, I wanted to be frivolous.

"So here he is."

To my horror I saw that several people had come into the solarium, and my apprehension did not lessen when I saw the flame-coloured gown of Lady Treslyn among them, for I was sure that wherever that flame-coloured dress was there Connan TreMellyn would be.

Somebody started to clap; others took it up. Then *The Blue Danube* ended.

I put my hand to my hair in my acute embarrassment. I knew that dancing had loosened the pins.

I thought: I shall be dismissed to-morrow for my irresponsibility, and perhaps I deserve it.

"What an excellent idea," said someone. "Dancing in

moonlight. What could be more agreeable? And one can hear the music up here almost as well as down there."

Someone else said : "This is a beautiful ballroom, Connan."

"Then let us use it for that purpose," he answered.

He went to the peep and shouted through it : "Once more —*The Beautiful Blue Danube.*"

Then the music started.

I turned to Alvean and I gripped Gilly by the hand. People were already beginning to dance. They were talking together and they did not bother to lower their voices. Why should they? I was only the governess.

I heard a voice : "The governess. Alvean's, you know."

"Forward creature! I suppose another of Peter's light ladies."

"I'm sorry for the poor things. Life must be dull for them."

"But in broad moonlight! What could be more depraved?"

"The last one had to be dismissed, I believe."

"This one's turn will come."

I was blushing hotly. I wanted to face them all, to tell them that my conduct was very likely less depraved than that of some of them.

I was furiously angry and a little frightened. I was aware of Connan's face in moonlight for he was standing near to me, looking at me, I feared, in a manner signifying the utmost disapproval, which I was sure he was feeling.

"Alvean," he said, " go to your room and take Gillyflower with you."

She dared not disobey when he spoke in those tones.

I said as coolly as I could : "Yes, let us go."

But as I was about to follow the children I found my arm gripped and Connan had come a little closer to me.

He said : "You dance extremely well, Miss Leigh. I could never resist a good dancer. Perhaps it is because I scarcely excel in the art myself."

"Thank you," I said. But he still held my arm.

"I am sure," he went on, " that *The Blue Danube* is a favourite of yours. You looked . . . enraptured." And with that he swung me into his arms and I found that I was dancing with him among his guests . . . I in my lavender cotton and my turquoise brooch, they in their chiffons and velvets, their emeralds and diamonds.

I was glad of the moonlight. I was so overcome with shame, for I believed that he was angry and that his intention was to shame me even further.

My feet caught the rhythm and I thought to myself: Always in future *The Blue Danube* will mean to me a fantastic dance in the solarium with Connan TreMellyn as my partner.

"I apologise, Miss Leigh," he said, "for my guests' bad manners."

"It is what I must expect and no doubt what I deserve."

"What nonsense," he said, and I told myself that I was dreaming, for his voice which was close to my ear sounded tender.

We had come to the end of the room and, to my complete astonishment, he had whirled me through the curtains and out of the door. We were on a small landing between two flights of stone stairs in a part of the house which I had not seen before.

We stopped dancing, but he still kept his arms about me. On the wall a paraffin lamp of green jade burned; its light was only enough to show me his face. It looked a little brutal I thought.

"Miss Leigh," he said, "you are very charming when you abandon your severity."

I caught my breath with dismay for he was forcing me against the wall and kissing me.

I was horrified as much by my own emotions as by what was happening. I knew what that kiss meant: You are not averse to a mild flirtation with Peter Nansellock; therefore why not with me?

My anger was so great that it was beyond my control. With all my might I pushed him from me and he was so taken by surprise that he reeled backwards. I lifted my skirts and began to run as fast as I could down the stairs.

I did not know where I was but I went on running blindly and eventually found the gallery and so made my way back to my own room.

There I threw myself on to my bed and lay there until I recovered my breath.

There is only one thing I can do, I told myself, and that is get away from this house with all speed. He has now made his intentions clear to me. I have no doubt at all that Miss Jansen was dismissed because she refused to accept his attentions. The man is a monster. He appeared to think that anyone whom he employed belonged to him completely. Did he imagine he was an eastern pasha? How dared he treat me in such a way!

There was a constricted feeling in my throat which made me feel as though I were going to choke. I was more desperately unhappy that I had ever been in my life. It was due to him. I would not face the truth, but I really cared more deeply than I had about anything else that he should regard me with such contempt.

These were the danger signals.

I had need now of my common sense.

I rose from my bed and locked my door. I must make sure that my door was locked during the last night I would spend in this house. The only other way to my room would be through Alvean's room and the schoolroom, and I knew he would not attempt to come that way.

Nevertheless I felt unsafe.

Nonsense, I said to myself, you can protect yourself. If he should dare enter your room you could pull the bell rope immediately.

The first thing I would do would be to write to Phillida. I sat down and tried to do this but my hands were trembling and my handwriting was so shaky that the note looked ridiculous.

I could start packing.

I did this.

I went to the cupboard and pulled open the door. For a moment I thought someone was standing there, and I cried out in alarm; which showed the nervous state to which I had been reduced. I saw what it was almost immediately: The riding habit which Alvean had procured for me. She must have hung it in my wardrobe herself. I had forgotten all about this afternoon's little adventure for what had happened in the solarium and after had temporarily obliterated everything else.

I packed my trunk in a very short time, for my possessions were not many. Then, as I was more composed, I sat down and wrote the letter to Phillida.

When I had finished writing I heard the sound of voices below and I went to my window. Some of the guests had come out on to the lawn, and I saw them dancing down there. More came out.

I heard someone say: " It's such a heavenly night. That moon is too good to miss."

I stood back in the shadows watching, and eventually I saw what I had been waiting for. There was Connan. He was dancing with Lady Treslyn; his head was close to hers. I imagined the sort of things he was saying to her.

Then I turned angrily from the window and tried to tell myself that the pain I felt within me was disgust.

I undressed and went to bed. I lay sleepless for a long time and when I did sleep I had jumbled dreams that were of Connan, myself and Lady Treslyn. And always in the background of these dreams was that shadowy figure who had haunted my thoughts since the day I had come here.

I awoke with a start. The moon was still visible and in the room in my half awakened state I seemed to see the dark shape of a woman.

I knew it was Alice. She did not speak yet she was telling me something. " You must not go from here. You must stay. I cannot rest. You can help me. You must help us all."

I was trembling all over. I sat up in bed. Now I saw what had startled me. When I had packed I had left the door of the cupboard open, and what appeared to be the ghost of Alice was only her riding habit.

I was late up next morning because when I had slept I had done so deeply, and it was Kitty banging on the door with my hot water who awakened me. She could not get in and clearly she wondered what was wrong.

I leaped out of bed and unlocked the door.

" Anything wrong, Miss?" she asked.

" No," I answered sharply, and she waited a few seconds for my explanation of the locked door.

I was certainly not going to give it to her, and she was so full of last night's ball that she was not as interested as she would have been had there been nothing else to absorb her.

" Wasn't it lovely, Miss? I watched from my room. They danced on the lawn in the moonlight. My dear life, I never saw such a sight. It was like it used to be when the mistress was here. You look tired, Miss. Did they keep you awake?"

" Yes," I said, " they did."

" Oh, well, it's all over now. Mr. Polgrey's already having the plants taken back. Fussing over them like a hen with her chicks, he be. The hall do look a sorry mess this morning, I can tell 'ee. It's going to take Daisy and me all day to get it cleared up, you see."

I yawned and she put my hot water by the hip bath and went out. In five minutes' time she was back again.

I was half clothed, and wrapped a towel about me to shield myself from her too inquisitive eyes.

" It's Master," she said. " He's asking for you. Wants to see you right away. In the punch room. He said, ' Tell Miss Leigh it is most urgent.' "

" Oh," I said.

" Most urgent, Miss," Kitty repeated, and I nodded.

I finished washing and dressed quickly. I guessed what this meant. Very likely there would be some complaint. I would be given my notice because I was inefficient in some way. I began to think of Miss Jansen, and I wondered whether something of this nature had happened in her case. " Here one day and gone the next." Some trumped-up case against her. What if he should trump up a case against me?

That man is quite unscrupulous! I thought.

Well, I would be first. I would tell of my decision to leave, before he had a chance to dismiss me.

I went down to the punch room prepared for battle.

He was wearing a blue riding jacket and he did not look as though he had been up half the night.

" Good morning, Miss Leigh," he said, and to my astonishment he smiled.

I did not return the smile. " Good morning," I said. " I

have already packed my bags and should like to leave as soon as possible."

" Miss Leigh!" His voice was reproachful, and I felt an absurd joy rising within me. I was saying to myself : He doesn't want you to go. He's not asking you to go. He's actually going to apologise.

I heard myself say in a high, prim voice, which I should have hated in anyone else as selfrighteous and priggish : " I consider it the only course open to me after——"

He cut in : " After my outrageous conduct of last night. Miss Leigh, I am going to ask you to forget that. I fear the excitement of the moment overcame me. I forgot with whom I was dancing. I have asked you to overlook my depravity on this occasion, and to say generously—I am sure you are generous, Miss Leigh—we will draw a veil over that unpleasant little incident and go on as we were before."

I had a notion that he was mocking me but I was suddenly so happy that I did not care.

I was not going. The letter to Phillida need not be posted. I was not to leave in disgrace.

I inclined my head and I said: " I accept your apology, Mr. TreMellyn. We will forget this unpleasant and unfortunate incident."

Then I turned and went out of the room.

I found that I was taking the stairs three at a time; my feet were almost dancing as they had been unable to resist dancing last night in the solarium.

The incident was over. I was going to stay. The whole house seemed to warm to me. I knew in that moment that if I had to leave this place I should be quite desolate.

I had always been given to self-analysis and I said to myself, Why this elation? Why would you be so wretched if you had to leave Mount Mellyn?

I had the answer ready : Because there is some secret here. Because I want to solve it. Because I want to help those two bewildered children; for Alvean is as bewildered as poor little Gillyflower.

But perhaps that was not the only reason. Perhaps I was a little more than interested in the Master of the house.

Perhaps had I been wise I should have recognised the danger signals. But I was not wise. Women in my position rarely are.

That day Alvean and I took our riding lesson as usual. It went off well and the only remarkable thing about it was that I wore the new riding habit. It was different from the other, for it consisted of the tightly fitting dress of light-weight material and with it was a jacket, tailored almost like a man's.

I was delighted that Alvean showed no sign of fear after her small mishap of the day before, and I said that in a few days' time we might attempt a little jumping.

We arrived back at the house and I went to my room to change before tea.

I took off the jacket, thinking of the shock these things had given me in the night, and I laughed at my fears, for I was in very high spirits that day. I slipped out of the dress with some difficulty (Alice had been just that little bit more slender than I), put on my grey cotton—Aunt Adelaide had warned me that it was advisable not to wear the same dress two days running— and was about to hang up the riding habit in the cupboard when I felt something in the pocket of the coat.

I thrust in my hand in surprise, for I was sure I had had my hands in the pockets before this and nothing had been there.

There was nothing actually in the pocket now but there was something beneath the silk lining. I laid the jacket on the bed and examining it soon discovered the concealed pocket. I merely had to unhook it and there it was; in it was a book, a small diary.

My heart beat very fast as I took it out because I knew that this belonged to Alice.

I hesitated for a moment but I could not resist the impulse to look inside. Indeed I felt in that moment that it was my duty to look inside.

On the fly leaf was written in a rather childish hand " Alice TreMellyn." I looked at the date. It was the previous year so I knew that she had written in that diary during the last year of her life.

I turned the leaves. If I had expected a revelation of character I was soon disappointed. Alice had merely used this as a record for her appointments. There was nothing in this book to make me understand her more.

I looked at the entries. " Mount Widden to tea." " The Trelanders to dine." " C to Penzance." " C due back."

Still it was written in Alice's handwriting and that made it exciting to me.

I turned to the last entry in the book. It was under the twentieth of August. I looked back to July. Under the fourteenth was written : " Treslyns and Trelanders to dine at M.M." " See dressmaker about blue satin." " Do not forget to see Polgrey about flowers." " Send Gilly to dressmaker." " Take Alvean for fitting." " If jeweller has not sent brooch by sixteenth go to see him." And on the sixteenth : " Brooch not returned must go along to-morrow morning. Must have it for dinner party at Trelanders on eighteenth."

It all sounded very trivial. What I had believed might be a great discovery was nothing very much. I put the book back into the pocket and went along to have tea in the schoolroom.

While Alvean and I were reading together a sudden thought struck me. I didn't know the exact date of Alice's death but it must have been soon after she was writing those trivial things in her diary. How odd that she should have thought it worth while to make those entries when she was planning to leave her husband and daughter for another man.

It suddenly became imperative to know the exact date of her death.

Alvean had had tea with her father because several people had come to pay duty calls and compliment Connan on last night's ball.

Thus I was free to go out alone. So I made my way down to Mellyn village and to the churchyard where I presumed Alice's remains would have been buried.

I had not seen much of the village before as I had had little opportunity of going so far except when we went to church on Sunday, so it was an interesting tour of exploration.

I ran almost all the way downhill and was very soon in the village. I reminded myself that it would be a different matter toiling uphill on my way back.

The village in the valley nestled about the old church, the grey tower of which was half covered in ivy. There was a pleasant little village green and a few grey stone houses clustered round it among which was a row of very ancient cottages which I guessed were of the same age as the church. I promised myself that I would make a closer examination of the village later. In the meantime I was most eager to find Alice's grave.

I went through the lych gate and into the churchyard. It was very quiet there at this time of the day. I felt I was surrounded by the stillness of death and I almost wished that I had brought Alvean with me. She could have pointed out her mother's grave.

How could I find it among these rows of grey crosses and headstones, I wondered as I looked about me helplessly. Then I thought, the TreMellyns would no doubt have some grand memorial to their dead; I must look for the most splendid vault, and I am sure I shall quickly find it that way.

I saw a huge vault of black marble and gilt not far off. I made for this and quickly discovered it to be that of the Nansellock family.

A sudden thought occurred to me. Geoffry Nansellock would lie here, and he died on the same night as Alice. Were they not found dead together?

I discovered the inscription engraved on the marble. This tomb contained the bones of defunct Nansellocks as far back as the middle seventeen hundreds. I remembered that the family had not been in Mount Widden as early as there had been TreMellyns at Mount Mellyn.

It was not difficult to find Geoffry's name for his was naturally the last entry on the list of the dead.

He died last year, I saw, on the 17th of July.

I was all eagerness to go back and look at the diary and check up that date.

I turned from the tomb and as I did so I saw Celestine Nansellock coming towards me.

"Miss Leigh," she cried. "I thought it was you."

I felt myself flush because I remembered seeing her last

night among the guests in the solarium, and I wondered what she was thinking of me now.

"I took a stroll down to the village," I answered, "and found myself here."

"I see you're looking at my family tomb."

"Yes. It's a beautiful thing."

"If such a thing can be beautiful. I come here often," she volunteered. "I like to bring a few flowers for Alice."

"Oh, yes," I stammered.

"You saw the TreMellyn vault, I suppose?"

"No."

"It's over here. Come and look."

I stumbled across the long grass to the vault which rivalled that of the Nansellocks in its magnificence.

On the black slab was a vase of Michaelmas daisies—large perfect blooms that looked like mauve stars.

"I've just put them there," she said. "They were her favourite flowers."

Her lips trembled, and I thought she was going to burst into tears.

I looked at the date and I saw it was that on which Geoffry Nansellock had died.

I said: "I shall have to go back now."

She nodded. She seemed too moved to be able to speak. I thought then: She loved Alice. She seems to have loved her more than anyone else.

It was on the tip of my tongue to tell her about the diary I had discovered, but I hesitated. The memory of last night's shame was too near to me. I might be reminded that I was, after all, only the governess. And what right had I, in any case, to meddle in their affairs?

I left her there and as I went away I saw her sink to her knees. I turned again later and saw that her face was buried in her hands and her shoulders were heaving.

I hurried back to the house and took out the diary. So on the 16th of July last year, on the day before Alice was supposed to have eloped with Geoffry Nansellock, she had written in her diary that if her brooch was not returned on the next day she must go along to the jeweller as she needed it for a dinner party to be held on the 18th.

That entry had not been made by a woman who was planning to elope.

I felt that I had almost certain proof in my hands that the body which had been found with Geoffry Nansellock's on the wrecked train was not Alice's.

I was back at the old question. What had happened to Alice? If she was not lying inside the black marble vault, where was she?


## V

I felt I had discovered a vital clue but it took me no further. Each day I woke up expectant, but of the days which passed one was very like another. Sometimes I pondered on several courses of action. I wondered whether I would go to Connan TreMellyn and tell him that I had seen his wife's diary and that it clearly showed she had not been planning to leave.

Then I told myself I did not quite trust Connan TreMellyn, and there was one thought concerning him which I did not want to explore too thoroughly. I had already begun to ask myself the question : Suppose Alice was not on the train, and something else happened to her, who would be most likely to know what that was? Could it be Connan TreMellyn?

There was Peter Nansellock. I might discuss this matter with him, but he was too frivolous; he turned every line of conversation towards the flirtatious.

There was his sister. She was the most likely person. I knew that she had been fond of Alice; they must have been the greatest friends. Celestine was clearly the one in whom I could best confide. And yet I hesitated. Celestine belonged to that other world into which I had been clearly shown on more than one occasion, I had no right to intrude. It was not for me, a mere governess, to set myself up as investigator.

The person in whom I might confide was Mrs. Polgrey, but

again I shrank from doing this. I could not forget her spoonfuls of whisky and her attitude towards Gilly.

So I decided that for the time being I would keep my suspicions to myself. October was upon us. I found the changing seasons delightful in this part of the world. The blustering south-west wind was warm and damp, and it seemed to carry with it the scent of spices from Spain. I had never seen so many spiders' webs as I did that October. They draped themselves over the hedges like gossamer cloth sewn with brilliants. When the sun came out it was almost as warm as June. " Summer do go on a long time in Cornwall," Tapperty told me.

The sea mist would come drifting in, wrapping itself about the grey stone of the house so that from the arbour in the south gardens it would sometimes be completely hidden. The gulls seemed to screech on a melancholy note on such days as though they were warning us that life was a sorrowful affair. And in the humid climate the hydrangeas continued to flower —blue, pink and yellow—in enormous masses of bloom such as I would not have expected to find outside a hot-house. The roses went on flowering, and with them the fuchsias.

When I went down to the village one day I saw a notice outside the church to the effect that the date of the horse show was fixed for the 1st of November.

I went back and told Alvean. I was delighted that she had lost none of her enthusiasm for the event. I had been afraid that, as the time grew near, her fear might have returned.

I said to her: " There's only three weeks. We really ought to get in a little more practice."

She was quite agreeable.

We could, I suggested, rearrange our schedule. Perhaps we could ride for an hour both in the mornings and the afternoons.

She was eager. " I'll see what can be done," I promised.

Connan TreMellyn had gone down to Penzance. I discovered this quite by accident. Kitty told me, when she brought in my water, one evening.

" Master have gone off this afternoon," she said. " 'Tis thought he'll be away for a week or more."

" I hope he's back in time for the show," I said.

"Oh, he'll be back for that. He be one of the judges. He'm always here for that."

I was annoyed with the man. Not that I expected him to tell me he was going; but I did feel he might have had the grace to say good-bye to his daughter.

I thought a good deal about him and I found myself wondering whether he had really gone to Penzance. I wondered whether Lady Treslyn was at home, or whether she had found it necessary to pay a visit to some relative.

Really! I admonished myself. "Whatever has come over you? How can you entertain such thoughts? It's not as though you have any proof!

I promised myself that while Connan TreMellyn was away there was no need to think of him, and that would be a relief.

I was not entirely lying about that. I did feel relaxed by the thought that he was out of the house. I no longer felt it necessary to lock my door; but I continued to do so, purely on account of the Tapperty girls. I did not want them to know that I locked it for fear of the Master—and although they were quite without education, they were sharp enough where such matters were concerned.

"Now," I said to Alvean, "we will concentrate on practising for the show."

I procured a list of the events. There were two jumping contests for Alvean's age group, and I decided that she should take the elementary one, for I felt that she had a good chance of winning a prize in that; and of course the whole point of this was that she *should* win a prize and astonish her father.

"Look, Miss," said Alvean, "there's this one. Why don't *you* go in for this?"

"Of course I shall do no such thing."

"But why not?"

"My dear child, I am here to teach you, not to enter for competitions.

A mischievous look came into her eyes. "Miss," she said, "I'm going to enter you for that. You'd win. There's nobody here can ride as well as you do. Oh, Miss, you must!"

She was looking at me with what I construed as shy pride,

and I felt a thrill of pleasure. I enjoyed her pride in me. She wanted me to win.

Well, why not? There was no rule about social standing in these contests, was there?

I fell back on my stock phrase for ending an embarrassing discussion :

" We'll see," I said.

One afternoon we were riding close to Mount Widden and met Peter Nansellock.

He was mounted on a beautiful bay mare, the sight of which made my eyes glisten with envy.

He came galloping towards us and pulled up, dramatically removing his hat and bowing from the waist.

Alvean laughed delightedly.

" Well met, dear ladies," he cried. " Were you coming to call on us?"

" We were not," I answered.

" How unkind! But now you are here you must come in for a little refreshment."

I was about to protest when Alvean cried : " Oh, do let's, Miss. Yes, please, Uncle Peter, we'll come in."

" I had hoped you would call before this," he said reproach-fully.

" We had received no definite invitation," I reminded him.

" For you there is always welcome at Mount Widden. Did I not make that clear?"

He had turned his mare and we all three walked our horses side by side. He followed my gaze, which was fixed on the mare.

" You like her?" he said.

" Indeed I do. She's a beauty."

" She's a real beauty, are you not, Jacinth my pet?"

" Jacinth. So that's her name."

" Pretty, you're thinking. Pretty name for a pretty creature. She'll go like the wind. She's worth four of that lumbering old cart horse you're riding, Miss Leigh."

" Lumbering old cart hourse? How absurd! Dion is a very fine horse."

"Was, Miss Leigh. *Was!* Do you not think that the creature has seen better days? Really, I should have thought Connan could have given you something better from his stables than poor old Dion."

"It was not a matter of his giving her any horse to ride," said Alvean in hot defence of her father. "He does not know what horses we ride, does he, Miss. These are the horses which Tapperty said we could have."

"Poor Miss Leigh! She should have a mount worthy of her. Miss Leigh, before you go, I would like you to take a turn on Jacinth. She'll quickly show you what it feels like to be on a good mount again."

"Oh," I said lightly, "we're satisfied with what we have. They serve my purpose—which is to teach Alvean to ride."

"We're practising for the show," Alvean told him. "I'm going in for one of the events, but don't tell Papa; it's to be a surprise."

Peter put his finger to his lips. "Trust me. I'll keep your secret."

"And Miss is entering for one of the events too. I've made her!"

"She'll be victorious," he cried. "I'll make a bet on it."

I said curtly: "I'm not at all sure about this. It is only an idea of Alvean's."

"But you must, Miss!" cried Alvean. "I insist."

"We'll both insist," added Peter.

We had reached the gates of Mount Widden which were wide open. There was no lodge here as at Mount Mellyn. We went up the drive—where the same types of flowers grew in profusion—the hydrangeas, fuchsias and fir trees which were indigenous to this part of the country.

I saw the house, grey stone as Mount Mellyn was, but much smaller and with fewer outbuildings. I noticed immediately that it was not so well cared for as what in that moment I presumptuously called " our " house and I felt an absurd thrill of pleasure because Mount Mellyn compared so favourably with Mount Widden.

There was a groom in the stables and Peter told him to take charge of our horses. He did so and we went into the house.

Peter clapped his hands and shouted: "Dick! Where are you, Dick?"

The houseboy, whom I had seen when he had been sent over to Mount Mellyn with messages, appeared; and Peter said to him: "Tea, Dick. At once, in the library. We have guests."

"Yes, Master," said Dick and hurried away.

We were in a hall which seemed quite modern when compared with our own hall. The floor was tessellated and there was a wide staircase at one end of it which led to a gallery containing oil paintings, presumably of the Nansellock family.

I laughed at myself for scorning the place, which was very much larger and much grander than the vicarage in which I had spent my childhood. But it had a neglected air—one might almost say one of decay.

Peter took us into the library, a huge room, the walls of which were lined with books on three sides. I noticed that the furniture was dusty and that dirt was visible in the heavy curtains. What they need, I thought, is a Mrs. Polgrey with her beeswax and turpentine.

"I pray you sit down, dear ladies," said Peter. "It is to be hoped that tea will not long be delayed, although I must warn you that meals are not served with the precision which prevails in our rival across the cove."

"Rival?" I said in surprise.

"Well, how could there fail to be a little rivalry? Here we stand, side by side. But the advantages are all with them. They have the grander house, and the servants to deal with it. Your father, dear Alvean, is a man of property. We Nansellocks are his poor relations."

"You are not our relations," Alvean reminded him.

"Now is that not strange? One would have thought that, living side by side for generations, the two families would have mingled and become one. There must have been charming TreMellyn girls and charming Nansellock men. How odd that they did not join up and become relations! I suppose the mighty TreMellyns always looked down their arrogant noses at the poor Nansellocks and went farther afield to make their marriages. But now there is the fair Alvean. How maddening that we have no boy of your age to marry you, Alvean. I shall have to wait for you. There is nothing for it but that."

Alvean laughed delightedly. I could see that she was quite fascinated by him; and I thought, Perhaps he is more serious than he pretends. Perhaps he has already begun courting Alvean in a subtle way.

Alvean began to talk about the show and he listened attentively. I occasionally joined in, and so the time passed until tea was brought to us.

"Miss Leigh, will you honour us by pouring out?" Peter asked me.

I said I should be happy to do so, and I placed myself at the head of the tea table.

Peter watched me with attention which I found faintly embarrassing because, not only was it admiring, but contented.

"How glad I am that we met," he murmured as Alvean handed him his cup of tea. "To think that, if I had been five minutes earlier or five minutes later, our paths might not have crossed. What a great part chance plays in our lives."

"Possibly we should have met at some other time."

"There may not be much more time left to us."

"You sound morbid. Do you think that something is going to happen to one of us?"

He looked at me very seriously. "Miss Leigh," he said, "I am going away."

"Where," Uncle Peter?" demanded Alvean.

"Far away, my child, to the other side of the world."

"Soon?" I asked.

"Possibly with the New Year."

"But where are you going?" cried Alvean in dismay.

"My dearest child, I believe you are a little hurt at the thought of my departure."

"Uncle, where?" she demanded imperiously.

"To seek my fortune."

"You're teasing. You're always teasing."

"Not this time. I have heard from a friend who was at Cambridge with me. He is in Australia, and there he has made a fortune. Gold! Think of it, Alvean. You too, Miss Leigh. Lovely gold . . . gold which can make a man . . . or woman . . . rich . And all one has to do is pluck it out of the ground."

"Many go in the hope of making fortunes," I said, "but are they all successful?"

"There speaks the practical woman. No, Miss Leigh, they are not all successful; but there is something named hope which, I believe, springs eternal in the human breast. All may not have gold but they can all have hope."

"Of what use is hope if it is proved to be false?"

"Until she is proved false she can give so much pleasure, Miss Leigh."

"Then I wish that your hopes may not prove false."

"Thank you."

"But I don't want you to go, Uncle Peter."

"Thank *you*, my dear. But I shall come back a rich man. Imagine it. Then I shall build a new wing on Mount Widden. I will make the house as grand as—no, grander than—Mount Mellyn. And in the years to come people will say it was Peter Nansellock who saved the family fortunes. For, my dear young ladies, someone has to save them . . . soon."

He then began to talk of his friend who had gone to Australia a penniless young man and who, he was sure, was now a millionaire, or almost.

He began planning how he would rebuild the house, and we both joined in. It was a pleasant game—building a house in the mind, to one's own desires.

I felt exhilarated by his company. He at least, I thought, has never made me feel my position. The very fact of his poverty —or what to him seemed poverty—endeared him to me.

It was an enjoyable tea time.

Afterwards he took us out to the stables and both he and Alvean insisted on my mounting Jacinth, and showing them what I could do with her. My saddle was put on her, and I galloped her and jumped with her, and she responded to my lightest touch. She was a delicious creature and I envied him his possession of her.

"Why," he said, "she has taken to you, Miss Leigh. Not a single protest at finding a new rider on her back."

I patted her fondly and said : "She's a beauty."

And the sensitive creature seemed to understand.

We then mounted our horses, and Peter came to the gates of Mount Mellyn with us, riding Jacinth.

As we went up to our rooms I decided that it had indeed been a very enjoyable afternoon.

Alvean came to my room and stood for a while, her head on one side. She said : " He likes you, I think, Miss."

" He is merely polite towards me," I replied.

" No, I think he likes you rather specially . . . in the way he liked Miss Jansen."

" Did Miss Jansen go to tea at Mount Widden?"

" Oh yes. I didn't have riding lessons with her, but we used to walk over there. And one day we had tea just as we did this afternoon. He'd just bought Jacinth then and he showed her to us. He said he was going to change her name to make her entirely his. Then he said her name was to be Jacinth. That was Miss Jansen's name."

I felt foolishly deflated. Then I said : " He must have been very sorry when she left so suddenly."

Alvean was thoughtful. " Yes, I think he was. But he soon forgot all about her. After all——"

I finished the sentence for her : " She was only the governess, of course."


It was later that day when Kitty came up to my room to tell me that there was a message for me from Mount Widden.

" And something more too, Miss," she said; it was clearly something which excited her, but I refrained from questioning her since I should soon discover what this was.

" Well," I said, " where is the message?"

" In the stables, Miss." She giggled. " Come and see."

I went to the stables, and Kitty followed at a distance.

When I arrived there I saw Dick, The Mount Widden houseboy; and, to my astonishment, he had the mare, Jacinth, with him.

He handed me a note.

I saw that Daisy, her father, and Billy Trehay were all watching me with amused and knowing eyes.

I opened the note and read it. It said :

*Dear Miss Leigh,*

You could not hide from me your admiration for Jacinth. I believe she reciprocates your feelings. That is why I am making you a present of her. I could not bear to see such a fine and graceful rider as yourself on poor old Dion. So pray accept this gift.

Your admiring neighbour,
*Peter Nansellock*

In spite of efforts to control myself I felt the hot colour rising from my neck to my forehead. I knew that Tapperty found it hard to repress a snigger.

How could Peter be so foolish! Was he laughing at me? How could I possibly accept such a gift, even if I wanted to? Horses have to be fed and stabled. It was almost as though he had forgotten this was not my home.

" Is there an answer, Miss?" asked Dick.

" Indeed there is," I said. " I will go to my room at once, and you may take it back with you."

I went with as much dignity as I could muster in front of such an array of spectators back to the house, and in my room I wrote briefly :—

*Dear Mr. Nansellock,*

Thank you for your magnificent gift which I am, of course, quite unable to accept. I have no means of keeping a horse here. It may have escaped you that I am employed in this house as a governess. I could not possibly afford the upkeep of Jacinth. Thank you for the kind thought.

Yours truly,
*Martha Leigh*

I went straight back to the stables. I could hear them all laughing and talking excitedly as I approached.

" Here you are, Dick," I said. " Please take this note to your master with Jacinth."

" But . . ." stammered Dick. " I was to leave her here."

I looked straight into Tapperty's lewd old face. " Mr. Nansellock," I said, " is fond of playing jokes."

Then I went back to the house.

The next day was Saturday and Alvean said that, as it was a half holiday, could we not take the morning off and go to the moors. Her Great-Aunt Clara had a house there, and she would be pleased to see us.

I considered this. I thought it would be rather pleasant to get away from the house for a few hours. I knew that they must all be talking about me and Peter Nansellock.

I guessed that he had behaved with Miss Jansen as he was behaving with me, and it amused them all to see the story of one governess turning out so much like another.

I wondered about Miss Jansen. Had she perhaps been a little frivolous? I pictured her stealing, whatever she was supposed to have stolen, that she might buy herself fine clothes to appear beautiful in the sight of her admirer.

And he had not cared when she was dismissed. A fine friend he would be!

We set out after breakfast. It was a beautiful day for riding for the October sun was not fierce and there was a soft south-west wind. Alvean was in high spirits, and I thought this would be a good exercise in staying power. If she could manage the long ride to her great aunt's house and back without fatigue I should be delighted.

I felt it was pleasant to get away from the watchful eyes of the servants, and it was delightful to be in the moorland country.

I found the great tracts of moor fitted my mood. I was enchanted by the low stone walls, the grey boulders and the gay little streams which trickled over them.

I warned Alvean to be watchful of boulders, but she was sure-seated and alert now, so I did not feel greatly concerned.

We studied the map which would guide us to Great-Aunt Clara's house—a few miles south of Bodmin. Alvean had travelled there in a carriage once or twice and she thought she would know the road; but the moor was the easiest place in the world in which to lose oneself, and I thought that we could profit by the occasion to learn a little map-reading.

But I had left a great deal of my severity behind and I found myself laughing with Alvean when we took the wrong road and had to retrace our steps.

But at length we reached The House on the Moors which was the pictureseque name of Great-Aunt Clara's home.

And a charming house it was, set there on the outskirts of a moorland village. There was the church, the little inn, the few houses and The House on the Moors which was like a small manor house.

Great-Aunt Clara lived here with three servants to minister to her wants, and when we arrived there was great excitement as we were quite unexpected.

" Why, bless my soul if it b'aint Miss Alvean!" cried an elderly housekeeper. " And who be this you have brought with 'ee, my dear?"

" It is Miss Leigh, my governess," said Alvean.

" Well now! And be there just the two on you? And b'aint your papa here?"

" No. Papa has gone to Penzance."

I wondered then whether I had been wrong in acceding to Alvean's wishes, and had forgotten my position by imposing myself on Great-Aunt Clara without first asking permission.

I wondered if I should be banished to the kitchen to eat with the servants. Such a procedure did not greatly disturb me and I would rather have done that than sit down with a haughty, disapproving old woman.

But I was soon reassured. We were taken into a drawing room and there was Great-Aunt Clara, a charming old lady seated in an armchair, white-haired, pink-cheeked with bright friendly eyes. There was an ebony stick beside her, so I guessed she had difficulty in walking.

Alvean ran to her and she was warmly embraced.

Then the lively blue eyes were on me.

" So you are Alvean's governess, my dear," she said. " Well, that is nice. And how thoughtful of you to bring her to see me. It is particularly fortunate, for I have my grandson staying with

me and I fear he grows a little weary of having no playmates of
his own age. When he hears Alvean has arrived he'll be
quite excited."

I did not believe that the grandson could be any more excited
than Great-Aunt Clara herself. She was certainly charming to
me, so much so that I forgot my diffidence and I really did feel
like a friend calling on a friend, rather than a governess
bringing her charge to see a relative.

Dandelion wine was brought out and we were pressed to take
a glass. There were wine cakes with it and I must say I found
the wine delicious. I allowed Alvean to take a very small glass
of it but when I had taken mine I wondered whether I had
been wise, for it was certainly potent.

Great-Aunt Clara wished to hear all the news of Mount
Mellyn; she was indeed a garrulous lady, and I guessed it was
due to the fact that she lived a somewhat lonely life in her
house on the moors.

The grandson appeared—a handsome boy a little younger
than Alvean—and the pair of them went off to play, although
I warned Alvean not to go too far away as we must be home
before dark.

As soon as Alvean had left us I saw that Great-Aunt Clara
was eager for a real gossip; and whether it was due to the fact
that I had taken her potent dandelion wine or whether I
believed her to be a link with Alice, I am not sure; but I found
her conversation fascinating.

She spoke of Alice as I had not until now heard her spoken
of—with complete candour; and I quickly realised that from
this gossipy lady I was going to discover a great deal more
than I could from anyone else.

As soon as we were alone she said : " And now tell me how
things really are at Mount Mellyn."

I raised my eyebrows as though I did not fully comprehend
her meaning.

She went on : " It was such a shock when poor Alice died.
It was so sudden. Such a tragic thing to happen to such a
young girl—for she was little more than a girl."

" Is that so?"

" Don't tell me you haven't heard what happened."

"I know very little about it."

"Alice and Geoffry Nansellock, you know. They went off together . . . eloped. And then this terrible accident."

"I have heard that there was an accident."

"I think of them—those two young people—quite often, in the dead of the night. And then I blame myself."

I was astonished. I did not understand how this gentle talkative old lady could blame herself for Alice's infidelity to her husband.

"One should never interfere in other people's lives. Or should one? What do you think, my dear? If one can be helpful——"

"Yes," I said firmly, "if one can be helpful I think one should be forgiven for interference."

"But how is one to know whether one is being helpful or the reverse?"

"One can only do what one thinks is right."

"But one might be doing right and yet be quite unhelpful?"

"Yes, I suppose so."

"I think of her so much . . . my poor little niece. She was a sweet creature. But, shall I say, not equipped to face the cruelties of fate."

"Oh, was she like that?"

"I can see that you, Miss Leigh, are so good for that poor child. Alice would be so happy if she could see what you've done for her. The last time I saw her she was with her . . . with Connan. She was not nearly so happy . . . so relaxed as she is to-day."

"I'm so glad of that. I am encouraging her to ride. I think that has done her a world of good." I was loath to interrupt that flow of talk from which I might extract some fresh evidence about Alice. I was afraid that at any moment Alvean and the grandson would return, and I knew that in their presence there would be no confidences. "You are telling me about Alvean's mother. I am sure you have nothing with which to reproach yourself."

"I wish I could believe that. It worries me sometimes. Perhaps I shouldn't weary you. But you seem so sympathetic, and you are there, living in the house. You are looking after little Alvean like . . . like a mother. It makes me feel very grateful to you, my dear."

"I am paid for doing it, you know." I could not resist that remark, and I thought of the smile it would have brought to Peter Nansellock's lips.

"There are some things in this world which cannot be bought. Love . . . devotion . . . they are some of them. Alice stayed with me before her marriage. Here . . . in this house. It was so convenient, you see. It was only a few hours' ride from Mount Mellyn. It gave the young people a chance to know each other."

"The young people?"

"The engaged pair."

"Did they not know each other then?"

"The marriage had been arranged when they were in their cradles. She brought him a lot of property. They were well matched. Both rich, both of good families. Connan's father was alive then and, you know, Connan was a wild boy with a will of his own. The feeling was that they should be married as soon as possible."

"So he allowed this marriage to be arranged for him?"

"They both took it as a matter of course. Well, she stayed with me several months before the wedding. I loved her dearly."

I thought of little Gilly and I said : " I think a great many people loved her dearly."

Great-Aunt Clara nodded; and at that moment Alvean and the grandson came in.

"I want to show Alvean my drawings," he announced.

"Well, go and get them," said his grandmother. "Bring them down and show her here."

I believed that she realised she had talked a little too much and was afraid of her own garrulity. It was clear to me that she was the sort of woman who could never keep a secret; how could she when she was ready to confide secret family history to me, a stranger?

The grandson returned with his portfolio, and the children sat at the table. I went over to them and I was so proud of

Alvean's attempts at drawing that I determined to speak to her father about that at the first opportunity.

Yet as I watched, I felt frustrated. I was sure that Great-Aunt Clara had been on the point of confiding something to me which was of the utmost importance.

Aunt Clara gave us luncheon and we left immediately after.

We found our way back with the utmost care, but I was determined to ride out again, and that before long, to the house on the moors.

When I was strolling through the village one day I passed the little jeweller's shop there. But perhaps that was scarcely the term to use when describing it. There were no valuable gems in the window; but a few silver brooches and plain gold rings, some engraved with the word Mizpah, or studded with semi-precious stones such as turquoises, topaz, and garnets. I guessed that the villagers bought their engagement and wedding rings here and that the jeweller made a living by doing repairs.

I saw in the window a brooch in the form of a whip. It was of silver, and quite tasteful, I decided, although it was by no means expensive.

I wanted to buy that whip for Alvean and give it to her the night before the horse show, telling her that it was to bring her luck.

I opened the door and went down the three steps into the shop.

Seated behind the counter was an old man wearing steel-rimmed spectacles. He let his glasses fall to the tip of his nose as he peered at me.

" I want to see the brooch in the window," I said. " The silver one in the form of a whip."

" Oh yes, Miss," he said, " I'll show it to you with pleasure."

He brought it from the window and handed it to me.

" Here," he said, " pin it on and have a look at it." He indicated the little mirror on the counter. I obeyed him and decided that the brooch was neat, not gaudy, and in the best of taste.

E

As I was looking at it I noticed a tray of ornaments with little tickets attached to them. They were clearly jewellery which he had received for repair. Then I wondered whether this was the jeweller to whom Alice had brought her brooch last July.

The jeweller said to me: "You're from Mount Mellyn, Miss?"

"Yes," I said; and I smiled encouragingly. I was becoming very ready to talk to anyone who I thought might have any information to offer me on this subject which appeared to obsess me. "As a matter of fact I want to give the brooch to my pupil."

Like most people in small villages he was very interested in those living around him.

"Ah," he said, "poor motherless little girl. It's heartening to think she has a kind lady like yourself to look after her now."

"I'll take the brooch," I told him.

"I'll find a little box for it. A nice little box makes all the difference when it be a matter of a present, don't you agree, Miss?"

"Most certainly."

He bent down and from under the counter brought a small cardboard-box which he began to stuff with cotton-wool.

"Make a little nest for it, Miss," he said with a smile.

I fancied that he was loth to let me go.

"Don't see much of them from the Mount these days. Mrs. TreMellyn, her was often in."

"Yes, I suppose so."

"See a little trinket in the window and she'd buy it . . . sometimes for herself, sometimes for others. Why, she was in here the day she died."

His voice had sunk to a whisper and I felt excitement grip me. I thought of Alice's diary which was still in the concealed pocket of her habit.

"Really?" I said encouragingly.

He laid the brooch in the cotton-wool and looked at me. "I thought 'twas a little odd at the time. I remember it very clearly. She came in here and said to me: ' Have you got the brooch done, Mr. Pastern? It's very important that I should have it. I'm anxious to wear it to-morrow. I'm going to a dinner party at Mr. and Mrs. Trelanders', and Mrs. Trelander gave me that brooch as a Christmas present so you see it's most important I should wear it to show her I appreciate it.' " His eyes were puzzled as they looked into mine. " She were a lady who talked like that. She'd tell you where she was going, why she wanted a thing. I couldn't believe my ears when I heard she'd left home that very evening. Didn't seem possible that she could have been telling me about the dinner party she was going to the next day, you see."

" No," I said, " it was certainly very strange."

" You see, Miss, there was no need for her to say anything to me like. If she'd said it to some it might seem as though she was trying to pull the wool over their eyes. But why should she say such a thing to me, Miss? That's what I've been wondering. Sometimes I think of it . . . and still wonder."

" I expect there's an answer," I said. " Perhaps you misunderstood her."

He shook his head. He did not believe that he had misunderstood. Nor did I. I had seen the entry in her diary and what I had read there confirmed what the jeweller had said.

Celestine Nansellock rode over next day to see Alvean. We were about to go for our riding lesson, and she insisted on coming with us.

" Now, Alvean," I said, " is the time to have a little rehearsal. See if you can surprise Miss Nansellock as you hope to surprise your father."

We were going to practise jumping, and we rode down through the Mellyn village and beyond.

Celestine was clearly astonished by Alvean's progress.

" But you've done wonders with her, Miss Leigh."

We watched Alvean canter round the field. " I hope her father is going to be pleased. She has entered for one of the events in the show."

" He'll be delighted, I'm sure."

" Please don't say anything to him beforehand. We do want it to be a surprise."

Celestine smiled at me. "He'll be very grateful to you, Miss Leigh. I'm sure of that."

"I'm counting on his being rather pleased."

I was conscious of her eyes upon me as she smiled at me benignly. She said suddenly: "Oh, Miss Leigh, about my brother Peter. I did want to speak to you confidentially about that matter of Jacinth."

I flushed faintly, and I was annoyed with myself for doing so.

"I know he gave you the horse and you returned it as too valuable a gift."

"Too valuable a gift to accept," I answered, "and too expensive for me to be able to maintain."

"Of course. I'm afraid he is very thoughtless. But he is the most generous man alive. He's rather afraid he has offended you."

"Please tell him I'm not offended, and if he thinks awhile he will understand why I can't accept such a gift."

"I explained to him, He admires you very much, Miss Leigh, but there was an ulterior motive behind the gift. He wanted a good home for Jacinth. You know that he plans to leave England."

"He did mention it."

"I expect he will sell some of the horses. I shall keep a couple for myself, but there is no point in keeping an expensive stable with only myself at the house."

"No, I suppose not."

"He saw you on Jacinth and thinks you'd be a worthy mistress for her. That was why he wanted you to have her. He's very fond of that mare."

"I see."

"Miss Leigh, you would like to possess a horse like that?"

"Who wouldn't?"

"Suppose I asked Connan if it could be taken into his stables and kept there for you to ride. How would that be?"

I replied emphatically: "It is most kind of you, Miss Nansellock, and I do appreciate your desire—and that of your brother—to please me. But I do not wish for any special favours here. Mr. TreMellyn has a full and adequate stable for the needs of us all. I should be very much against asking for special favours for myself."

"I see," she said, "that you are very determined and very proud."

She leaned forward and touched my hand in a very friendly manner. There was a faint mist of tears in her eyes. She was touched by my position, and understood how desperately I clung to my pride because it was my only possession.

I thought her kind and considerate, and I could understand why Alice had made a friend of her. I felt that I too could easily become her friend, for she had never made me in the least conscious of my social position in the house.

One day, I thought, I'll tell her what I've discovered about Alice.

But not yet. I was, as her brother had said, as spiky as a hedgehog. I did not think for a moment that I should be rebuffed by Celestine Nansellock, but just at this time I was not going to run any risk.

Alvean joined us, and Celestine complimented her on her riding. Then we went back to the house, and tea, over which I presided, was served in the punch room.

I thought what a happy afternoon that was.

Connan TreMellyn came back the day before the show. I was glad he had not returned before, because I was afraid that Alvean might betray her excitement.

I was entered for one of the early events in which points were scored, particularly for jumping. It was what they called a mixed event which meant that men and women competed together.

Tapperty, who knew I was going to enter, wouldn't hear of my riding on Dion.

"Why, Miss," he said, the day before the show, "if you'd have took Jacinth when she was offered you, you would have got first prize. That mare be a winner and so would you be, Miss, on her back. Old Dion, he's a good fellow, but he ain't no prize winner. How'd you say to taking Royal Rover?"

"What if Mr. TreMellyn objected?"

Tapperty winked. "Nay, he'd not object. He'll be riding

out to the show on May Morning, so old Royal 'ull be free. I'll tell 'ee what, just suppose master was to say to me ' Saddle up Royal Rover for me, Tapperty.' Right, then I'd saddle the Rover for him and it would be May Morning for you, Miss. Nothing 'ud please master more than for to see his horse win a prize."

I was anxious to show off before Connan TreMellyn and I agreed to Tapperty's suggestion. After all, I was teaching his daughter to ride and that meant that I could, with the approval of his head stable man, make my selection from the stables.

The night before the show I presented Alvean with the brooch.

She was extremely delighted.

" It's a whip! " she cried.

" It will pin your cravat," I said, " and I hope bring you luck."

" It will, Miss. I know it will."

" Well, don't rely on it too much. Remember luck only comes to those who deserve it." I quoted the beginning of an old rhyme which Father used to say to us.

" Your head and your heart keep boldly up,

Your chin and your heels keep down." I went on : " And when you take your jump together . . . go with Prince."

" I'll remember."

" Excited?"

" It seems so long in coming."

" It'll come fast enough."

That night when I went in to say good night to her I sat on her bed and we talked about the show.

I was a little anxious about her, because she was too excited, and I tried to calm her down. I told her she must go to sleep for if she did not she would not be fresh for the morning.

" But how does one sleep, Miss," she asked, " when sleep won't come?"

I realised then the magnitude of what I had done. A few months before, when I had come to this house, this girl had been afraid to mount a horse; now she was looking forward to competing at the horse show.

That was all well and good. I would have preferred her interest not to have been centred so wholeheartedly on her father. It was his approval which meant so much to her.

She was not only eager; she was apprehensive, so desperately did she long for his admiration.

I went to my room and came back with a book of Mr. Longfellow's poems.

I sat down by her bed and began to read to her, for I knew of nothing to turn the mind to peace than his narrative poem, " Hiawatha."

I often quoted it when I was trying to sleep and then I would feel myself torn from the events of this world in which I lived and in my imagination I would wander along through the primeval forests with the " rushings of great rivers . . . and their wild reverberations."

The words flowed from my lips. I knew I was conjuring up visions for Alvean. She had forgotten the show . . . her fears and her hopes. She was with the little Hiawatha sitting at the feet of the good Nokomis and—she slept.

I woke up on the day of the horse show to find the mist had penetrated my room. I got out of bed and went to the window. Little wisps of it encircled the palm trees and the feathery leaves of the evergreen pines were decorated with little drops of moisture.

" I hope the mist lifts before the afternoon," I said to myself.

But all through the morning it persisted, and there were anxious looks and whispers throughout the house where everyone was thinking of the show. Most of the servants were going. They always did, Kitty told me, because the master had special interest in it as one of the judges, and Billy Trehay and some of the stable boys were entrants.

" It do put master in a good mood to see his horses win," said Kitty : " but they say he's always harder on his own than on others."

Immediately after luncheon Alvean and I set out; she was riding Black Prince and I was on Royal Rover. It was exhilarating to be on a good horse, and I felt as excited as

Alvean; I fear I was just as eager to shine in the eyes of
Connan TreMellyn as she was.

The show was being held in a big field close to the village
church, and when we arrived the crowds were already
gathering.

Alvean and I parted company when we reached the field and
I discovered that the event in which I was competing was one
of the first.

The show was intended to start at two-fifteen, but there was
the usual delay, and at twenty past we were still waiting to
begin.

The mist had lifted slightly, but it was a leaden day; the sky
was like a grey blanket and everything seemed to have
accumulated a layer of moisture. The sea smell was strong
but the waves were silent to-day and the cry of the gulls was
more melancholy than ever.

Connan arrived with the other judges; there were three of
them, all local worthies. Connan, I saw, had come on May
Morning, as I expected, since I had been given Royal Rover.

The village band struck up a traditional air and everyone
stood still and sang.

It was very impressive, I thought, to hear those words sung
with such fervour in that misty field:

> *And shall they scorn Tre Pol and Pen,*
> *And shall Trelawney die?*
> *Then twenty thousand Cornish men*
> *Will know the reason why."*

A proud song, I thought, for an insular people; and they
stood at attention as they sang. I noticed little Gillyflower
standing there, singing with the rest, and I was surprised to see
her; she was with Daisy and I hoped the girl would look after
her.

She saw me and I waved to her, but she lowered her eyes at
once, yet I could see that she was smiling to herself and I was
quite pleased.

A rider came close to me and a voice said: " Well, if it is
not Miss Leigh, herself ! "

I turned and saw Peter Nansellock; he was mounted on
Jacinth.

"Good afternoon," I said, and my eyes lingered on the perfections of Jacinth.

I was wearing a placard with a number on my back which had been put there by one of the organisers.

"Don't tell me," said Peter Nansellock, "that you and I are competitors in this first event."

"Are you in it then?"

He turned, and I saw the placard on his back.

"I haven't a hope," I said.

"Against me?"

"Against Jacinth," I answered.

"Miss Leigh, you could have been riding her."

"You must have been mad to do what you did. You set the stables talking."

"Who cares for stable boys?"

"I do."

"Then you are not being your usual sensible self."

"A governess has to care for the opinions of all and sundry."

"You are not an ordinary governess."

"Do you know, Mr. Nansellock," I said lightly, "I believe all the governesses in your life were no ordinary governesses. If they had been, perhaps they would have had no place in your life."

I gave Royal Rover a gentle touch on the flank and he responded immediately.

I did not see Peter again until he was competing. He went before I did. I watched him ride round the field. He and Jacinth seemed like one animal. Like a centaur, I thought. Were they the creatures with the head and shoulders of a man and the body of a horse?

"Oh, perfect," I explained aloud as I watched him take the jumps and canter gracefully round the field. And who couldn't, I said to myself maliciously, on a mare like that!

A round of applause followed him as he finished his turn.

Mine did not come until some time later.

I saw Connan TreMellyn in the judges' stand. And I whispered: "Royal Rover, help me. I want you to beat Jacinth. I want you to win this prize. I want to show Connan

TreMellyn that there is one thing I can do. Help me, Royal Rover."

The sensitive ears seemed to prick up as Royal Rover moved daintily forward and I knew that he heard me, and would respond to the appeal in my voice:

"Come on, Rover," I whispered. "We can do it."

And we went round as faultlessly, I hoped, as Jacinth had. I heard the applause burst out as I finished, and walked my horse away.

We waited until the rest of the competitors were finished and the results were called. I was glad that they were announced at the end of each event. People were more interested immediately after they had seen a performance. The practice of announcing all winners at the end of the meeting I had always thought to be a sort of anti-climax.

"This one is a tie," Connan was saying. "Two competitors scored full marks in this one. It's most unusual, but I am happy to say that the winners are a lady and a gentleman: Miss Martha Leigh on Royal Rover, and Mr. Peter Nansellock on Jacinth."

We trotted up to take our prizes.

Connan said: "The prize is a silver rose bowl. How can we split it? Obviously we cannot do that so the lady gets the bowl."

"Of course," said Peter.

"But you get a silver spoon," Connan told him. "Consolation for having tied with a lady."

We accepted our prizes, and as Connan gave me mine he was smiling, very well pleased.

"Good show, Miss Leigh. I did not know anyone could get so much out of Royal Rover."

I patted Royal Rover and said, more for his hearing than anyone else's: "I couldn't have had a better partner."

Then Peter and I trotted off; I with my rose bowl, he with his spoon.

Peter said: "If you had been on Jacinth you would have been the undisputed winner."

"I should still have had to compete against you on something else."

" Jacinth would win any race . . . just look at her. Isn't she perfection? Never mind, you got the rose bowl."

" I shall always feel that it is not entirely mine."

" When you arrange your roses you will aways think, Part of this belonged to that man . . . what was his name? He was always charming to me, but I was a little acid with him. I'm sorry now."

" I rarely forget people's names, and I feel I have nothing to regret in my conduct towards you."

" There is a way out of this rose bowl situation. Suppose we set up house together. It could have a place of honour there. ' Ours,' we could say, and both feel happy about it."

I was angry at this flippancy, and I said : " We should, I am sure, feel far from happy about everything else."

And I rode away.

I wanted to be near the judges' stand when Alvean appeared. I wanted to watch Connan's face as his daughter performed. I wanted to be close when she took her prize—which I was sure she would, for she was eager to win and she had worked hard. The jumps should offer no difficulty to her.

The elementary jumping contest for eight-year-olds began and I was feverishly impatient, waiting for Alvean's turn as I watched those little girls and boys go through their performances. But there was no Alvean. The contest was over and the results announced.

I felt sick with disappointment. So she had panicked at the last moment. My work had been in vain. When the great moment came her fears had returned.

When the prizes were being given I went in search of Alvean, but I could not find her, and as the more advanced jumping contest for the eight-year-old group was about to begin, it occurred to me that she must have gone back to the house. I pictured her abject misery because after all our talk, all our practice, her courage had failed her at the critical moment.

I wanted to get away, for now my own petty triumph meant nothing to me, and I wanted to find Alvean quickly, to comfort her if need be, and I felt sure she would need my comfort.

I rode back to Mount Mellyn, hung up my saddle and bridle, gave Royal Rover a quick rub-down and a drink, and left him munching an armful of hay in his stall while I went into the house.

The back door was unlatched and I went in. The house seemed very quiet. I guessed that all but Mrs. Polgrey were at the horse show. Mrs. Polgrey would probably be in her room having her afternoon doze.

I went up to my room and called Alvean as I went.

There was no answer so I hurried through the schoolroom to her room which was deserted. Perhaps she had not come back to the house. I then remembered that I had not seen Prince in the stables. But then I had forgotten to look in his stall.

I came back to my room and stood uncertainly at the window. I thought, I'll go back to the show. She's probably still there.

And as I stood at the window I knew that someone was in Alice's apartments. I was not sure how I knew. It may only have been a shadow across the window-pane. But I was certain that someone was there."

Without thinking very much of what I would do when I discovered who was there I ran from my room, through the gallery to Alice's rooms. My riding-boots must have made a clatter along the gallery. I threw open the door of the room and shouted : " Who is here? Who is it?"

No one was in the room, but I saw in that fleeting second, the communicating door between the two rooms close.

I had a feeling that it might be Alvean who was there, and I was sure that Alvean needed me at this moment. I had to find her, and any fear I might have had, disappeared. I ran across the dressing room and opened the door of the bedroom. I looked round the room. I ran to the curtains and felt them. There was no one there. Then I ran to the other door and opened it. I was in another dressing room and the communicating door—similar to that in Alice's—was open. I went through and immediately I knew that I was in Connan's bedroom for I saw a cravat, which he had been wearing that morning, flung on the dressing table. I saw his dressing gown and slippers.

The sight of these made me blush and realise that I was trespassing in a part of the house where I had no right to be.

But someone other than Connan had been there before me. Who was it?

I went swiftly across the bedroom, opened the door and found myself in the gallery.

There was no sign of anyone there so I went slowly back to my room.

Who had been in Alice's room? Who was it who haunted the place?

"Alice," I said aloud. "Is it you, Alice?"

Then I went down to the stables. I wanted to get back to the show and find Alvean.

I had saddled Royal Rover and was riding out of the stable yard when I saw Billy Trehay hurrying towards the house.

He said: "Oh Miss, there's been an accident. A terrible accident."

"What?" I stammered.

"It's Miss Alvean. She took a toss in the jumping."

"But she wasn't in the jumping!" I cried.

"Yes she were. In the eight-year-olds. Advanced class. It was the high jump. Prince stumbled and fell. They went rolling over and over. . . ."

For a moment I lost control of myself; I covered my face with my hands and cried out in protest.

"They were looking for you, Miss," he said.

"Where is she then?"

"She were down there in the field. They'm afraid to move her. They wrapped her up and now they'm waiting for Dr. Pengelly to come. They think she may have broken some bones. Her father's with her. He kept saying, 'Where's Miss Leigh?' And I saw you leave so I came after you. I think perhaps you'd better be getting down there, Miss . . . since he was asking for you like."

I turned away and rode as fast as I dared down the hill into the village, and as I rode I prayed, and scolded:

"Oh God, let her be all right. Oh Alvean, you little fool! It would have been enough to take the simple jumps. That would have pleased him enough. You could have done the high jumps next year. Alvean, my poor, poor child." And then: "It's his fault. It's all his fault. If he had been a human parent this wouldn't have happened."

And so I came to the field. I shall never forget what I saw there: Alvean lying unconscious on the grass, and the group round her and others standing about. There would be no more competitions that day.

For a moment I was terrified that she had been killed.

Connan's face was stern as he looked at me.

"Miss Leigh," he said, "I'm glad you've come. There's been an accident. Alvean . . ."

I ignored him and knelt down beside her.

"Alvean . . . my dear . . ." I murmured.

She opened her eyes then . She did not look like my arrogant little pupil. She was just a lost and bewildered child.

But she smiled.

"Don't go away . . ." she said.

"No, I'll stay here."

"You did go . . . before . . ." she murmured, and I had to bend low to catch her words.

And then I knew. She was not speaking to Martha Leigh, the governess. She was speaking to Alice.

## VI

Dr. Pengelly had arrived on the field and had diagnosed a broken tibia; but he could not say if any further damage had been done. He set the fractured bone and drove Alvean back to Mount Mellyn in his carriage while Connan and I rode back together in silence.

Alvean was taken to her room and given a sedative by the doctor.

"Now," he said, "there is nothing we can do but wait. I'll come back again in a few hours' time. It may be that the child is suffering acute shock. In the meantime we will keep her warm and let her sleep. She should sleep for several hours, and at the end of that time we shall know how deeply she has suffered from this shock."

When the doctor had left, Connan said to me: " Miss Leigh, I want to have a talk with you. Come to the punch room . . . now, will you please."

I followed him there and he went on:

" There is nothing we can do but wait, Miss Leigh. We must try to be calm."

I realised that he could never have seen me agitated as I was now, and he had probably considered me incapable of such deep feeling.

Impulsively I said : " I find it hard to be as calm about my charge as you are about your daughter, Mr. TreMellyn."

I was so frightened and worried that I wanted to blame someone for what had happened so I blamed him.

" Whatever made the child attempt such a thing?" he demanded.

" You made her," I retorted. " You!"

" I! But I had no idea that she was so advanced in her riding."

I realised later that I was on the verge of hysteria. I believed that Alvean might have done herself some terrible injury and I felt almost certain that a child of her temperament would never want to ride again. I believed I had been wrong in my methods. I should not have tried to overcome her fear of horses; I had tried to win my way into her affections by showing her the way to win those of her father.

I could not rid myself of a terrible sense of guilt, and I was desperately trying to. I was saying to myself, This is a house of tragedy. Who are you to meddle in the lives of these people? What are you trying to do? To change Alvean? To change her father? To discover the truth about Alice? What do you think you are? God?

But I wouldn't blame myself entirely. I was looking for a scapegoat. I was saying to myself, He is to blame. If he had been different, none of this would have happened. I'm sure of that.

I had lost control of my feelings and on the rare occasions when people like myself do that, they usually do it more competely than those who are prone to hysterical outbursts.

"No," I cried out, "of course you had no idea that she was so advanced. How could you when you had never shown the slightest interest in the child? She was breaking her heart through your neglect. It was for that reason that she attempted this thing of which she was not capable."

"My dear Miss Leigh," he murmured. "My dear Miss Leigh." And he was looking at me in complete bewilderment.

I thought to myself, What do I care! I shall be dismissed, but in any case I have failed. I had hoped to do the impossible —to bring this man out of his own selfishness to care a little for his lonely daughter. And what have I done—made a complete mess of it and perhaps maimed the child for life. A fine one I was to complain of the conduct of others.

But I continued to blame him, and I no longer cared what I said.

"When I came here," I went on, "it did not take me long to understand the state of affairs. That poor motherless child was starved . . . Oh, I know she had her broth and her bread and butter at regular intervals. But there is another starvation besides that of the body. She was starved of the affection which she might expect from a parent and, as you see, she was ready to risk her life to win it."

"Miss Leigh, please, I beg of you, do be calm, do be reasonable. Are you telling me that Alvean did that . . ."

But I would not let him speak. "She did that for you. She thought it would please you. She has been practising for weeks."

"I see," he said. Then he look his handkerchief from his pocket and wiped my eyes. "You do not realise it, Miss Leigh," he went on almost tenderly, "but there are tears on your cheeks."

I took the handkerchief from him and angrily wiped my tears away.

"They are tears of anger," I said.

"And of sorrow. Dear Miss Leigh, I think you care very much for Alvean."

" She is a child," I said, " and it was my job to care for her. God knows, there are few others to do it."

" I see," he answered, " that I have been behaving in a very reprehensible manner."

" How could you . . . if you had any feeling? Your own daughter! She lost her mother. Don't you see that because of that she needed special care?"

Then he said a surprising thing: " Miss Leigh, you came here to teach Alvean, but I think you have taught me a great deal too."

I looked at him in amazement; I was holding his hand-kerchief a few inches from my tear-stained face; and at that moment Celestine Nansellock came in.

She looked at me in some astonishment, but only for a second. Then she burst out: " What is this terrible thing I've heard?"

" There's been a accident, Celeste," said Connan. " Alvean was thrown."

" Oh . . . no!" Celestine uttered a piteous cry. " And what . . . and where . . . ?"

" She's in her room now," Connan explained. " Pengelly's set the leg. Poor child. At the moment she is asleep. He gave her something to make her sleep. He's coming again in a few hours' time."

" But how badly . . . ?"

" He's not sure. But I've seen accidents like this before. I think she'll be all right."

I was not sure whether he meant that or whether he was trying to soothe Celestine who was so upset. I felt drawn towards her; she was the only person, I believed, who really cared about Alvean.

" Poor Miss Leigh is very distressed," said Connan. " I think she fancies it is her fault. I do want to assure her that I don't think that at all."

My fault! But how could I be blamed for teaching the child to ride? And having taught her, what harm was there in her entering for a competition? No, it was his fault, I wanted to shout. She would have been content to do what she was capable of, but for him.

I said with defiance in my voice : " Alvean was so anxious to impress her father that she undertook more than she could do. I am sure that had she believed her father would be content to see her victorious in the elementary event she would not have attempted the advanced."

Celestine had sat down and covered her face with her hands. I thought fleetingly of the occasion when I had seen her in the churchyard, kneeling by Alice's grave. I thought, Poor Celestine, she loves Alvean as her own child, because she has none of her own and perhaps believes she never will have.

" We can only wait and see," said Connan.

I rose and said : " There is no point in my remaining here. I will go to my room."

But Connan put out a hand and said almost authoritatively : " No, stay here, Miss Leigh. Stay with us. You care for her deeply, I know."

I looked down at my riding habit—Alice's riding habit— and I said : " I think I should change."

It seemed that in that moment he looked at me in a new light—and perhaps so did Celestine. If they did not look at my face I must have appeared to be remarkably like Alice.

I knew it was important that I change my clothes, for in my grey cotton dress with its severe bodice I should be the governess once more and that would help me to control my feelings.

Connan nodded. He said : " But come back when you've changed, Miss Leigh. We have to comfort each other, and I want you to be here when the doctor returns."

So I went to my room and I took off Alice's riding habit and put on my own grey cotton.

I was right. The cotton did help to restore my equilibrium. I began to wonder, as I buttoned the bodice, what I had said, in my outburst, to Connan TreMellyn.

The mirror showed me a face that was ravaged by grief and anxiety, eyes which burned with anger and resentment, and a mouth that was tremulous with fear.

I sent for hot water. Daisy wanted to talk, but she saw that I was too upset to do so and she went quickly away.

I bathed my face and when I had done so I went down to the

punch-room and rejoined Connan and Celestine, there to await the coming of Dr. Pengelly.

It seemed a long time before the doctor returned. Mrs. Polgrey made a pot of strong tea and Connan, Celestine and I sat together drinking it. I did not feel astonished then, but I did later, because the accident seemed to have made them both forget that I was merely the governess. But perhaps I mean it made Connan forget; Celestine had always treated me without that condecension which I thought I had discerned in others.

Connan seemed to have forgotten my outburst and treated me with a courtly consideration and a new gentleness. I believed he was anxious that I should not blame myself in any way, and he knew that the reason I had turned on him so vehemently was because I wondered whether I had been at fault.

" She'll get over this," he said. " And she'll want to ride again. Why, when I was a little older than herself I had an accident which I'm sure was worse than this one. I got it in the collar-bone and was unable to ride for weeks. I could scarcely wait to get back on a horse."

Celestine shivered. " I shall never have a moment's peace if she rides again after this."

" Oh Celeste, you would wrap her in cotton wool. And then what would happen? She would go out and catch her death of cold. You must not coddle children too much. After all, they've got to face the world. They must be prepared for it in some way. What does the expert have to say to that?"

He was looking at me anxiously. I knew he was trying to keep up our spirits. He knew how deeply Celestine and I felt about this, and he was trying to be kind.

I said : " I believe one shouldn't coddle. But if children are really set against something I don't think they should be forced to do it."

" But she was not forced to ride."

" She did it most willingly," I answered. " But I cannot be sure whether she did it from a love of riding or from an intense desire to please you."

"Well," he said almost lightly, "is it not an excellent thing that a child should seek to please a parent?"

"But it should not be necessary to risk a life for the sake of a smile."

My anger was rising again and my fingers gripped the cotton of my skirt as though to remind me that I was not in Alice's riding habit now. I was the governess in my cotton gown, and it was not for me to press forward my opinions.

Both Celestine and Connan were surprised at my remark, and I went on quickly: "For instance, Alvean's talents may lie in another direction. I think she has artistic ability. She has done some good drawings. Mr. TreMellyn, I have been going to ask you for some time whether you would consider letting her have drawing lessons."

There was a tense silence in the room and I wondered why they both looked so startled.

I blundered on: "I am sure there is great talent there, and I do not feel that it should be ignored."

Connan said slowly: "But Miss Leigh, you are here to teach my daughter. Why should it be necessary to engage other teachers?"

"Because," I replied boldly, "I believe she has a special talent. I believe it would be an added interest in her life if she were to be given drawing lessons. These should be given by a specialist in the art. She is good enough for that. I'm merely a governess, Mr. TreMellyn, I am not an artist as well."

He said rather gruffly: "Well, we shall have to go into this at some time."

He changed the subject, and shortly afterwards the doctor arrived.

I waited outside in the corridor while Connan and Celestine were with Alvean and the doctor.

A hundred images of disaster crowded into my mind. I imagined that she died of her injuries. I saw myself leaving the place, never to return. If I did that I should feel that my life had been incomplete in some way. I realised that if I had to go away I should be a very unhappy woman. Then I thought of her, maimed for life, more difficult than she had been previously, a wretched and unhappy little girl; and myself devoting my life to her. It was a gloomy picture.

Celestine joined me.

" This suspense is terrible," she said. " I wonder whether we ought to get another doctor. Dr. Pengelly is sixty. I am afraid . . ."

" He seemed efficient," I said.

" I want the best for her. If anything happens to her . . ."

She was biting her lips in anguish, and I thought how strange it was that she, who always seemed so calm about everything else, should be so emotional over Alice and her daughter.

I wanted to put my arm about her and comfort her, but of course, remembering my position, I did no such thing.

Doctor Pengelly came out with Connan, and the doctor was smiling.

" Injuries," he said, " a fractured tibia. Beyond that . . . there's very little wrong."

" Oh, thank God!" cried Celestine, and I echoed her words.

" A day or so and she'll be feeling better. It'll just be a matter of mending that fracture. Children's bones mend easily. There's nothing for you two ladies to worry about."

" Can we see her?" asked Celestine eagerly.

" Yes, of course you can. She's awake now, and she asked for Miss Leigh. I'm going to give her another dose in half an hour, and that will ensure a good night's sleep. You'll see a difference in her in the morning."

We went into the room. Alvean was lying on her back looking very ill, poor child; but she gave us a wan smile when she saw us.

" Hallo, Miss," she said. " Hallo, Aunt Celestine."

Celestine knelt by the bed, took her hand and covered it with kisses. I stood on the other side of the bed and the child's eyes were on me.

" I didn't do it," she said.

" Well, it was a good try."

Connan was standing at the foot of the bed.

I went on : " Your father was proud of you."

"He'll think I was silly," she said.

"No, he doesn't," I cried vehemently. "He is here to tell you so."

Connan came round to the side of the bed and stood beside me.

"He's proud of you," I said. "He told me so. He said it didn't matter that you fell. He said all that mattered was that you tried; and you'd do it next time."

"Did he? Did he?"

"Yes, he did," I cried; and there was an angry note in my voice because he still said nothing and the child was waiting for him to confirm my words.

Then he spoke. "You did splendidly, Alvean. I *was* proud of you."

A faint smile touched those pale lips. Then she murmured: "Miss . . . oh Miss . . ." And then: "Don't go away, will you. Don't *you* go away."

I sank down on my knees then. I took her hand and kissed it. The tears were on my cheeks again.

I cried: "I'll stay, Alvean. I'll stay with you always . . ."

I looked up and saw Celestine watching me from the other side of the bed. I was aware of Connan, standing beside me. Then I amended those words, and the governess in me spoke. "I'll stay as long as I'm wanted," I said firmly.

Alvean was satisfied.

When she was sleeping we left her and, as I was about to go to my room, Connan said: "Come into my library a moment with us, Miss Leigh. The doctor wants to discuss the case with you."

So I went into his library with him, Celestine and the doctor, and we talked of the nursing of Alvean.

Celestine said: "I shall come over every day. In fact I wonder, Connan, whether I won't come over and stay while she's ill. It might make things easier."

"You ladies must settle that," answered Dr. Pengelly. "Keep the child amused. We don't want her getting depressed while those bones are knitting together."

"We'll keep her amused," I said. "Any special diet, Doctor?"

"For a day or so, light invalid foods. Steamed fish, milk puddings, custards and so on. But after a few days let her have what she wants."

I was almost gay, and this swift reversal of feelings made me slightly light-headed.

I listened to the doctor's instructions and Connan's assurance that there was no need for Celestine to stay at the house; he was sure Miss Leigh would manage and it would be wonderfully comforting for Miss Leigh to know that in any emergency she could always ask for Celestine's help.

"Well Connan," said Celestine, "perhaps it's as well. People talk. And if I stayed here . . . Oh, people are so ridiculous. But they are always ready to gossip."

I saw the point. If Celestine lived at Mount Mellyn, people would begin to couple her name with Connan's; whereas the fact that I, an employee of the same age, lived in the house aroused no comment. I was not of the same social standing.

Connan laughed and said: "How did you come over, Celeste?"

"I rode over on Speller."

"Right. I'll ride back with you."

"Oh, thank you, Connan. It's nice of you. But I can go alone if you'd rather . . ."

"Nonsense! I'm coming." He turned to me. "As for you, Miss Leigh, you look exhausted. I should advise you to go to bed and have a good night's sleep."

I was sure I could not rest, and my expression must have implied this for the doctor said: "I'll give you a draught, Miss Leigh. Take it five minutes before retiring for the night. I think I can promise you a good night's sleep."

"Thank you," I said appreciatively, for I suddenly realised how exhausted I was.

I believed that to-morrow I should wake up my usual calm self, able to cope with whatever new situation should be the result of all that had happened to-day.

I went to my room, where I found a supper tray waiting for

me. It contained a wing of cold chicken, appetising enough on most occasions, but to-night I had no appetite.

I toyed with it for a while and ate a few mouthfuls, but I was too upset to eat.

I thought it would be an excellent idea to take Dr. Pengelly's sleeping draught and retire for the night.

I was about to do so when there was a knock on my door.

"Come in," I called; and Mrs. Polgrey came. She looked distraught. No wonder, I thought. Who in this household isn't?

"It's terrible," she began.

But I cut in quickly: "She'll be all right, Mrs. Polgrey. The doctor said so."

"Oh yes, I heard the news. It's Gilly, Miss. I'm worried about her."

"Gilly!"

"She didn't come back from the show, Miss. I haven't seen her since this afternoon."

"Oh, she's wandering about somewhere, I expect. I wonder if she saw. . . ."

"I can't understand it, Miss. I can't understand her being at the show. She'm afeared of going near the horses. You could have knocked me down with a feather when I heard she was there. And now . . . she's not come in."

"But she does wander off alone, doesn't she?"

"Yes, but she'll always be in for her tea. I don't know what can have become of her."

"Has the house been searched?"

"Yes, Miss. I've looked everywhere. Kitty and Daisy have helped me. So's Polgrey. The child's not in the house."

I said: "I'll come and help look for her."

So instead of going to bed I joined in the search for Gillyflower.

I was very worried because on this day of tragedy I was prepared for anything to happen. What could have happened to little Gilly? I visualised a thousand things. I thought she might have wandered on to the beach and been caught by the tide, and I pictured her little body thrown up by the waves in Mellyn Cove as her mother's had been eight years ago.

That was morbid. No, Gilly had gone wandering and had fallen asleep somewhere. I remembered that I had seen her often in the woods. But she would not be lost if she were in the woods. She knew every inch of them.

I nevertheless made my way to the woods, calling "Gilly! Gilly!" as I went; and the mist, which was rising again with the coming of evening, seemed to catch my voice and muffle it as though it were cotton wool.

I searched those woods thoroughly because my intuition told me that she was there, and that she was not lost but hiding.

I was right. I came across her lying in a clearing surrounded by small conifers.

I had seen her in this spot once or twice and I guessed it was a haven to her.

"Gilly!" I called. "Gilly!" And as soon as she heard my voice she sprang to her feet. She was poised to run but she hesitated when I called to her: "Gilly, it's all right. I'm here all alone and I won't hurt you."

She looked like a wild fairy child, her extraordinary white hair hanging damply about her shoulders.

"Why, Gilly," I said, "You'll catch cold, lying on that damp grass. Why are you hiding, Gilly?"

Her big eyes watched my face, and I knew that it was fear of something which had driven her to this refuge in the woods.

If only she would talk to me! I thought. If only she would explain.

"Gilly," I said, "we're friends, aren't we? You know that. I'm your friend—as Madam was."

She nodded and the fear slipped from her face. I thought, she has seen me in Alice's well-cut riding clothes and, I believe, in her confused little mind she had bracketed us together in some way.

I put my arm about her; her dress was damp and I could see the mist on her pale brows and lashes.

"Why, Gilly, you are cold."

She allowed me to cuddle her. I said: "Come on, Gilly, we're going back. Your grandmamma is very anxious. She is wondering what has become of you."

She allowed me to lead her from the clearing, but I was aware of the reluctant drag of her feet.

I kept my arm firmly about her, and I said : " You were at the horse show this afternoon."

She turned to me and as she buried her face against me, her little hands gripped the cloth of my dress. I was conscious of her trembling.

Then in a flash of understanding I began to see what had happened. This child, like Alvean, was terrified of horses. Of course she was. Had she not been almost trampled to death by one?

I believed that, as Alvean had been suffering from temporary shock, so was this child ; but the shock which had come to her was of longer duration, and she had never known anyone who had been able to help her fight the darkness which had descended upon her.

In that misty wood I felt like a woman who has a mission. I was not going to turn my face from a poor child who needed help.

She was suffering from a return of that earlier shock. This afternoon she had seen Alvean beneath a horse's hoofs as she herself had been—after all it had happened only four years ago.

At that moment I heard the sound of horse's hoofs in the wood, and I shouted : " Hallo, I've found her."

" Hallo! Coming, Miss Leigh." And I was exhilarated— almost unbearably so—because that was Connan's voice.

I guessed that he had returned from Mount Widden to discover that Gilly was lost, and that he had joined the search party. Perhaps he knew that I had come to the woods and decided to join me.

He came into sight and Gilly shrank closer to me, keeping her face hidden.

" She's here," I called. He came close to us and I went on : " She is exhausted, poor child. Take her up with you."

He leaned forward to take her, but she cried out : " No! No!"

He was astonished to hear her speak, but I was not. I had already discovered that in moments of stress she did so.

I said: " Gilly. Go up there with the master. I'll walk beside you and hold your hand."

She shook her head.

I went on: " Look! This is May Morning. She wants to carry you, because she knows you're tired."

Gilly's eyes turned to look at May Morning, and, in the fear I saw there, was the clue.

" Take her," I said to Connan, and he stooped and swung her up in his arms and set her in front of him.

She tried to fight, but I kept on talking to her soothingly. " You're safe up there. And we'll get back more quickly. You'll find a nice bowl of bread and milk waiting for you, and then there'll be your warm cosy bed. I'll hold your hand all the time and walk beside you."

She no longer struggled but kept her hand in mine.

And so ended that strange day, with myself and Connan bringing in the lost child.

When she was lifted from the horse and handed to her grandmother, Connan gave me a smile which I thought was infinitely charming. That was because it held none of the mockery which I had seen hitherto.

I went up to my room, exultation wrapped me as the mist wrapped itself about the horse. It was tinged with melancholy but the joy was so strong that the mingling of my feelings was difficult to understand.

I knew of course what had happened to me. To-day had made it very clear. I had done a foolish thing—perhaps the most foolish thing I had ever done in my life.

I had fallen in love for the first time, and with someone who was quite out of my world. I was in love with the master of Mount Mellyn, and I had an uneasy feeling that he might be aware of it.

On the table by my bed was the draught which Dr. Pengelly had given me.

I locked the door, undressed, drank the draught and went to bed.

But before I got into bed I looked at myself in my pink flannelette nightdress, primly buttoned up to the throat. Then I laughed at the incongruity of my thoughts and said aloud in

my best governess's tones : " In the morning, after the good
night's rest Dr. Pengelly's potion will give you, you'll come to
your senses."

The next few weeks were the happiest I had so far spent in
Mount Mellyn. It soon became clear that Alvean had suffered
no great harm. I was delighted to find that she had lost none
of her keenness for riding and asked eager questions about
Black Prince's slight injuries, taking it for granted that she
would soon ride him again.

We resumed school after the first week; she was pleased to
do so. I also taught her to play chess, and she picked up the
game with astonishing speed; and if I handicapped myself by
playing without my queen she was even able to checkmate me.

But it was not only Alvean's progress which made me so
happy. It was the fact that Connan was in the house; and what
astonished me was that, although he made no reference to my
outburst on the day of the accident, he had clearly noted it and
would appear in Alvean's room with books and puzzles which
he thought would be of interest to her.

In the first days I said to him : " There is one thing that
pleases her more than all the presents you bring; that is your
own company."

He had answered : " What an odd child she must be to
prefer me to a book or a game."

I smiled at him and he returned my smile; and again I was
aware of that change in his expression.

Sometimes he would sit down and watch our game of chess.
Then he would range himself on Alvean's side against me.
I would protest and demand I be allowed to have my
queen back.

Alvean would sit smiling, and he would say : " Look,
Alvean. We'll put our bishop there, and that'll make our dear
Miss Leigh look to her defences."

Alvean would giggle and throw me a triumphant glance,
and I would be so happy to be with the two of them that I
grew almost careless and nearly lost the game. But not quite.
I never forgot that between Connan and me there was a certain
battle in progress and I always wanted to prove my mettle.

Though it was only a game of chess I wanted to show him I was his match.

He said one day: "When Alvean's movable we'll drive over to Fowey and have a picnic."

"Why go to Fowey," I asked, "when you have a perfect picnic beach here?"

"My dear Miss Leigh"—he had acquired a habit of calling me his dear Miss Leigh—"do you not know that other people's beaches are more exciting than one's own?"

"Oh yes, Papa," cried Alvean. "Do let's have a picnic."

She was so eager to get well for the picnic that she ate all the food which was brought to her and talked of the expedition continually. Dr. Pengelly was delighted with her; so were we all.

I said to Connan one day: "But you are the real cure. You have made her so happy, because at last you let her see that you are aware of her existence."

Then he did a surprising thing. He took my hand and lightly kissed my cheek. It was very different from that kiss which he had given me on the night of the ball. This was swift, friendly, passionless yet affectionate.

"No," he said, "it is you who are the real cure, my dear Miss Leigh."

I thought he was going to say something more. But he did not do so. Instead he left me abruptly.

I did not forget Gilly. I determined to fight for her as I had for Alvean, and I thought the best way of doing so was to speak to Connan about it. He was in that mood, I believed, to grant me what I asked. I should not have been surprised if, when Alvean was about again, he changed to his old self—forgetful of her, full of mockery for me. So I decided to strike my blow for Gilly while I had a chance of success.

I boldly went down to the punch room, when I knew he was there one morning, and asked if I might speak to him.

"But of course, Miss Leigh," he replied. "It is always a pleasure to speak to you."

I came straight to the point. "I want to do something for Gilly."

" Yes?"

" I do not believe she is half-witted. I think that no one
has made any attempt to help her. I have heard about her
accident. Before that, I understand, she was quite a normal
little girl. Don't you see that it might be possible to make her
normal once again?"

I saw a return of that mockery to his eyes as he said lightly :
" I believe that as with God, so with Miss Leigh, all things are
possible."

I ignored the flippancy. " I am asking your permission to
give her lessons."

" My dear Miss Leigh, does not the pupil you came here to
teach take up all your time?"

" I have a little spare time, Mr. TreMellyn. Even governesses
have that. I would be ready to teach Gilly in my own time,
providing of course you do not expressly forbid it."

" If I forbade you I am sure you would find some way of
doing it, so I think it would be simpler if I say : ' Go ahead
with your plans for Gilly. I wish you all success.' "

" Thank you," I said ; and turned to go.

" Miss Leigh," he called. I stood waiting.

" Let us go on that picnic soon. I could carry Alvean if
necessary to and from the carriage."

" That would be excellent, Mr. TreMellyn. I'll tell her at
once. I know it will delight her."

" And you, Miss Leigh, does it delight you?"

For a moment I thought he was coming towards me and I
started back. I was suddenly afraid that he would place his
hands on my shoulders and that at his touch I might betray
myself.

I said coolly : " Anything which is going to be so good for
Alvean delights me, Mr. TreMellyn."

And I hurried back to Alvean to tell her the good news.


So the weeks passed—pleasurable, wonderful weeks which I
sometimes felt could never be repeated.

I had taken Gilly to the schoolroom and I had even managed
to teach her a few letters. She delighted in pictures and quickly
became absorbed in them. I really believed she enjoyed our

lessons for she would present herself at the schoolroom each day at the appointed time.

She had been heard to speak a few words now and then and I knew that the whole household was watching the experiment with amusement and interest.

When Alvean was well enough to take lessons in the schoolroom I should have to be prepared for opposition. Alvean's aversion to Gilly was apparent. I had brought the child into the sick-room on one occasion and Alvean had immediately become sulky. I thought, when she is quite well I shall have to reconcile her to Gilly. But that was one of the problems of the future. I knew very well that when life returned to normal I could not expect these days of pleasure to continue.

There were plenty of visitors for Alvean. Celestine was there every day. She brought fruit and other presents for her. Peter came and she was always pleased to see him.

Once he said to her: " Do you not think I am a devoted uncle to call and see you so often, Alvean?"

She had retorted: " Oh, but you don't come to see me only, do you, Uncle Peter. You come mainly for Miss."

He had replied in characteristic style: " I come to see you both. How fortunate I am to have two such charming ladies on whom to call."

Lady Treslyn called with expensive books and flowers for Alvean, but Alvean received her sullenly and would scarcely speak to her.

" She is an invalid still, Lady Treslyn," I explained; and the smile which was flashed upon me almost took my breath away, so beautiful was it.

" Of course I understand," Lady Treslyn told me. " Poor child! Mr. TreMellyn tells me that she has been brave and you have been wonderful. I tell him how lucky he is to have found such a treasure. 'They are not easy to come by,' I said. I reminded him of how my last cook walked out in the middle of a dinner party. She was another such treasure."

I bowed my head and hated her—not because she had linked me in her mind with her cook, but because she was so beautiful, and I knew that rumours persisted about her and Connan and I feared that there was truth in them.

Connan seemed different when this woman was in the house. I felt he scarcely saw me. I heard the sounds of their laughter and I wondered sadly what they said to each other. I saw them in the gardens and I told myself there was an unmistakable intimacy in the very way they walked together.

Then I realised what a fool I had been, for I had been harbouring thoughts which I would not dare express, even to myself. I tried to pretend they did not exist. But they did— and in spite of my better sense they kept intruding.

I dared not look into the future.

Celestine one day suggested that she should take Alvean over to Mount Widden for the day and look after her there.

" It would be a change," she said.

" Connan," she added, " you shall come to dinner, and you can bring her back afterwards."

He agreed to do so. I was disappointed not to be included in the invitation; which showed what a false picture I had allowed myself to make of the situation during these incredible weeks. Imagine myself—the governess—invited to dine at Mount Widden!

I laughed at my own foolishness, but there was a note of bitterness and sadness. It was like waking up to a chilly morning after weeks of sunshine so brilliant that you thought it was going to last for ever; it was like the gathering of storm clouds in a summer sky.

Connan drove Alvean over in the carriage and I was left alone, for the first time since I arrived here without any definite duties.

I gave Gilly her lesson but I did not believe in taxing the child too much and when I had returned her to her grandmother I wondered what I was going to do.

Then an idea struck me. Why should I not go for a ride, a long ride? Perhaps on the moors.

I immediately remembered that day when Alvean and I had ridden to her Great-Aunt Clara. I began to feel rather excited. I was remembering the mystery of Alice again, which I had forgotten during those halcyon weeks of Alvean's convalescence. I began to wonder whether I had been so interested in Alice's story because I needed some interest to prevent me from brooding on my own.

I thought to myself, Great-Aunt Clara will want to hear how Alvean is getting on. In any case she had made it clear that I should be welcomed any time I called. Of course it would be different, calling without Alvean; but then I believed that she had been more interested to talk to me than to the child.

So I made up my mind.

I went to Mrs. Polgrey and said : " Alvean will be away all day. I propose to take a day's holiday."

Mrs. Polgrey had become very fond of me since I had taken such an interest in Gilly. She really did love the child, I believed. It was merely because she had assumed that Gilly's strangeness had been the price which had to be paid for her parents' sins that she had accepted her as *non compos mentis*.

" And none deserves a holiday more, Miss," she said to me. " Where are you going?"

" I think I'll go on to the moors. I'll take luncheon at an inn."

" Do you think you should, Miss, by yourself?"

I smiled at her. " I am very well able to take care of myself, Mrs. Polgrey."

" Well, there be bogs on the moor and mists and the Little People, some say."

" Little People indeed!"

" Ah, don't 'ee laugh at 'em, Miss. They don't like people to laugh at 'em. There's some as say they've seen 'em. Little gnome-like men in sugarloaf hats. If they don't like 'ee they'll lead 'ee astray with their fairy lanterns, and afore you knows where you be you'm in the middle of a bog that sucks 'ee down and won't let 'ee go however much you do struggle."

I gave a shiver. " I'll be careful, and I wouldn't dream of offending the Little People. If I meet any I'll be very polite."

" You'm mocking, Miss, I do believe."

" I'll be all right, Mrs. Polgrey. Don't have any fears about me."

I went to the stables and asked Tapperty which horse I could have to-day.

" There's May Morning if you'd like her. She be free."

F

I told him I was going to the moors. " A good chance to see the country," I added.

" Trust you, Miss. Bain't much you miss." And he laughed to himself as though enjoying some private joke.

" You be going with a companion, Miss?" he asked slyly.

I said that I was going alone, but I could see that he did not believe me.

I felt rather angry with him because I guessed that his thoughts were on Peter Nansellock. I believed that my name had been coupled with his since he had been so foolish as to send Jacinth over for me.

I wondered too if my growing friendship with Connan had been noted. I was horrified at the possibility. Oddly enough I could bear to contemplate their sly remarks which I was sure were exchanged out of my hearing, about Peter and me; it would be a different matter if they talked in that way of me and Connan.

How ridiculous! I told myself as I walked May Morning out of the stables and down to the village.

There is nothing to talk about between you and Connan. But there is, I answered myself; and I fell to thinking of those two occasions when he had kissed me.

I looked across the cove at Mount Widden. Wistfully I hoped that I should meet Connan coming back. But I didn't of course; he would stay there with Alvean and his friends. Why should I imagine that he would want to come back to be with me? I was letting this foolish habit of day dreaming get the better of my common sense.

But I continued to hope until I had left the village well behind me and I came to the first grey wall and boulders of the moor.

It was a sparkling December morning and there were great golden patches of gorse dotted over the moor.

I could smell the peaty soil, and the wind which had veered a little to the north was fresh and exhilarating.

I wanted to gallop across the moor with that wind in my face. I gave way to my desire and while I did so I imagined that Connan was riding beside me and that he called me to stop that he might tell me what a difference I had made to his life as well as Alvean's, and that, incongruous as it seemed, he was in love with me.

In this moorland country it was possible to believe in fantastic dreams; as some told themselves that these tracts of land were inhabited by the Little People, so I told myself that it was not impossible that Connan TreMellyn would fall in love with me.

At midday I arrived at The House on the Moor. It was very like that other occasion; the elderly housekeeper came out to welcome me and I was taken into Great-Aunt Clara's sitting room.

" Good day to you, Miss Leigh! And all alone to-day?"

So no one had told her of Alvean's accident. I was astonished. I should have thought Connan would have sent someone over to explain, since the old lady was obviously interested in her great-niece.

I told her about the accident and she looked very concerned. I hastily added that Alvean was getting on well and would soon be about again.

" But you must be in need of some refreshment, Miss Leigh," she said. " Let us have a glass of my elderberry wine; and will you stay to luncheon?"

I said it was most kind of her to invite me and if it were not causing too much inconvenience I should be delighted to do so.

We sipped our elderberry wine, and once more I was conscious of that heady feeling which I had experienced after her dandelion wine on the previous occasion. Luncheon consisted of mutton with caper sauce exceedingly well cooked and served; and afterwards we retired to the drawing room for what she called a little chat.

This was what I had been hoping for, and I was not to be disappointed.

" Tell me," she said, " how is dear little Alvean? Is she happier now?"

" Why . . . yes, I think she is very much happier. In fact I think she has been more so since her accident. Her father has been so attentive, and she is so fond of him."

" Ah," said Great-Aunt Clara, " her father." She looked at

me, and her bright blue eyes showed her excitement. I knew she was one of those women who cannot resist talking; and since she spent so much of her time with only her own household, the coming of a visitor such as myself was an irresistible temptation.

I was determined to make the temptation even more irresistible. I said tentatively: "There is not the usual relationship between them, I fancy."

There was a slight pause, and then she said quickly : "No. I suppose it is inevitable."

I did not speak. I waited breathlessly, afraid that she might change her mind. She was hovering on the edge of confidences and I felt that she could give me some vital clue to the situation at Mount Mellyn, to the story of the TreMellyns which I was beginning reluctantly to admit might very well become my story.

"I sometimes blame myself," she said, as though she were talking to herself; and indeed her blue eyes looked beyond me as though she were looking back over the years and was quite unconscious of my presence.

"The question is," she went on, "how much should one interfere in the lives of others."

It was a question which had often interested me. I had certainly tried to interfere in the lives of people I had met since I entered Mount Mellyn.

"Alice was with me after the engagement," she went on. "Everything could have changed then. But I persuaded her. You see, I thought *he* was the better man."

She was being a little incoherent, and I was afraid to ask her to elucidate lest I broke the spell. She might remember that she was betraying confidences to a young woman who was more curious than she should be.

"I wonder what would have happened if she had acted differently then. Do you ever play that game with yourself, Miss Leigh? Do you ever say, now if at a certain point I . . . or someone else . . . had done such and such . . . the whole tenor of life for that person would have changed?"

"Yes," I said. "Everybody does. You think that things would have been different for your niece and for Alvean."

"Oh yes . . . for her—Alice—more than most. She had come to a real turning-point. A cross-roads, one might say. Go this way and you have such and such a life. Go that way and everything will be quite different. It frightens me sometimes because if she had turned to the right instead of the left . . . as it were . . . she might be here to-day. After all, if she had married Geoffry there would not have been any need to run away with him, would there?"

"I see you were in her confidence."

"Indeed yes. I'm afraid I had quite a big part in shaping what happened. That's what alarmed me. Did I do right?"

"I am sure you did what you thought was right, and that is all any of us can do. You loved your niece very much, did you not?"

"Very much. My children were boys, you see, and I'd always wanted a girl. Alice used to come and play with my family . . . three boys and no girl. I used to hope that she might marry one of them. Cousins though. Perhaps that would not have been so good. I didn't live in this house then. We were in Penzance. Alice's parents had a big estate some few miles inland. That's her husband's now of course. She had a good fortune to bring to a husband. All the same, perhaps it would not have been good for cousins to marry. In any case they were set on the marriage with the TreMellyns."

"So that was arranged."

"Yes. Alice's father was dead, and her mother—she was my sister—had always been very fond of Connan TreMellyn . . . the elder I mean. There have been Connans in that family for centuries. The eldest son was aways given the name. I think my sister would have liked to marry the present Connan's father, but other marriages were arranged for them, and so they wanted their children to marry. They were betrothed when Connan was twenty and Alice eighteen. The marriage was to take place a year later."

"So it was indeed a marriage of convenience."

"How odd it is! Marriages of convenience often turn out to be marriages of inconvenience, do they not? They thought it would be a good idea if she came to stay with me. You see, I was within a few hours' riding distance from Mount Mellyn, and the young people could meet often like that . . . without her staying at the house. Of course you might say, why did not her mother take her to stay at Mount Mellyn? My sister was very ill at that time and not able to travel. In any case it was arranged that she should stay with me."

" And I suppose Mr. TreMellyn rode over to see her often."

" Yes. But not as often as I should have expected. I began to suspect that they were not as well matched as their fortunes were."

" Tell me about Alice," I said earnestly. " What sort of girl was she?"

" How can I explain her to you. The word light comes to my mind. She was light-hearted, light-minded. I do not mean she was light in her morals—which is a sense in which some people use the word. Although of course, after what happened . . . But who shall judge? You see, he came over here to paint. He did some peautiful pictures of the moors."

" Who? Connan TreMellyn?"

" Oh, dear me, no! Geoffry. Geoffry Nansellock. He was an artist of some reputation. Did you not know that?"

" No," I said. " I know nothing of him except that he was killed with Alice last July twelvemonth."

" He came over here often while she was with me. In fact he came more often than Connan did. I began to wonder how matters stood. There was something between them. They would go off together and he'd have his painting things with him. She used to say she was going to watch him at work. She would be a painter herself one day. But of course it was not painting they did together."

" They were . . . in love?" I asked.

" I was rather frightened when she told me. You see, there was going to be a child."

I caught my breath in surprise. Alvean, I thought. No wonder he could not bring himself to love her. No wonder my statement that she possessed artistic talent upset him and Celestine.

" She told me two weeks before the day fixed for her wedding. She was almost certain, she said. She did not think she could be mistaken. She said, 'What shall I do, Aunt Clara? Shall I marry Geoffry?'

" I said : 'Does Geoffry want to marry you, my dear?' And she answered : 'He would have to, would he not, if I told him.'

" I know now that she should have told him. It was only right that she should. But her marriage was already arranged, Alice was an heiress and I wondered whether Geoffry had hoped for this. You see the Nansellocks had very little and Alice's fortune would have been a blessing to them. I wondered . . . as one does wonder. He had a certain reputation too. There had been others who found themselves in Alice's condition, and it was due to him. I did not think she would be very happy with him for long."

There was silence, and I felt as though vital parts of a puzzle were being fitted together to give my picture meaning.

" I remember her . . . that day," the old lady continued. " It was in this very room. I often go over it. She talked to me about it . . . unburdening herself as I'm unburdening myself to you. It's been on my conscience for the last year . . . ever since she died. You see, she said to me : 'What shall I do, Aunt Clara? Help me. . . . Tell me what I should do.'

" And I answered her. I said : 'There's only one thing you can do, my dear; and that is go on with your marriage to Connan TreMellyn. You're betrothed to him. You must forget what happened with Geoffry Nansellock.' And she said to me : 'Aunt Clara, how can I forget? There'll be a living reminder, won't there?' Then I did this terrible thing. I said to her : 'You must marry. Your child will be born prematurely.' Then she threw back her head and laughed and laughed. It was hysterical laughter. Poor Alice, she was near breaking-point."

Great-Aunt Clara sat back in her chair; she looked as though she had just come out of a trance. I really believe she had been seeing, not me sitting opposite her, but Alice.

She was now a little frightened because she was wondering whether she had told me too much.

I said nothing. I was picturing it all; the wedding which

would have been a ceremonial occasion; the death of Alice's mother almost immediately afterwards; and Connan's father had died the following year. The marriage had been to please them and they had not lived long to enjoy it. And Alice was left with Connan—my Connan—and Alvean, the child of another man, whom she had tried to pass off as his. She had not succeeded—that much I knew.

He had kept up the pretence that Alvean was his daughter, but he had never accepted her as such in his mind. Alvean knew it; she admired him so much; but she suspected something was wrong and she was uncertain; she longed to be accepted as his daughter. Perhaps he had never really discovered whether she was or not.

The situation was fraught with drama. And yet, I thought, what good can come of brooding on it? Alice is dead; Alvean and Connan are alive. Let them forget what happened in the past. If they were wise they would try to make happiness for each other in the future.

" Oh, my dear," sighed Great-Aunt Clara, " how I talk! It is like living it all again. I have wearied you." A little fear crept into her voice. " I have talked too much and you, Miss Leigh, have played no part in all this. I trust you will keep what I have said, to yourself."

" You may trust me to do so," I assured her.

" I knew it. I would not have told you otherwise. But in any case, it is all so long ago. It has been a comfort to talk to you. I think about it all sometimes during the night. You see, it might have been right for her to marry Geoffry. Perhaps she thought so, and that was why she tried to run away with him. To think of them on that train! It seems like the judgment of God, doesn't it?"

" No," I said sharply. " There were many other people on that train who were killed. They weren't all on the point of leaving their husbands with other men."

She laughed on a high note. " How right you are! I knew you had lots of common sense. And you don't think I did wrong? You see, I sometimes tell myself that, if I had persuaded her not to marry Connan, she wouldn't. That is what frightens me. I pointed the way to her destiny."

" You must not blame yourself," I said. " Whatever you did you did because you thought it was best for her. And we after all make our own destinies. I am sure of that."

" You do comfort me, Miss Leigh. You will stay and have tea with me, won't you?"

" It is kind of you, but I think I should be back before dark."

" Oh yes, you must be back before dark."

" It grows dark so early at this time of year."

" Then I must not be selfish and keep you. Miss Leigh, when Alvean is well enough, you will bring her over to see me?"

" I promise I shall."

" And if you yourself feel like coming over before that. . . ."

" Depend upon it, I shall come. You have given me a very pleasant and interesting time."

The fear came back into her eyes. " You will remember it was in confidence?"

I reassured her. I knew that this charming old lady's greatest pleasure in life must have been sharing confidences, telling a little more than was discreet. Well, I thought, we all have our little vices.

She came to the door to wave me on when I left.

" It's been so pleasant," she reiterated. " And don't forget." She put her finger to her lips and her eyes sparkled.

I imitated the gesture and, waving, rode off.

I was very thoughtful on the way home. This day I had learned so much.

I was nearly at Mellyn village when the thought struck me that Gilly was Alvean's half-sister. I remembered then the drawings I had seen of Alvean and Gilly combined.

So Alvean knew. Or did she merely fear? Was she trying to convince herself that her father was not Geoffry Nansellock —which would make her Gilly's half-sister? Or did her great desire for Connan's approval really mean that she was longing for him to accept her as his daughter?

I felt a great desire to help them all out of this morass of tragedy into which Alice's indiscretion had plunged them.

I can do it, I told myself. I will do it.

Then I thought of Connan with Lady Treslyn, and I was

filled with disquiet. What absurd and impossible dreams I was indulging in. What chance had I—a governess—of showing Connan the way to happiness?

Christmas was rapidly approaching, and it brought with it all that excitement which I remembered so well from the old days in my father's vicarage.

Kitty and Daisy were constantly whispering together, and Mrs. Polgrey said that they nearly drove her crazy, and that their work was more skimped than usual, though that had to be seen to be believed. She went about the house sighing " Nowadays. . . ." and shaking her head in sorrow. But even she was excited.

The weather was warm, more like the approach of spring than of winter. On my walks in the woods I noticed that the primroses had begun to bloom.

" My dear life," said Tapperty, " primroses in December be nothing new to we. Spring do come early to Cornwall."

I began to think about Christmas presents and I made a little list. There must be something for Phillida and her family, and Aunt Adelaide; but I was mainly concerned with the people at Mount Mellyn. I had a little money to spend, as I used very little and had saved most of what I had earned since I had taken my post at Mount Mellyn.

One day I went into Plymouth and did my Christmas shopping. I bought books for Phillida and her family and had them sent direct to her; I bought a scarf for Aunt Adelaide and that was sent direct too. I spent a long time choosing what I would give the Mellyn household. Finally, I decided on scarves for Kitty and Daisy, red and green which would suit them; and a blue one for Gilly to match her eyes. For Mrs. Polgrey I bought a bottle of whisky which I was sure would delight her more than anything else, and for Alvean some handkerchiefs in many colours, with A embroidered on them.

I was pleased with my purchases. I was beginning to grow as excited about Christmas as Daisy and Kitty were.

The weather continued very mild, and on Christmas Eve I helped Mrs. Polgrey and the girls to decorate the great hall and some of the other rooms.

The men had been out the previous day and brought in ivy, holly, box and bay. I was shown how the pillars in the great hall were entwined with these leaves and Daisy and Kitty taught me how to make Christmas bushes; they were delightedly shocked by an ignorance like mine. I had never before heard of a Christmas bush! We took two wooden hoops—one inserted into the other—and this ball-like framework we decorated with evergreen leaves and furze; then we hung oranges and apples on it; and I must say this made a pretty show. These we hung in some of the windows.

The biggest logs were carried in for the fireplaces, and the house was filled with laughter, while the servants' hall was decorated in exactly the same manner as the great hall.

"We do have our ball here while the family be having theirs," Daisy told me; and I wondered to which ball I should go. Perhaps to neither. A governess's position was somewhere in between, I supposed.

"My life!" cried Daisy, "I can scarcely wait for the day. Last Christmas was a quiet one . . . had to be on account of the house being in mourning. But we in the servants' hall managed pretty well. There was dash-an-darras and metheglin to drink, and Mrs. Polgrey's sloe gin had to be tasted to be believed. There was mutton and beef, I remember, and hog's pudding. No feast in these parts ain't complete without hog's pudding. You ask Father!"

All through Christmas Eve the smell of baking filled the kitchen and its neighbourhood. Tapperty, with Billy Trehay and some of the boys from the stables, came to the door just to smell it. Mrs. Tapperty was up at the house all day working in the kitchen. I scarcely recognised the usualy calm and dignified Mrs. Polgrey. She was bustling about, her face flushed, purring, stirring and talking ecstatically of pies which bore the odd names of squab and lammy, giblet, muggety and herby.

I was called in to help. "Do 'ee keep your eye on that saucepan, Miss, and should it come to the boil tell I quickly." Mrs. Polgrey's dialect became more and more broad as the excitement grew, and I could scarcely understand the language which was being bandied about in the kitchen that Christmas.

I was smiling fatuously at a whole batch of pasties which had just come out of the oven, golden-brown pastry with the smell of savoury meats and onions, when Kitty came in shouting: " M'am, the curl singers be here."

"Well, bring 'em, bring 'em in, ye daftie," cried Mrs. Polgrey, forgetting dignity in the excitement and wiping her hand across her sweating brow. "What be 'ee waiting for? Don't 'ee know, me dear, that it be bad luck to keep curl singers waiting?"

I followed her into the hall, where a company of village youths and girls had gathered. They were already singing when we arrived, and I understood that the curl singers were what were known in other parts of the country as carol singers.

They rendered " The Seven Joys of Mary," " The Holly and the Ivy," " The Twelve Days of Christmas " and " The First Noël." We all joined in.

Then the leader of the group began to sing:

> " *Come let me taste your Christmas beer*
> *That is so very strong,*
> *And I do wish that Christmas time,*
> *With all its mirth and song,*
> *Was twenty times as long.*"

Then Mrs. Polgrey signed to Daisy and Kitty, who were already on their way, I guessed, to bring refreshment to the party after this gentle reminder.

Metheglin was served to the singers with blackberry and elderberry wine, and into their hands were thrust great pasties, some containing meat, some fish. The satisfaction was evident.

And when they had finished eating and drinking, a bowl—which was tied with red ribbons and decorated with furze—was handed to Mrs. Polgrey who very majestically placed some coins in it.

When they had gone Daisy said: "Well, now that lot have come a-gooding, what's to be next?"

She delighted in my ignorance of course when I had to ask what a-gooding meant.

" My dear life, you don't know all, Miss, do 'ee now. To go

a-gooding means to go collecting for Christmas wine or a Christmas cake. What else?"

I realised that I had a great deal to learn concerning the habits of the Cornish, but I did feel that I was enjoying their way of celebrating Christmas.

" Oh, Miss, I forgot to tell 'ee," cried Daisy. " There be a parcel in your room. I took it up just afore them come a-gooding, and forgot to tell 'ee till now." She was surprised because I lingered. " A parcel, Miss! Don't 'ee want to see what it is? 'Twas so size, and 'twas a box like as not."

I realised that I had been in a dream. I felt that I wanted to stay here for ever, and learn all the customs of this part of the world. I wanted to make it my part of the world.

I shook myself out of that dream. What you really want, I told myself, is some fairy-tale ending to your story. You want to be the mistress of Mount Mellyn. Why not admit it?

I went up to my room, and there I found Phillida's parcel.

I took out a shawl of black silk on which was embroidered a pattern in green and amber. There was also an amber comb of the Spanish type. I stuck the comb in my hair and wrapped the shawl about me. I was startled by my reflection. I looked exotic, more like a Spanish dancer than an English governess.

There was something else in the parcel. I undid it quickly and saw that it was a dress—one of Phillida's which I had greatly admired. It was of green silk, the same shade of green as in the shawl. A letter fell out.

" *Dear Marty,*

How is the governessing? Your last letter sounded as though you found it intriguing. I believe your Alvean is a little horror. Spoilt child, I'll swear. Are they treating you well? It sounded as if that side of it was not too bad. What is the matter with you, by the way? You used to write such amusing letters. Since you've been in that place you've become uncommunicative. I suspect you either love it or hate it. Do tell.

The shawl and comb are my Christmas gift. I hope you like them because I spent a lot of time choosing. Are they too frivolous? Would you rather have had a set of woollen underwear or some improving book? But I heard from Aunt Adelaide that she was sending you the former. There is a distinctly governessy flavour in your letters. All sound and fury, Marty, my dear, signifying nothing. I am wondering whether you'll be sitting down to dine with the family this Christmas or presiding in the servants' hall. I'm sure it will be the former. They couldn't help but ask you. After all it is Christmas. You'll dine with the family even if there's one of those dinner parties where a guest doesn't turn up and they say, ' Send for the governess. We cannot be thirteen.' So our Marty goes to dine in my old green and her new scarf and comb, and there she attracts a millionaire and lives happily ever after.

Seriously, Marty, I did think you might need something for the festivities. So the green gown is a gift. Don't think of it as a cast-off. I love the thing and I'm giving it to you, not because I'm tired of it, but because it always suited you better than me.

I shall want to hear all about the Christmas festivities. And, dear sister, when you're the fourteenth at the dinner table don't freeze likely suitors with a look or give them one of your clever retorts. Be a nice gentle girl and, kind lady, I see romance and fortune in the cards for you.

Happy Christmas, dear Marty, and do write soon sending the real news. The children and William send their love. Mine to you also. *Phillida*."

I felt rather emotional. It was a link with home. Dear Phillida, she did think of me often then. Her shawl and comb were beautiful, even if a little incongruous for someone in my humble position; and it was good of her to send the dress.

I was startled by a sudden cry. I spun round and saw Alvean at the door which led to the schoolroom.

" Miss! " she cried. " So it's you! "

" Of course. Who did you think it was? "

She did not answer, but I knew.

" I've never seen you look like that, Miss."

" You've never seen me in a shawl and comb."

" You look . . . pretty."

" Thank you, Alvean."

She was a little shaken. I knew who she had thought it was standing in my room.

I was the same height as Alice, and if I were less slender that would not be obvious with the silk shawl round me.

Christmas Day was a day to remember all my life.

I awoke in the morning to the sounds of excitement . The servants were laughing and talking together below my window.

I opened my eyes and thought : Christmas Day. And then : My first Christmas at Mount Mellyn.

Perhaps, I said to myself trying to throw a cold douche over my exuberance which somehow made me apprehensive because it was so great, it will be not only your first but your last.

A whole year lay between this Christmas and the next. Who could say what would happen in that time?

I was out of bed when my water was brought up. Daisy scarcely stopped a moment, she was so full of excitement.

" I be late, Miss, but there be so much to do. You'd better hurry now or you'll not be in time to see the wassail. They'll be coming early, you can depend on that. They know the family 'ull be off to church, so they mustn't be late."

There was no time to ask questions so I washed and dressed and took out my parcels. Alvean's had already been put by her bed the previous night.

I went to the window. The air was balmy and it had that strong tang of spices in it. I drew deep breaths and listened to the gentle rhythm of the waves. They said nothing this morning; they merely swished contentedly. This was Christmas morning when for a day all troubles, all differences might be shelved.

Alvean came to my room. She was carrying her embroidered handkerchiefs rather shyly. She said : " Thank you, Miss. A happy Christmas ! "

I put my arms about her and kissed her, and although she seemed a little embarrassed by this demonstration she returned my kiss.

She had brought a brooch so like the silver whip I had given her that I thought for a moment that she was returning my gift.

"I got it from Mr. Pastern," she said. "I wanted one as near mine as possible, but not too near, so that we shouldn't get them mixed up. Yours has got a little engraving on the handle. Now we'll each have one when we go riding."

I was delighted. She had not ridden since her accident, and she could not have shown me more clearly that she was ready to start again.

I said: "You could not have given me anything I should have liked better, Alvean."

She was very pleased, although she murmured in an offhand way: "I'm glad you like it, Miss." Then she left me abruptly.

This, I told myself, is going to be a wonderful day. It's Christmas.

My presents proved to be a great success. Mrs. Polgrey's eyes glistened at the sight of the whisky; as for Gilly, she was delighted with her scarf. I suppose the poor child had never had anything so pretty before; she kept stroking it and staring at it in wonder. Daisy and Kitty were pleased with their scarves too; and I felt I had been clever in my choice.

Mrs. Polgrey gave me a set of doilies with a coy whisper: "For your bottom drawer, me dear." I replied that I would start one immediately, and we were very gay. She said that she would make a cup of tea and we'd sample my whisky, but there wasn't the time.

"My dear life, when I think of all there has to be done to-day!"

The wassail singers arrived in the morning and I heard their voices at the door of the great hall.

> "*The Master and Mistress our wassail begin*
> *Pray open your door and let us come in*
> *With our wassail, wassail, wassail.*
> *And joy come to our jolly wassail.*"

They came into the hall, and they also carried a bowl into which coins were dropped; and all the servants crowded in and, as Connan entered, the singing grew louder and the verse was repeated.

" The Master and the Mistress . . ."

I thought, Two years ago, Alice would have stood there with him. Does he remember? He showed no sign. He sang with them and ordered that the stirrup cup, the dash-an-darras, be brought out with the saffron cake and pasties and ginger-bread, which had been made for the occasion.

He moved nearer to me.

" Well, Miss Leigh," he said under cover of the singing, " what do you think of a Cornish Christmas?"

" Very interesting."

" You haven't seen half yet."

" I should hope not. The day has scarcely begun."

" You should rest this afternoon."

" But why?"

" For the feasting this evening."

" But I . . ."

" Of course you will join us. Where else would you spend your Christmas Day? With the Polgreys? With the Tappertys?"

" I did not know. I wondered whether I was expected to hover between the great hall and the servants' hall."

" You look disapproving."

" I am not sure."

" Oh, come, this is Christmas. Do not wonder whether you should be sure or not. Just come. By the way, I have not wished you a merry Christmas yet. I have something here . . . a little gift. A token of my gratitude, if you like. You have been so good to Alvean since her accident. Oh, and *before* of course, I have no doubt. But it has been brought to my notice so forcibly since . . ."

" But I have only done my duty as a governess. . . ."

" And that is something you would always do. I know it. Well, let's say this is merely to wish you a merry Christmas."

He had pressed a small object into my hand, and I was so overcome with pleasure that I felt it must show in my eyes and betray my feelings to him.

" You are very good to me," I said. " I had not thought . . ."

He smiled and moved away to the singers. I had noticed

Tapperty's eyes on us. I wondered whether he had seen the gift handed to me.

I wanted to be alone, for I felt so emotionally disturbed. The small case he had pressed into my hand was demanding to be opened. I could not do so here.

I slipped out of the hall and ran up to my room.

It was a small, blue plush case, the sort which usually contained jewellery.

I opened it. Inside, on oyster-coloured satin, lay a brooch. It was in the form of a horseshoe, and it was studded with what could only be diamonds.

I stared at it in dismay. I could not accept such a valuable object. I must return it of course.

I held it up to the light and saw the flash of red and green in the stones. It must be worth a great deal of money. I possessed no diamonds, but I could see that these were fine ones.

Why did he do it? If it had been some small token I should have been so happy. I wanted to throw myself on to my bed and weep.

I could hear Alvean calling me. " Miss, it's time for church. Come on, Miss. The carriage is waiting to take us to church."

I hastily put the brooch into its box and put on my cape and bonnet as Alvean came into the room.

I saw him after church. He was going across to the stables and I called after him.

He hesitated, looked over his shoulder and smiled at me.

" Mr. TreMellyn. It is very kind of you," I said as I ran up to him, " but this gift is far too valuable for me to accept."

He put his head on one side and regarded me in the old mocking manner.

" My dear Miss Leigh," he said lightly. " I am a very ignorant man, I fear. I have no notion how valuable a gift must be before it is acceptable."

I flushed hotly and stammered : " This is a very valuable ornament."

" I thought it so suitable. A horseshoe means luck, you know. And you have a way with horses, have you not?"

" I . . . I have no occasion to wear such a valuable piece of jewellery."

" I thought you might wear it to the ball to-night."

For a moment I had a picture of myself dancing with him. I should be wearing Phillida's green silk dress, which would compare favourably with those of his guests because Phillida had a way with clothes. I would wear my shawl, and my diamond brooch would be proudly flaunted on the green silk, because I treasured it so much, and I treasured it because he had given it to me.

" I feel I have no right."

" Oh," he murmured, " I begin to understand. You feel that I give the brooch in the same spirit as Mr. Nansellock offered Jacinth."

" So . . ." I stammered, "you knew of that?"

" Oh, I know most things that go on here, Miss Leigh. You returned the horse. Very proper and what I would expect of you. Now the brooch is given in a very different spirit. I give it to you for a reason. You have been good to Alvean. Not only as a governess but as a woman. Do you know what I mean? There is more to the care of a child, is there not, than arithmetic and grammar. You gave her that little extra. The brooch belonged to Alvean's mother. Look upon it like this, Miss Leigh : It is a gift of appreciation from us both. Does that make it all right?"

I was silent for a few moments. Then I said : " Yes . . . that is different, of course. I accept the brooch. Thank you very much, Mr. TreMellyn."

He smiled at me—it was a smile I did not fully understand, because it seemed to hold in it many meanings.

I was afraid to try to understand.

" Thank you," I murmured again; and I hurried back to the house.

I went up to my room and took out the brooch. I pinned it on my dress, and immediately my lavender cotton took on a new look.

I would wear the diamonds to-night. I would go in Phillida's dress and my comb and shawl, and on my breast I would wear Alice's diamonds.

So on this strange Christmas Day I had a gift from Alice.

I had dined in the middle of the day in the small dining room with Connan and Alvean, the first meal I had taken with them in this intimacy. We had eaten turkey and plum pudding and had been waited on by Kitty and Daisy. I could feel that certain significant looks were being directed towards us.

" On Christmas Day," Connan had said, " you could not be expected to dine alone. Do you know, Miss Leigh, I fear we have treated you rather badly. I should have suggested that you should go home to your family for Christmas. You should have reminded me."

" I felt I had been here too short a time to ask for a holiday," I answered. " Besides . . ."

" In view of Alvean's accident, you felt you should stay," he murmured. " It is good of you to be so thoughtful."

Conversation in the small dining room was animated. The three of us discussed the Christmas customs, and Connan told us stories of what had happened in previous years, how on one occasion the wassailers had arrived late so that the family had gone to church and they had to wait outside and serenade them all the way home.

I imagined Alice with him now. I imagined her sitting in the chair I now occupied. I wondered what the conversation was like then. I wondered if now, seeing me there, he was thinking of Alice.

I kept reminding myself that it was merely because it was Christmas that I was sitting here. That after the festivities were over I should revert to my old place.

But I was not going to think of that now. To-night I was going to the ball. Miraculously I had a dress worthy of the occasion. I had a comb of amber and a brooch of diamonds. I felt, To-night I shall mingle with these people on my own terms. It will be quite unlike that occasion when I danced in the solarium.

I took Connan's advice that afternoon and tried to rest so that I might stay fresh until the early morning. Much to my surprise I did manage to sleep. I must have slept lightly for I dreamed, and as so often in this house, my dreams were of

Alice. I thought that she came to the ball, a shadowy wraith of a figure whom no one but I could see, and she whispered to me as I danced with Connan: " This is what I want, Marty. I like to see this. I like to see you sitting in my chair at luncheon. I like to see your hand in that of Connan. You . . . Marty . . . you . . . not another. . . ."

I awoke with reluctance. That was a pleasant dream. I tried to sleep again, tried to get back to that half-world where ghosts came back from the tomb and told you that they longed for you to have all that you most wanted in life.

Daisy brought me a cup of tea at five o'clock. On Mrs. Polgrey's instructions, she told me.

" I've brought 'ee a piece of Mrs. Polgrey's fuggan to take with it," she said, indicating a slice of raisin cake. " If there's more you do want, 'tis only for you to say."

I said : " This will be ample."

" Then you'll be wanting to get ready for the ball, will 'ee not, Miss?"

" There's plenty of time," I told her.

" I'll bring 'ee hot water at six, Miss. That'll give 'ee plenty of time to dress. The Master 'ull be receiving the guests at eight. That's how it always was. And don't forget—'tis but buffet supper at nine, so there's a long time to go afore you get more to eat. Are you sure you wouldn't like something more than that there piece of fuggan?"

I was sure I was going to find it difficult to eat what she had brought so I said : " This is quite enough, Daisy."

" Well, 'tis for you to say, Miss."

She stood at the door a moment, her head on one side, watching me. Speculatively? Was she regarding me with a new interest?

I pictured them in the servants' hall, Tapperty leading the conversation.

Were they always wondering what new relationship had begun—or was about to begin—between the Master of the house and the governess?

I was at the ball in Phillida's green dress with the tight, low-cut bodice and the billowing skirt. I had dressed my hair differently, piling it high on my head; it was necessary to do so in order to do justice to the comb. On my dress sparkled the diamond brooch.

I was happy. I could mingle with the guests as one of them. No one would know, unless told, that I was only the governess.

I had waited until the ballroom was full before I went down. Then I could best mingle with the guests. I had only been there a few minutes when Peter was at my elbow.

"You look dazzling," he said.

"Thank you. I am glad to surprise you."

"I'm not in the least surprised. I always knew how you could look, given the chance."

"You always know how to pay the compliment."

"To you I always say what I mean. One thing I have not yet said to you, and that is ' A happy Christmas.' "

"Thank you. I wish you the same."

"Let us make it so for each other. I have brought no gift for you."

"But why should you?"

"Because it is Christmas, and a pleasant custom for friends to exchange gifts."

"But not for . . ."

"Please . . . please . . . no reminders of governessing to-night. One day I am going to give you Jacinth, you know. She is meant for you. I see Connan is about to open the ball. Will you partner me?"

"Thank you, yes."

"It's the traditional dance, you know."

"I don't know it."

"It's easy. You only have to follow me." He began humming the tune to me. "Haven't you seen it done before?"

"Yes, through the peep in the solarium at the last ball."

"Ah, that last ball! We danced together. But Connan cut in, didn't he?"

"It was somewhat unconventional."

"Very, for our governess. I'm really surprised at her."

The music had begun, and Connan was walking into the centre of the hall holding Celestine by the hand. To my horror

I realised that Peter and I would have to join them and dance those first few bars with them.

I tried to hold back, but Peter had me firmly by the hand.

Celestine was surprised to see me there; but if Connan was he gave no sign. I imagined that Celestine reasoned: It is all very well to ask the governess as it is Christmas. But should she immediately thrust herself into such a prominent position?

However, I believed her to be of too sweet a nature to show her astonishment after that first start of surprise. She gave me a warm smile.

I said: " I shouldn't be here. I don't really know the dance. I didn't realise . . ."

" Follow us," said Connan.

" We'll look after you," echoed Peter.

And in a few seconds the others were falling in behind us. Round the hall we went to the tune of *The Furry Dance*.

" You're doing excellently," said Connan with a smile as our hands touched.

" You will soon be a Cornishwoman," added Celestine.

" And why not?" demanded Peter. " Are we not the salt of the earth?"

" I am not sure that Miss Leigh thinks so," replied Connan.

" I am becoming very interested in all the customs of the country," I added.

" And in the inhabitants, I hope," whispered Peter.

We danced on. It was simple enough to learn, and when it was over I knew all the movements.

As the last bars were played I heard someone to say: " Who is the striking-looking young woman who danced with Peter Nansellock?"

I wanted for the answer to be: " Oh, that's the governess."

But it was different: " I've no idea. She certainly is . . . unusual."

I was exultant. I doubt that I had ever been so happy in my life.

I knew that in the time to come I should treasure every minute of that wonderful evening, for I was not only at the ball, I was a success at the ball.

I did not lack partners; and, even when I was forced to admit
that I was the governess, I continued to receive the homage
due to an attractive woman. What had happened to change me,
I wondered. Why couldn't I have been like this at Aunt
Adelaide's parties? But if I had, I should never have come to
Mount Mellyn.

Then I knew why I had not been like this. It was not only
the green dress, the amber comb and the diamond brooch; I
was in love, and love was the greatest beautifier of all.

Never mind if I was ridiculously, hopelessly in love. I was
like Cinderella at the ball, determined to enjoy myself until the
stroke of twelve.

A strange thing happened while I was dancing. I was with
Sir Thomas Treslyn, who turned out to be a courteous old
gentleman, a little wheezy during the dance so I suggested
that he might prefer to sit out the rest of it. He was very
grateful to me and I felt quite fond of him. I was ready to be
fond of anyone on that night.

He said: " I'm getting a little too old for the dance, Miss
er . . ."

" Leigh," I said. " Miss Leigh. I'm the governess here,
Sir Thomas."

" Oh indeed," he said. " I was going to say, Miss Leigh,
it is extremely kind of you to think of my comfort when you
must be longing to dance."

" I'm quite happy to sit for a while."

" I see that you are kind as well as very attractive."

I remembered Phillida's instructions and accepted the com-
pliments nonchalantly as though I had been accustomed to
them all my life.

He was relaxed and confidential. " It's my wife who likes to
come to these affairs. She has so much vitality."

" Ah yes," I said, " she is very beautiful."

I had noticed her, of course, the very moment I entered the
ballroom; she was in pale mauve chiffon over an underskirt of
green; she evidently had a passion for chiffon and such clinging
materials, and it was understandable considering her figure; she
wore quantities of diamonds. The mauve toning down the
green was exquisite and I wondered whether my own vivid

emerald was not a little blatant compared with hers. She looked
outstandingly beautiful, as she would in any assembly.

He nodded, a little sadly I thought.

And as I sat talking, my eyes, wandering round the hall,
went suddenly to the peep high in the wall, that star-shaped
opening which merged so perfectly into the murals that none
would have guessed it was there.

Someone was watching the ball through the peep, but it was
impossible to see who it was.

I thought: Of course it is Alvean. Did she not always
watch the ball through the peep? Then I was suddenly startled
for, as I was sitting there, watching the dancers, I saw Alvean.
I had forgotten that this was a special occasion—Christmas
Day—and just as, on such a day, the governess might come
to the ball, so might Alvean.

She was dressed in a white muslin dress with a wide blue
sash and I saw that she wore the silver whip pinned to the
bodice of her dress. All these things I noticed with half my
attention. I looked swiftly up to the peep. The face,
unrecognisable, indefinable, was still there.

Supper was served in the dining room and the punch room.
There was a buffet in both these rooms and guests helped themselves, for according to custom the servants on this day of days
were having their own ball in their own hall.

I saw that these people who so rarely waited on themselves
now found it quite good fun to do so. Piled on dishes were the
results of all that kitchen activity; small pies of various kinds,
called here pasties—not the enormous ones which were eaten
frequently in the kitchen, but dainty ones. There were slices of
beef, and chicken and fish of various descriptions. There was a
great bowl of hot punch; another of mulled wine; there was
mead, whisky and sloe gin.

Peter Nansellock, with whom I had had the supper dance,
led me into the punch room. Sir Thomas Treslyn was already
there with Celestine, and Peter led me to the table at which
they were sitting.

" Leave it to me," he said. " I'll feed you all."

I said: " Allow me to help you."

"Nonsense," he replied. "You remain with Celeste." He whispered banteringly: "You're not the governess to-night, Miss Leigh; you're a lady like the rest of them. Don't forget it; then no one else will."

But I was determined that I would not be waited on and I insisted on going to the buffet with him.

"Pride," he murmured, slipping his hand through my arm. "Wasn't that the sin by which fell the angels?"

"It may have been ambition; I am not sure."

"Well, I'll warrant you're not without a dash of that either. Never mind. What will you eat? Perhaps it is as well you came. Our Cornish food often seems odd to you foreigners from the other side of the Tamar."

He began loading one of the trays which had been put there in readiness.

"Which sort of pie will you have? Giblet, squab, nattling or muggety? Ha, here's taddage too. I can recommend the squab: layers of apple and bacon, onions and mutton and young pigeon. The most delicious Cornish fare."

"I'm ready to try it," I said.

"Miss Leigh," he went on, "Martha . . . has anyone ever told you that your eyes are like amber?"

"Yes," I answered.

"Has anyone ever told you you're beautiful?"

"No."

"Then that oversight should be and is recitified immediately."

I laughed and at that moment Connan came into the room with Lady Treslyn.

She sat down with Celestine, and Connan came over to the buffet.

"I am enlightening Miss Leigh about our Cornish food. She doesn't know what a 'fair maid' is. Is that not odd, Con, seeing that she is one herself?"

Connan looked excited; his eyes smiling into mine were warm. He said: "Fair maids, Miss Leigh, is another name for pilchards served like this with oil and lemon." He took a fork and put some on two plates. "It is a contraction of the old

Spanish fumado, and we always say here that it is food fit for a Spanish don."

"A relic, Miss Leigh," interrupted Peter, "of those days when the Spaniards raided our shores and took too great an interest in another kind of fair maid."

Alvean had come in and was standing beside me. I thought she looked tired.

"You should be in bed," I said.

"I'm hungry," she told me.

"After supper we'll go up."

She nodded and with sleepy pleasure she piled food on a plate.

We sat round the table, Alvean, Peter, Celestine, Sir Thomas, Connan and Lady Treslyn.

It seemed like a dream that I should be there with them. Alice's brooch glittered on my dress, and I thought : Thus, two years ago, she would have sat . . . as I am sitting now. Alvean would not have been here then; she would have been too young to have been allowed to come, but apart from that and the fact that I was in Alice's place, it must have been very like other occasions. I wondered if any of the others thought this.

I remembered the face I had seen at the peep, and what Alvean had said on the night of that other ball. I could not remember the exact words but I knew that it had been something about her mother's love of dancing and how, if she came back, she would come to a ball. Then Alvean had half-hoped to see her among the dancers. . . . What if she watched from another place? I thought of that ghostly solarium in moonlight and I said to myself : "Whose face did I see at the peep?"

Then I thought : Gilly! What if it were Gilly? It must have been Gilly. Who else could it have been?

My attention was brought back to the group at the table when Connan said : "I'll get you some more whisky, Tom." He rose and went to the buffet. Lady Treslyn got up quickly and went to him. I found it difficult to take my eyes from them. I thought how distinguished they looked—she in green shaded mauve draperies, the most beautiful woman at the ball and he, surely the most distinguished of the men.

"I'll help you, Connan," she said, and I heard them laughing together.

"Look out," said Connan, "we're spilling it."

They had their backs to us, and as I watched them I thought that with the slightest provocation I could have burst into tears because now I clearly saw the ridiculousness of my hopes.

She had slipped her arm through his as they came back to the table. The intimate gesture wounded me deeply. I suppose I had drunk too much of the mead, or metheglin as they called it. Mead. It was such a soft and gentle name. But the mead which was made at Mount Mellyn was very potent.

I said to myself coldly : It is time you retired.

As he gave the glass to Sir Thomas—who emptied it with a speed which surprised me—I noticed that there were smudges of shadow under Alvean's eyes, and I said : " Alvean, you look tired. You should be in bed."

"Poor child!" cried Celestine at once. "And she only just recovering. . . ."

I rose. "I will take Alvean to bed now," I said. "Come along, Alvean."

She was half-asleep already and made no protest but rose meekly to her feet.

"I will say good night to you all," I said.

Peter rose to his feet. "We'll see you later," he said.

I did not answer. I was desperately trying not to look at Connan, for I felt he was not aware of me; that he would never be aware of anyone when Lady Treslyn was near.

"*Au revoir*," said Peter, and as the others echoed the words absentmindedly I went out of the punch room, holding Alvean by the hand.

I felt as Cinderella must have felt with the striking of the midnight hour.

My brief glory was over. Lady Treslyn had made me realise how foolish I had been to dream.

Alvean was asleep before I felt her room. I tried not to think of Connan and Lady Treslyn while I went to my room and lighted the candles on my dressing table. I looked attractive;

there was no doubt of it. Then I said to myself, Anyone looks attractive by candlelight.

The diamonds winked back at me, and I was immediately reminded of the face I had seen at the peep.

I thought afterwards that I must have drunk too freely of the metheglin, because on impulse I went down to the landing below my own. I could hear the shouts coming from the servants' hall. So they were still merry-making down there. The door to Gilly's room was ajar, and I went in. There was enough moonlight for me to see that the child was in her bed, but sitting up, awake.

" Gilly," I said.

" Madam!" she cried and her voice was joyful. " I knew you'd come to-night."

" Gilly, you know who this is." What had made me say such a foolish thing?

She nodded.

" I'm going to light your candle," I said, and I did so.

Her eyes regarded my face with that blank blue stare, and came to rest on the brooch. I sat on the edge of the bed. I knew that when I had first come in she had thought I was someone else.

She was contented though, which showed the confidence she was beginning to feel in me.

I touched the brooch and said: " Once it was Mrs. Tre-Mellyn's."

She smiled and nodded.

I said: " You spoke when I came in. Why do you not speak to me now?"

She merely smiled.

" Gilly," I said, " were you at the peep in the solarium tonight? Were you watching the dancers?"

She nodded.

" Gilly, say ' Yes.' "

" Yes," said Gilly.

" You were up there all alone? You weren't afraid?"

She shook her head and smiled.

" You mean no, don't you, Gilly? Say ' no.' "

"No."

"Why weren't you afraid?"

She opened her mouth and smiled. Then she said: "Not afraid because . . ."

"Because?" I said eagerly.

"Because," she repeated.

"Gilly," I said. "Were you alone up there?"

She smiled and I could get her to say no more.

After a while I kissed her and she returned my kiss. She was fond of me, I knew. I believed that in her mind she confused me with someone else, and I knew who that person was.

Back in my room I did not want to take off my dress. I felt that as long as I wore it, I could still hope for what I knew to be impossible.

So I sat by my window for an hour or so. It was a warm night and I was comfortable with my silk shawl about me.

I heard some of the guests coming out to their carriages. I heard the exchange of good-byes.

And while I was there I heard Lady Treslyn's voice. Her voice was low and vibrant, but she spoke with such intensity that I caught every syllable and I knew to whom she was speaking.

She said: "Connan, it can't be long now. It won't be long."

Next morning when Kitty brought my water, she did not come alone. Daisy was with her. I heard their raucous voices mingling and, in my half-waking state, thought they sounded like the gulls.

"Morning, Miss."

They wanted me to wake up quickly; they had exciting news. I saw that in their faces.

"Miss . . ." they were both speaking together, both determined to be the one to impart the startling information, "last night . . . or rather this morning . . ."

Then Kitty rushed on ahead of her sister: "Sir Thomas Treslyn was taken bad on the way home. He was dead when they got to Treslyn Hall."

I sat up in bed, looking from one excited face to the other. One of the guests . . . dead! I was shocked. But this was no ordinary death, no ordinary death.

I realised, no less than Kitty and Daisy, what such news could mean to Mount Mellyn.

# VII

Sir Thomas Treslyn was buried on New Year's Day.

During the preceding week gloom had settled on the house, and it was all the more noticeable because it followed on the heels of the Christmas festivities. All the decorations had been left about the house, and there was divided opinion as to which was the more unlucky—to remove them before Twelfth Night or to leave them up and thereby show lack of respect.

They all appeared to consider that the death touched us closely. He had died between our house and his own; our table was the last at which he had sat. I realised that the Cornish were a very superstitious people, constantly on the alert for omens, eager to placate supernatural and malignant powers.

Connan was absentminded. I saw little of him, but when I did he seemed scarcely aware of my presence. I imagined he was considering all that this meant to him. If he and Lady Treslyn had been lovers there was no obstacle now to their regularising their union. I knew that this thought was in the minds of many, but no one spoke of it. I guessed that Mrs. Polgrey would consider it unlucky to do so until Sir Thomas had been buried for some weeks.

Mrs. Polgrey called me to her room and we had a cup of Earl Grey laced with a spoonful of the whisky I had given her.

" This is a shocking thing," she said. " Sir Thomas to die on Christmas Day as he did. Although 'tweren't Christmas Day but Boxing Day morning," she added in a slightly relieved tone, as though this made the situation a little less shocking. " And to think," she went on, reverting to her original gloom, " that ours was the last house he rested in, my food was the

last that passed his lips! The funeral is a bit soon, do you not
think, Miss?''

I began to count the days on my fingers. "Seven days," I
said.

"They could have kept him longer, seeing it's winter."

"I suppose they feel that the sooner it's over the sooner
they'll recover from the shock."

She herself looked shocked indeed. I think she thought it
was disrespectful or unlucky to suggest that anyone would want
to recover quickly from their grief.

"I don't know," she said, "you hear tales of people being
buried alive. I remember years ago, when I was a child, there
was a smallpox epidemic. People panicked and buried quick.
It was said that some was buried alive."

"There is surely no doubt that Sir Thomas is *dead*."

"Some seem dead and are not dead, after all. Still seven
days should be long enough to tell. You'll come to the funeral
with me, Miss?''

"I?"

"But why not? I think we should show proper respect to
the dead."

"I have no mourning clothes."

"My dear life, I'll find a bonnet for 'ee. I'll give 'ee a black
band to sew on your cloak. Reckon that 'ud be all right if we
were just at the grave. 'Twouldn't do for 'ee to go into the
church like, but then 'twouldn't be right either . . . you being
the governess here, and them having so many friends as will
attend to fill Mellyn Church to the full."

So it was agreed that I should accompany Mrs. Polgrey to the
churchyard.

I was present when Sir Thomas's body was lowered into the
tomb.

It was an impressive ceremony, for the funeral had been a
magnificent one in accordance with the Treslyn's rank in the
duchy. Crowds attended, but Mrs. Polgrey and I hovered only
in the distance. I was glad of this; she deplored it.

It was enough for me to see the widow in flowing black
draperies yet looking as beautiful as she ever had. Her lovely

face was just visible among the flowing black, which seemed to become her even as green and mauve had on the night of the Christmas ball. She moved with grace and she looked even more slender in her black than in the brilliant colours I had seen her wear, intensely feminine and appealing.

Connan was there, and I thought how elegant and distinguished he looked; I tried to fathom the expression on his face that I might discover his feelings. But he was determined to hide those feelings from the world; and I thought, in the circumstances, that was just as well.

I watched the hearse with the large waving black plumes and I saw the coffin, carried by six bearers and covered with velvet palls of deep purple and black, taken into the church. I saw the banks of flowers and the mourners in their deathly black, the only colour being the white handkerchiefs which the women held to their eyes—and they had wide black borders.

A cold wind had swept the mists away and the winter sun shone brightly on the gilt of the coffin as it was lowered into the grave.

There was a deep silence in the churchyard, broken only by the sudden cry of gulls.

It was over and the mourners, Connan, Celestine and Peter among them, went back to their carriages which wound their way to Treslyn Hall.

Mrs. Polgrey and I returned to Mount Mellyn, where she insisted on the usual cup of tea and its accompaniment.

We sat drinking, and her eyes glittered. I knew she was finding it difficult to restrain her tongue. But she said nothing of the effect this death might have on us all at Mount Mellyn. So great was her respect for the dead.

Sir Thomas was not forgotten. I heard his name mentioned often during the next few weeks. Mrs. Polgrey shook her head significantly when the Treslyns were mentioned, but her eyes were sharp and full of warning.

Daisy and Kitty were less discreet. When they brought my water in the mornings they would linger. I was a little cunning, I think. I longed to know what people were saying but I did not want to ask, yet I managed to draw them out without, I hoped, seeming to do so.

It was true they did not need a lot of encouragement.

"I saw Lady Treslyn yesterday," Daisy told me, one morning. "Her didn't look like a widow, in spite of the weeds."

"Oh? In what way?"

"Don't 'ee ask me, Miss. She was quite pale and not smiling, but I could see something in her face . . . if you do get my meaning."

"I'm afraid I don't."

"Kit were with me. She said the same. Like as though she were waiting and content because she wouldn't have to wait long. A year though. Seems a long time to *me*."

"A year? What for?" I asked, although I knew very well what for.

Daisy looked at me and giggled.

"'Twon't do for them to be seeing too much of each other for a bit, will it, Miss. After all, him dying here. . . almost on our doorstep. 'Twould seem as though they'd almost willed him to it."

"Oh, Daisy, that's absurd. How could anybody?"

"Well, that's what you can't say till you know, 'twould seem."

The conversation was getting dangerous. I dismissed her with "I must hurry. I see I'm rather late."

When she had gone, I thought : So there is talk about them. They are saying he was willed to die.

As long as that's all they say, that won't do much harm.

I wondered how careful they were being. I remembered hearing Phillida say that people in love behaved like ostriches. They buried their heads in the sand and thought, because they saw no one, no one saw them.

But they were not two inexperienced lovers.

No, I thought bitterly, it is clear that both are very experienced. They knew the people among whom they lived. They would be careful.

It was later that day, when I was in the woods, that I heard the sound of horses' hoofs walking nearby and then I heard Lady Treslyn say: "Connan. Oh, Connan!"

They had met then . . . and to meet as near the house as this was surely foolish.

In the woods their voices carried. The trees hid me, but snatches of their conversation came to me.

"Linda! You shouldn't have come."

"I know . . . I know. . . ." Her voice fell and I could not hear the rest.

"To send that message . . ." That was Connan. I could hear him more clearly than her, perhaps because I knew his voice so well. "Your messenger will have been seen by some of the servants. You know how they gossip."

"I know, but . . ."

"When did this come . . . ?"

"This morning. I had to show it to you right away."

"It's the first?"

"No, there was one two days ago. That's why I had to see you, Connan. No matter what . . . I'm frightened. . . ."

"It's mischief," he said. "Ignore it. Forget it."

"Read it," she cried. "Read it."

There was a short silence. Then Connan spoke. "I see. There's only one thing to be done. . . ."

The horses had begun to move. In a few seconds they might come past the spot where I was. I hurried away through the trees.

I was very uneasy.

That day Connan left Mount Mellyn.

"Called away to Penzance," Mrs. Polgrey told me. "He said he was unsure how long he would be away."

I wondered if his sudden departure had anything to do with the disquieting news which Lady Treslyn had brought to him that morning in the woods.

Several days passed. Alvean and I resumed our lessons and Gilly too came to the schoolroom.

I would give Gilly some small task while I worked with Alvean, such as trying to make letters in a tray of sand, or on a slate, or counting beads on an abacus. She was contented to do this and I believed that she was happy in my company, that from me she drew a certain comfort which had its roots in security. She had trusted Alice and she was transferring that trust to me.

Alvean had rebelled at first but I had pointed out the need to be kind to those less fortunate than ourselves, and at length I had worked on her sympathy so that she accepted Gilly's presence, although a little sullenly. But I had noticed that now and then she would throw a glance at the child, and I was sure that at least she was very interested in her.

Connan had been away a week and it was a cold February morning when Mrs. Polgrey came into the schoolroom. I was very surprised to see her, for she rarely interrupted lessons; she was holding two letters in her hand and I could see that she was excited.

She made no excuses for her intrusion and said: " I have heard from the Master. He wants you to take Miss Alvean down to Penzance at once. Here is a letter for you. No doubt he explains more fully in that."

She handed me the letter and I was afraid that she would see that my hand shook a little as I opened it.

*My dear Miss Leigh*, I read,

I will be here for a few weeks, I think, and I am sure you will agree that it would be very desirable for Alvean to join me here. I do not think she should miss her lessons, so I am asking you to bring her and be prepared to stay for a week or so.

Perhaps you could be ready to leave to-morrow. Get Billy Trehay to drive you to the station for the 2.30 train.

                                        Connan TreMellyn

I knew that the colour had rushed to my face. I hoped I had not betrayed the extreme joy which took possession of me.

I said: " Alvean, we are to join your father to-morrow."

Alvean leapt up and threw herself into my arms, a most unusual display, but it moved me deeply to realise how much she cared for him.

This helped me to regain my own composure. I said:

" That is for to-morrow. To-day we will continue with our lessons."

" But, Miss, there's our packing to do."

" We have this afternoon for that," I said primly. " Now, let us return to our work."

I turned to Mrs. Polgrey. " Yes," I said, " Mr. TreMellyn wishes me to take Alvean to him."

She nodded. I could see that she thought it very strange, and this was because he had never before shown such interest in the child.

" And you're leaving to-morrow."

" Yes. Billy Trehay is to be given instructions to drive us to the station in time for the 2.30 train."

She nodded.

When she had gone I sat down in a daze. I could not concentrate more than Alvean could. It was some time before I remembered Gilly. She was looking at me with that blank expression in her eyes which I had dreamed of banishing.

Gilly understood more than one realised.

She knew that we were going away and that she would be left behind.

I could scarcely wait to begin my packing. Alvean and I had luncheon together in the schoolroom but neither of us was interested in food, and immediately after the meal we went to our rooms to do the packing.

I had very little to pack. My grey and mauve dresses were clean, for which I was thankful, and I would wear my grey merino. It was not very becoming but it would be too difficult to pack.

I took out the green silk dress which I had worn at the Christmas ball. Should I take it? Why not? I had rarely possessed anything so becoming, and who knew, there might be an occasion when I could wear it.

I took out my comb and shawl, stuck the comb in my hair and let the shawl fall negligently about my shoulders.

I thought of the Christmas ball—that moment when Peter had taken my hand and had drawn me into the *Furry Dance*. I heard the tune in my head and began to dance, for the moment really feeling I was in the ballroom and that it was Christmas night again.

I had not heard Gilly come in, and I was startled to see her standing watching me. Really, the child did move too silently about the house.

I stopped dancing, flushing with embarrassment to have been caught in such silly behaviour. Gilly was regarding me solemnly.

She looked at the bag on my bed and the folded clothes beside it, and immediately my pleasure left me for I understood that Gilly was going to be very unhappy if we went away.

I stooped down and put my arms about her. " It'll only be for a little while, Gilly."

She screwed her eyes up tightly and would not look at me.

" Gilly," I said, " listen. We'll soon be back, you know."

She shook her head and I saw tears squeeze themselves out of her eyes.

" Then," I went on, " we'll have our lessons. You shall draw me more letters in the sand, and soon you will be writing your name."

But I could see that she refused to be comforted.

She tore herself from me and ran to the bed and began pulling the things out of my trunk.

" No, Gilly, no," I said. I lifted her up in my arms and went to a chair. I sat for a while rocking her. I went on : " I'm coming back, you know, Gilly. In less than no time I'll be here. It will seem as though I've never been away."

She spoke then : " You won't come back. She . . . She . . ."

" Yes, Gilly, yes?"

" She . . . went."

For the moment I forgot even the fact that I was going to Connan, because I was certain now that Gilly knew something, and what she knew might throw some light on the mystery of Alice.

" Gilly," I said, " did she say good-bye to you before she went?"

Gilly shook her head vehemently, and I thought she was going to burst into tears.

"Gilly," I pleaded, " try to talk to me, try to tell me. . . . Did you see her go?"

Gilly threw herself at me and buried her face against my bodice. I held her tenderly for a moment, then withdrew myself and looked into her face; but her eyes were tightly shut.

She ran back to the bed and again started to pull the things out of my trunk.

"No. . . ." she cried. "No . . . no. . . ."

Swiftly I went to her. "Look, Gilly," I said, " I'm coming back. I'll only be away a short time."

"She stayed away!"

We were back at that point where we started. I did not believe I could discover anything more from her at this stage.

She lifted her little face to mine and all the blankness had gone from the eyes; they were tragic.

I saw in that moment how much my care of her had meant to her, and that it was impossible to make her understand that if I went away it was not for ever. Alice had been kind to her and Alice had gone. Her experiences had taught her that that was the way of life.

A few days . . . a week in the life of Gilly . . . would be like a year to most of us. I knew then that I could not leave Gilly behind.

Then I asked myself what Connan would say if I arrived with both children.

I believed that I could adequately explain my reasons. However, I was not going to leave Gilly behind. I could let Mrs. Polgrey know that the master expected the two children; she would be pleased; she trusted Gilly with me, and she had been the first to admit that the child had improved since I had tried to help her.

"Gilly," I said. "I'm going away for a few days. Alvean and you are coming with me." I kissed her upturned face. And I repeated because she looked so bewildered: "You are coming with me. You'll like that, won't you."

It was still some seconds before she understood, and then she shut her eyes tightly and lowered her head; I saw she smiled. That moved me more than any words could have done.

I felt I was ready to brave Connan's displeasure to bring such happiness to this poor child.

The next morning we set out early, and the whole household turned out to see us go. I sat in the carriage with a child on either side of me, and Billy Trehay in TreMellyn's livery sat jauntily in the driver's seat talking to the horses.

Mrs. Polgrey stood, her arms folded across her bosom, and her eyes were on Gilly. It was clear that she was delighted to see her little granddaughter riding with myself and Alvean.

Tapperty stood with his daughters on either side of him; and their twinkling eyes, all so much alike, were full of speculation.

I did not care. I felt so light-headed as we drove off that it was all I could do to prevent myself breaking into song.

It was a bright sunny morning and there was a slight frost in the air which sparkled on the grass, and the thin layer of ice on the ponds and streams.

We rattled along at a good speed over the rough roads. The children were in high spirits; Alvean chattered a good deal, and Gilly sat contentedly beside me. I noticed that she clutched my skirt with one hand, and the gesture filled me with tenderness for her. I was deeply aware of my responsibility towards this child.

Billy was talkative, and when we passed a grave at a cross-roads, he uttered a prayer for the poor lost soul who was buried there.

" Not that the soul will rest, me dears. A person who meets death that way never rests. 'Tis the same if they meet death any way violent like. They can't stay buried underground. They *walks*."

" What nonsense! " I said sharply.

" Them that knows no better call wisdom nonsense," retorted Billy, piqued.

" It seems to me that many people have too lively imaginations."

The children's eyes I noticed were fixed on my face.

" Why," I said quickly as we passed a cob cottage with

beehives in the garden, " look at those hives! What's that over them?"

" 'Tis black crêpe," said Billy. " It means death in the family. Bees would take it terrible hard if they weren't told of the death and helped to share in the mourning."

I was glad when we arrived in the station.

We were met at Penzance by a carriage and then began the journey to Penlandstow. It was growing dark when we turned into a drive and I saw a house loom up before us. There was a man in the porch with a lantern who called out : " They be here. Run and tell master. He did say to let him know the minute they did come."

We were a little stiff and both children were half-asleep. I helped them down and as I turned, I saw Connan standing beside me. I could not see him very clearly in the dim light but I did know that he was very pleased to see me. He took my hand and pressed it warmly.

Then he said an astonishing thing. " I've been anxious. I visualised all sorts of mishaps. I wished I'd come and brought you here myself."

I thought : He means Alvean, of course. He is not really talking to me.

But he was facing me, and smiling; and I felt I had never been quite so happy in the whole of my life.

I began : " The children . . ."

He smiled down at Alvean.

" Hallo, Papa," she said. " It's lovely to be here with you."

He laid a hand on her shoulder, and she looked up at him almost pleadingly, as though she were asking him to kiss her. That, it seemed, was asking too much.

He merely said : " I'm glad you've come, Alvean. You'll have some fun here."

Then I brought Gilly forward.

" What . . ." he began.

" We couldn't leave Gilly behind," I said. " You know you gave me your permission to teach her."

He hesitated for a moment. Then he looked at me and laughed. I knew in that moment that he was so pleased to see

me—me, not the others—that he would not have cared whom I
brought with me as long as I came myself.

It was no wonder that as I walked into Alice's old home I
felt as though I were entering an enchanted place.

During the next two weeks it seemed that I had left behind me
the cold hard world of reality and stepped into one of my own
making, and that everything I desired was to be mine.

From the moment I arrived at Penlandstow Manor I was
treated, not as a governess, but as a guest. In a few days I had
lost my sensitivity on this point and, when I had cast that off,
I was like the high-spirited girl who had enjoyed life in the
country vicarage with her father and Phillida.

I was given a pleasant room next to Alvean's and when I
asked that Gilly should be put near me this was done.

Penlandstow was a house of great charm which had been
built in the Elizabethan era. It was almost as large as Mount
Mellyn and as easy to lose oneself in.

My room was large and there were padded window seats
upholstered in red velvet, and dark red curtains. My bed was a
fourposter hung with silk embroidered curtains. The carpet
was of the same deep red, and this would have given warmth to
the room even if there had not been a log fire burning in the
open grate.

My bag was brought up to this room and one of the maids
proceeded to unpack while I stood by the fire watching the blue
flames dart among the logs.

The maid curtsied when she had laid my things on the bed,
and asked if she might put them away. This was not the
manner in which to treat a governess, I thought. Kind and
friendly as Daisy and Kitty had been, they had not been ready
to wait on me like this.

I said I would put my things away myself but would like hot
water to wash.

"There be a little bathroom at the end of the landing,
Miss," I was told. "Shall I show it to 'ee and bring 'ee hot
water up there?"

I was taken along to the room in which there was a big bath;
there was also a hip bath.

" Miss Alice had the room done afore her married and went away," I was told; and with a little shock I remembered that I was in Alice's old home.

When I had washed and changed my dress—I put on the lavender cotton—I went along to see Alvean. She had fallen asleep on her bed so I left her. Gilly was also asleep in her room. And when I returned to my own the maid who had shown me the bathroom came in and said that Mr. TreMellyn had asked that, when I was ready, I would join him in the library.

I said I was ready then and she took me to him.

" It is indeed pleasant to see you here, Miss Leigh," he said.

" It will be very agreeable for you to have your own daughter here. . . ." I began.

And he interrupted me with a smile. " I said it was pleasant to see you here, Miss Leigh. I meant exactly that."

I flushed. " That is kind of you. I have brought certain of the children's lesson books along. . . ."

" Let us give them a little holiday, shall we? Lessons I suppose there must be, if you say so, but need they sit at their desks all the time?"

" I think their lessons might be curtailed on an occasion like this."

He came and stood close to me. " Miss Leigh," he said, " you are delightful."

I drew back startled, and he went on : " I'm glad you came so promptly."

" Those were your orders."

" I did not mean to order, Miss Leigh. Merely to request."

" But . . ." I began; and I was apprehensive because he seemed different from the man I had known. He was almost like a stranger—a stranger who fascinated me no less than that other Connan TreMellyn, a stranger who frightened me a little, for I was unsure of myself, unsure of my own emotions.

" I was so glad to escape," he said. " I thought you would be too."

" Escape . . . from what?"

" From the gloom of death. I hate death. It depresses me."

" You mean Sir Thomas. But . . ."

"Oh, I know. A neighbour merely. But still it did depress me. I wanted to get right away. I am so glad you have joined me . . . with Alvean and the other child."

I said on impulse: "I hope you did not think it was presumptuous of me to bring Gillyflower. She would have been heartbroken if I had not brought her."

Then he said a thing which set my senses swimming: "I can understand her being heartbroken if she had to part from you."

I said quickly: "I suppose the children should have a meal of some sort. They are exhausted and sleeping now. But I do feel they need some refreshment before they go to bed. It has been a tiring day for them."

He waved a hand. "Order what you wish for them, Miss Leigh. And when you have seen to them, you and I will dine together."

I said: "Alvean dines with you . . . does she not?"

"She will be too tired to-night. We will have it alone."

So I ordered what I wanted for the children, and I dined with Connan in the winter parlour. It was a strange and exhilarating experience to dine with that man in candlelight. I kept telling myself that it could not be real. If ever anything was the stuff that dreams were made of, this was.

He talked a great deal; there was no sign of the taciturn Connan that evening.

He told me about the house, how it had been built in the shape of an E as a compliment to the queen who had been reigning when it was built. He drew the shape to show me. "Two three-sided courtyards," he said, "and a projecting centre block, if you see what I mean. We are in the central block now. The main feature of it is the hall, the staircase and the gallery, and these smaller rooms such as the winter parlour which, I think you will agree, is ideally suited for a small company."

I said I thought it was a delightful house, and how fortunate he was to possess two such magnificent places.

"Stone walls do not bring satisfaction, Miss Leigh. It is the life one lives within those walls which is of the greatest importance."

" Yet," I retaliated, " it is some comfort to have charming surroundings in which to live one's life."

" I agree. And I cannot tell you how glad I am that you find my homes so charming."

When we had eaten he took me to the library and asked me if I would play a game of chess with him. I said I would be delighted.

And we sat there in that beautiful room with its carved ceiling and thick piled carpet, lighted by lamps the bowls of which were made of artistically painted china of oriental origin. I was happier than I had ever dreamed I could be.

He had set out the ivory pieces on the board, and we played in silence.

It was a deep, contented silence, or so it seemed to me. I knew I should never forget the flickering firelight, the ticking of the gilded clock which looked as though it might have belonged to Louis XIV, as I watched Connan's strong lean fingers on the ivory pieces.

Once, as I frowned in concentration, I was conscious of his eyes fixed on me and, lifting them suddenly, I met his gaze. It was of amusement, and yet of speculation. In that moment I thought : He has asked me here for a purpose. What is it?

I felt a shiver of alarm, but I was too happy to entertain such feelings.

I moved my piece and he said : " Ah!" And then : " Miss Leigh, oh my dear Miss Leigh, you have, I think, walked straight into the trap I have set for you."

" Oh . . . no!" I cried.

He moved a knight which immediately menaced my king. I had forgotten that knight.

" I believe it is . . ." he said. " Oh no, not entirely. Check, Miss Leigh. But not checkmate."

I saw that I had allowed my attention to wander from the game. I sought hurriedly to save myself, but I could not. With every move the inevitable end was more obvious.

I heard his voice, gentle, full of laughter. " Checkmate, Miss Leigh."

I sat for a few seconds staring at the board. He said : " I took an unfair advantage. You were tired after the journey."

" Oh no," I said quickly. " I suspect you are a better player than I am."

" I suspect," he replied, " that we are very well matched."

I retired to my room soon after that game.

I went to bed and tried to sleep, but couldn't. I was too happy. I kept going over in my mind his reception of me, our meal together, his words : " We are very well matched."

I even forgot that the house in which I now lay had been Alice's home—a fact which at one time would have seemed of utmost interest to me—I forgot everything but that Connan had sent for me and, now that I was here, seemed so delighted to have me.


The next day was as pleasant and unpredictable as the first. I did a few lessons with the children in the morning and in the afternoon Connan took us for a drive. How different it was, riding in his carriage than jogging along behind Tapperty or Billy Trehay.

He drove us to the coast and we saw St. Michael's Mount rising out of the water.

" One day," he said, " when the spring comes, I'll take you out there and you can see St. Michael's chair."

Can we sit in it, Papa?" asked Alvean.

" You can if you are prepared to risk a fall. You'll find your feet dangling over a drop of seventy feet or so. Nevertheless, many of your sex think it worth while."

" But why, Papa, why?" demanded Alvean, who was always delighted when she had his undivided attention.

" Because," he went on, " there is an old saying that if a woman can sit in St. Michael's chair before her husband, she will be the master of the house.

Alvean laughed with pleasure and Gilly, who I had insisted on bringing with us, stood there smiling.

Connan looked at me. " And you, Miss Leigh," he said, " would you think it worth while to try?"

I hesitated for a second, and then met his gaze boldly. " No, Mr. TreMellyn, I don't think I should."

"Then you would not desire to be the master in the house?"

"I do not think that either a husband or his wife should be master in that sense. I think they should work together and, if one has an opinion which he or she feels to be the only right one, he or she should adhere to it."

I flushed a little; I imagined how Phillida would smile if she heard that.

"Miss Leigh," said Connan, "your wisdom puts our foolish folklore to shame."

We drove back in winter sunshine and I was happy.

I did not dine with him that evening because I had asked that I might have my meals in the schoolroom with Gilly. Alvean dined with her father. And afterwards I sat in my room reading. He did not ask me to join him that evening.

I went to bed early and lay for a long time thinking of the strange turn life had taken, and I knew that when I awoke next morning I should do so with a feeling of expectation, because I believed that something wonderful was about to happen to me.

I awoke with a start. Someone was in my room. There was a movement by my bed. I started up. It was early morning. I knew this because I could see that the sky was streaked with pale pink light.

"Who is there?" I cried.

Then I saw Gilly.

She was wearing one of Alvean's old dressing gowns which I had altered to fit her, and her feet were in a pair of slippers which I had bought for her.

I said: "What are you doing here, Gilly?"

She opened her mouth as though to speak. I waited, but she smiled at me and nodded.

I said: "What has happened, Gilly? It is something, I know. You must tell me."

She pointed to the door and stared at it.

I felt a shiver run down by spine because Gilly often made me think that she could see things which I could not.

"There's nothing there," I said.

She nodded again and then she spoke : " She's here. She's here."

I felt my heart beat fast. I thought : She means that Alice is here. This was Alice's home. She has found Alice here.

" Mrs. TreMellyn . . ." I whispered.

She smiled rapturously and continued to nod.

" You . . . you've seen her?"

Gilly nodded again.

" In this house?"

Again the nod.

" I'll take you to her." The words tumbled out. " She wants me to."

I got out of bed and with trembling fingers wrapped my dressing gown about me and put my feet into my slippers.

Gilly took my hand.

We went through a gallery and down a short staircase. Gilly rapped with her fingers on the door and appeared to listen.

She looked up at me and nodded as though she had heard someone tell her to enter. I had heard nothing. It was very uncanny.

Then she opened the door. We were in a room which was shadowy, for the day was young yet.

Gilly pointed, and for a few seconds I thought I saw a woman standing there. She was dressed in a ball dress and her fair hair fell about her shoulders in long silken curls.

I stared, and then I saw that I was looking at a life-size oil painting.

I knew I was face to face with Alice.

I went close to the painting and looked up at it. The blue eyes looked straight out of the picture at me and it seemed as though words were forming themselves on those red lips.

I forced myself to say : " What a good artist must have painted that picture ! "

But perhaps because it was not yet quite light, because this grey house was sleeping, because Gilly had brought me here in her own strange way, I felt that this was more than a picture.

" Alice," I whispered. And I stared at that painted face,

and, practical woman that I was, I half expected her to step out of the frame and talk to me.

I wondered when that had been painted . . . before or after the disastrous marriage, before she had known she was to have Geoffry's child or after.

"Alice," I said to myself, "where are you now, Alice? You are haunting me, Alice. Since I have known you I have known what haunting means."

Gilly was holding my hand.

I said: "It's only a picture, Gilly."

She reached out a small finger and touched the white ball-dress.

Gilly had loved her. I looked into that soft young face and thought I understood why.

Poor Alice, who had been caught up in too many emotions, what had become of her?

I suddenly realised that it was a winter's morning and I was lightly clad.

"We'll catch our deaths," I said practically; and taking Gilly's hand in mine I firmly shut the door on Alice.


I had been at Penlandstow a week, and I was wondering how much longer this idyllic interlude could last, when Connan spoke to me of what was in his mind.

The children were in bed and Connan asked me if I would join him in a game of chess in the library.

There I found him, the pieces set out on the board, sitting looking at them.

The curtains had been drawn and the fire burned cheerfully in the great fireplace. He rose as I entered and I quickly slipped into my place opposite him.

He smiled at me and I thought his eyes took in every detail of my appearance, in a manner which I might have found offensive in anyone else.

I was about to move king's pawn when he said: "Miss Leigh, I did not ask you down here to play. There is something I have to say to you."

"Yes, Mr. TreMellyn?"

"I feel I have known you a very long time. You have made such a difference to us both—Alvean and myself. If you went away, we should miss you very much. I am certain that we should both want to ensure that you do not leave us."

I tried to look at him and failed because I was afraid he would read the hopes and fears in my eyes.

"Miss Leigh," he went on, "Will you stay with us . . . always?"

"I . . . I don't understand. I . . . can't believe . . ."

"I am asking you to marry me."

"But . . . but that is impossible."

"Why so, Miss Leigh?"

"Because . . . because it is so incongruous."

"Do you find me incongruous . . . repulsive? Do please be frank."

"I . . . No indeed not! But I am the governess here. . . ."

"Precisely. That is what alarms me. Governesses sometimes leave their employment. It would be intolerable for me if you went away."

I felt I was choking with my emotions. I could not believe this was really happening to me. I remained silent. I dared not try to speak.

"I see that you hesitate, Miss Leigh."

"I am so surprised."

"Should I have prepared you for the shock?" His lips twitched slightly at the corner. "I am sorry, Miss Leigh. I thought I had managed to convey to you something of my feelings in this matter."

I tried to picture it all in those few seconds—myself going back to Mount Mellyn as the wife of the Master, slipping from the role of governess to that of Mistress of the house. Of course I would do it and in a few months they would forget that I had once been the governess. Whatever else I lacked I had my dignity—perhaps a little too much of it, according to Phillida. But I should have thought that a proposal would have been made in a different way. He did not take my hand; he did not touch me; he merely sat at the table watching me in an almost cool and calculating manner.

He went on : " Think of how much good this could bring to us all, my dear Miss Leigh. I have been so impressed by the manner in which you have helped Alvean. The child needs a mother. You would supply that need . . . admirably."

" Should two people marry for the sake of a child, do you think?"

" I am a most selfish man. I never would." He leaned forward across the table and his eyes were alight with something I did not understand. " I would marry for my own satisfaction."

" Then . . ." I began.

" I confess I was not considering Alvean alone. We are three people, my dear Miss Leigh, who could profit from this marriage. Alvean needs you. And I. . . I need you. Do you need us? Perhaps you are more self-sufficient than we are, but what will you do if you do not marry? You will go from post to post, and that is not a very pleasant life. When one is young, handsome and full of spirit it is tolerable . . . but sprightly governesses become ageing governesses."

I said acidly : " Do you suggest that I should enter into this marriage as an insurance against old age?"

" I suggest only that you do what your desires dictate, my dear Miss Leigh."

There was a short silence during which I felt an absurd desire to burst into tears. This was something I had longed for, but a proposal of marriage should have been an impassioned declaration, and I could not rid myself of the suspicion that there was something other than Connan's love for me which had inspired it. It seemed to me as though he were offering me a list of reasons why we should marry, for fear I should discover the real one.

" You put it on such a practical basis," I stammered. " I had not thought of marriage in that way."

His eyebrows lifted and he laughed, looking suddenly very gay. " How glad I am. I thought of you always as such a practical person, so I was trying to put it to you in the manner in which I felt it would appeal to you most."

" Are you seriously asking me to marry you?"

"I doubt if I have ever been so serious in my life as I am at this moment. What is your answer? Please do not keep me in suspense any longer."

I said I must have time to consider this.

"That is fair enough. You will tell me to-morrow?"

"Yes," I said. "I will tell you to-morrow."

I rose and went to the door. He was there before me. He laid his fingers on the door handle and I waited for him to open it, but he did no such thing. He stood with his back to the door and caught me up in his arms.

He kissed me as I had never been kissed, never dreamed of being kissed; so that I knew that there was a life of the emotions of which I was totally ignorant. He kissed my eyelids, my nose, my cheeks, my mouth and my throat until he was breathless, and I was too.

Then he laughed.

"Wait until the morning!" he mocked. "Do I look the sort of man who would wait until the morning? Do you think I am the sort of man who would marry for the sake of his daughter? No, Miss Leigh . . ." he mocked again, "my dear, *dear* Miss Leigh . . . I want to marry you because I want to keep you a prisoner in my house. I don't want you to run away from me, because, since you came, I have thought of little else but you, and I know I am going on thinking of you all my life."

"Is this true?" I whispered. "Can this be true?"

"Martha!" he said. "What a stern name for such an adorable creature! And yet, how it fits!"

I said: "My sister calls me Marty. My father did too."

"Marty," he said. "That sounds helpless, clinging . . . feminine. . . . You can be a Marty sometimes. For me you will be all three. Marty, Martha and Miss Leigh, my very dear Miss Leigh. You see you *are* all three, and my dearest Marty would always betray Miss Leigh. I knew from her that you were interested in me. Far more interested than Miss Leigh would think proper. How enchanting! I shall marry not one woman but three!"

"Have I been so blatant?"

"Tremendously so . . . adorably so."

I knew that it was foolish to pretend. I gave myself up to his embrace, and it was wonderful beyond my imaginings.

At length I said: "I have a terrible feeling that I shall wake up in bed at Mount Mellyn and find I have dreamed all this."

"Do you know," he said seriously, "I feel exactly the same."

"But it is so different for you. You can do as you will . . . go where you will . . . dependent on no one."

"I am dependent no longer. I depend on Marty, Martha, my dear Miss Leigh."

He spoke so seriously that I could have wept with tenderness. The changing emotions were almost too much for me to bear.

This is love! I thought. The emotion which carries one to the very heights of human experience and, because it can carry one so high, one is in continual danger of falling; and one must never forget, the higher the delight, the more tragic the fall.

But this was not the moment to think of tragedy. I loved, and miraculously I was loved. I had no doubt in that library of Penlandstow that I was loved.

For love such as this, one would be prepared to risk everything.

He put his hands on my shoulders and looked long into my face.

He said: "We'll be happy, my darling. We'll be happier than either you or I ever dreamed possible."

I knew that we should be. All that had gone before would give us a finer appreciation of this joy we could bring each other.

"We should be practical," he said. "We should make our plans. When shall we marry? I do not like delay. I am the most impatient man alive, where my own pleasures are concerned. We will go home to-morrow, and there we will announce our engagement. No, not to-morrow . . . the day after. I have one or two little commitments here to-morrow. And as soon as we are home we will give a ball to announce our engagement. I think that in a month after that we should be setting out on our honeymoon. I suggest Italy, unless you have any other ideas?"

I sat with my hands clasped. I must have looked like an ecstatic schoolgirl.

"I wonder what they will think at Mount Mellyn."

"Who, the servants? You may be sure they have a pretty shrewd idea of the way things are; servants have, you know. Servants are like detectives in the house. They pick up every little clue. You shiver. Are you cold?"

"No, only excited. I still believe I'm going to wake up in a moment."

"And you like the idea of Italy?"

"I would like the idea of the North Pole in some company."

"By which, my darling, I hope you mean mine."

"That was my intention."

"My dear Miss Leigh," he said, "how I love your astringent moods. They are going to make conversation throughout our lives so invigorating." I had an idea then that he was making comparisons between Alice and myself, and I shivered again as I had when he had made that remark about the detectives.

"You are a little worried about the reception of the news," he went on. "The servants . . . the countryside. . . . Who cares? Do you? Of course you do not. Miss Leigh has too much good sense for that. I am longing to tell Peter Nansellock that you are to be my wife. To tell the truth I have been somewhat jealous of that young man."

"There was no need to be."

"Still I was anxious. I had visions of his persuading you to go to Australia with him. That was something I should have gone to great lengths to prevent."

"Even so far as asking me to marry *you*?"

"Farther than that if the need had arisen. I should have abducted you and locked you up in a dungeon until he was far away."

"There was no need for the slightest apprehension."

"Are you quite sure? He is very handsome, I believe."

"Perhaps he is. I did not notice."

"I could have killed him when he had the effrontery to offer you Jacinth."

" I think he merely enjoys being outrageous. He probably
knew I should not accept it."

" And I need not fear him?"

" You need never fear anyone," I told him.

Then once more I was in that embrace, and I was oblivious
of all but the fact that I had discovered love, and believed, as
doubtless hosts of lovers have before, that there was never love
such as that between us two.

At length he said : " We'll go back the day after to-morrow.
We'll start making arrangements immediately. In a month
from now we'll be married. We'll put up the banns as soon as
we return. We will have a ball to announce our engagement
and invite all our neighbours to the wedding."

" I suppose it must be done in this way?"

" Tradition, my darling. It is one of the things we have to
bow down to. You'll be magnificent, I know. You're not
nervous?"

" Of your country neighbours, no."

" You and I will open the ball this time together, dearest
Miss Leigh."

" Yes," I said; and I pictured myself in the green dress
wearing the amber comb in my hair with the diamond horseshoe glittering on the green background.

I had no qualms about taking my place in his circle.

Then he began to talk of Alice. " I have never told you," he
said, " of my first marriage."

" No," I answered.

" It was not a happy one."

" I'm sorry."

" A marriage which was arranged. This time I shall marry
my own choice. Only one who has suffered the first can realise
the joy of the second. Dearest, I have not lived the life of a
monk, I fear."

" I guessed it."

" I am a most sinful man, as you will discover."

" I am prepared for the worst."

" Alice . . . my wife . . . and I were most unsuited, I
suppose."

" Tell me about her."

" There is little to tell. She was a gentle creature, quiet, anxious to please. She seemed to have little spirit. I understood why. She was in love with someone else when she married me."

" The man she ran away with?" I asked.

He nodded. " Poor Alice! She was unfortunate. She chose not only the wrong husband but the wrong lover. There is little to choose between us . . . myself and Geoffry Nansellock. We were of a kind. In the old days there was a tradition of the *droit de seigneurs* in these parts. Geoffry and I did our best to maintain that."

" You are telling me that you have enjoyed many love affairs."

" I am a dissolute, degenerate philanderer. I am going to say *was*. Because from this moment I am going to be faithful to one woman for the rest of my life. You do not look scornful or sceptical. Bless you for that. I mean it, dearest Marty. I swear I mean it. It is because of those experiences of the past that I know the difference between them and this. This is love."

" Yes," I said slowly, " you and I will be faithful together because that is the only way we can prove to each other the depth and breadth of our love."

He took my hands and kissed them, and I had never known him so serious. " I love you," he said. " Remember that . . . always remember it."

" I intend to."

" You may hear gossip."

" One does hear gossip," I admitted.

" You have heard of Alice and that Alvean is not my daughter? Oh, darling, someone told you and you do not want to betray the teller. Never mind. You know. It is true. I could never love the child. In fact I avoided the sight of her. She was an unpleasant reminder of much that I wished to forget. But when you came I felt differently. You made me see her as a lonely child, suffering from the sins of grown-up people. You see, you changed me, Marty dear. Your coming changed the whole household. That is what confirms me in my belief that with us it is going to be different from anything that has ever happened to me before."

"Connan, I want to make that child happy. I want to make her forget that there is a doubt as to her parentage. Let her be able to accept you as her father. It is what she needs."

"You will be a mother to her. Then I must be her father."

"We are going to be so happy, Connan."

"Can you see into the future?"

"I can see into ours, for our future is what we make it, and I intend that it shall be one of complete happiness."

"And what Miss Leigh decides shall be, will be. And you will promise me not to be hurt if you hear gossip about me?"

"You are thinking of Lady Treslyn, I know. She has been your mistress."

He nodded."

Then I said : "She will never be again. That is all over."

He kissed my hand. "Have you not sworn eternal fidelity?"

"But, Connan," I said, "she is so beautiful and she will still be there."

"But I am in love," he answered, "for the first time in my life."

"And you were not in love with her?"

"Lust, passion," he answered, "they sometimes wear the guise of love; but when one meets true love one recognises them for what they are. Dearest, let us bury all that is past. Let us start afresh from this day forth . . . you and I . . . for better for worse. . . ."

I was in his arms again. "Connan," I said, "I am not dreaming, am I? Please say I am not dreaming."

It was late when I left him. I went to my room in a haze of happiness. I was afraid to sleep for fear I should wake up and find it had all been a dream.

In the morning I went to Alvean's room and told her the news.

For a few seconds a satisfied smile appeared at the corners of her mouth; then she assumed indifference, but it was too late. I knew that she was pleased.

"You'll stay with us all the time now, Miss," she said.

"Yes," I assured her.

" I wonder if I shall ever ride as well as you."

" Probably better. You'll be able to have more practice than I ever could."

Again that smile touched her lips. Then she was serious.

" Miss," she said, " what shall I call you? You'll be my step-mother, won't you?"

" Yes, but you can call me what you like."

" Not Miss ! "

" Well, hardly. I shan't expect Miss any more."

" I expect I shall have to call you Mamma." Her mouth hardened a little.

" If you do not like that you could call me Martha in private. Or Marty. That's what my father and sister always called me."

" Marty," she repeated. " I like that. It sounds like a horse."

" What could be better praise," I cried, and she regarded my amusement with continued seriousness.

I went to Gilly's room.

" Gilly," I said, " I'm going to be Mrs. TreMellyn."

The blankness left the blue eyes and her smile was dazzling.

Then she ran to me and buried her head in my bodice. I could feel her body shaking with laughter.

I could never be quite sure what was going on among all the shadowy vagueness of Gilly's mind, but I knew she was contented. She had bracketed me with Alice in her mind and I felt that she was less surprised than I or Alvean, or anyone else, would be.

To Gilly it was the most natural thing in the world that I should take Alice's place.

I believe that, from that moment, for Gilly I became Alice.

It was a merry journey home. We sang Cornish songs all the way to the station. I had never seen Connan so happy. I thought, this is how it will be all the rest of our lives.

Alvean joined in the singing, so did Gilly; and it was astonishing to hear that child, who scarcely ever spoke, singing quietly as though to herself.

We sang the " Twelve Days of Christmas." Connan had a rich baritone voice which was very pleasant to hear and I felt

I had reached the very peak of happiness as he sang the first lines.

> "*The first day of Christmas my true love sent to me*
> *A partridge in a pear tree.*"

We went through the song and I had difficulty in remembering all the gifts after the five golden rings; and we laughed together hilariously while we argued as to how many maids there were a-milking, and how many geese a-laying were sent.

"But they were not very sensible things," said Alvean, "except of course the five gold rings. I think he was pretending he loved her more than he really did."

"But he was her true love," I protested.

"How could she be sure?" asked Alvean.

"Because he told her so," answered Connan.

"Then he ought to have given her something better than a partridge in a pear tree. I expect the partridge flew away and the pears were those hard ones which are used for stewing."

"You must not be hard on lovers," Connan cried. "All the world loves them, and you have to keep in step."

And so we laughed and bantered until we boarded the train.

Billy Trehay met us with the carriage and I was astonished when we reached the house, for I then realised that Connan must have sent a message to arrive before we did. He wanted me to be received with honours. Even so I was unprepared for the reception which was waiting for us in the hall.

The servants were all there—the Polgrey and Tapperty families and others from the gardens and stables, and even the village boys and girls who came to help and whom I scarcely knew.

They were lined up ceremoniously, and Connan took my arm as we entered the hall.

"As you know," he said, "Miss Leigh has promised to marry me. In a few weeks' time she will be your Mistress."

The men bowed and the women curtsied, but I was conscious, as I smiled at them and walked along the line with Connan, that there was a certain wariness in their eyes.

As I had guessed, they were not ready to accept me as mistress of the house . . . yet.

There was a big fire in my room and everything looked cosy and welcoming. Daisy brought my hot water. She was a little remote, I thought. She did not stop and chat with me as she had hitherto.

I thought : I will regain their confidence, but of course I had to remember that, as the future Mistress of the house, I must not gossip as I once had.

I dined with Connan and Alvean and afterwards I went up with Alvean; and when I had said good night to her I joined Connan in the library.

There were so many plans to make, and I gave myself up to the complete joy of contemplating the future.

He asked me if I had written to my family, and I told him that I had not yet done so. I still could not quite believe this was really happening to me.

"Perhaps this token will help you to remember," he said. Then he took a jewel case from a drawer in the bureau and showed me a beautiful square-cut emerald set in diamonds.

"It's . . . quite beautiful, far too beautiful for me."

"Nothing is too beautiful for Martha TreMellyn," he said, and he took my left hand and put the ring on the third finger.

I held it out and stared at it.

"I never thought to possess anything so lovely."

"It's the beginning of all the beautiful things I shall bring to you. It's the partridge in the pear tree, my darling."

Then he kissed my hand and I told myself that, whenever I doubted the truth of all that was happening to me, I could look at my emerald and know I was not dreaming.

Next morning when I went down Connan had gone out on business, and after I had given Alvean and Gilly their lessons —for I was eager that everything should go on as before—I went to my room, and I had not been there for more than a few minutes when there was a discreet knock.

"Come in," I said; and Mrs. Polgrey entered.

She looked a little furtive, and I knew that something significant had happened.

"Miss Leigh," she said, "there will be things which we have to discuss. I was wondering if you would come to my room. I have the kettle on. Could you drink a cup of tea?"

I said I would like that. I was very anxious that there should be no difference in our relationship which, from my point of view, had always been a very pleasant and dignified one.

In her room we drank tea. There was no suggestion of whisky this time, and this secretly amused me although I made no reference to it. I should be the mistress of the house, and it was very different for *her* to know of the tea-tippling than the mere governess.

She again congratulated me on my engagement and told me how delighted she was. "In fact," she said, "the whole household is delighted." She asked me then if I intended to make changes, and I answered that, while the household was so efficiently run by herself, I should make none at all.

This was a relief to her, I could see, and she settled down to come to the point.

"While you've been away, Miss Leigh, there's been a bit of excitement in these parts."

"Oh?" I said, feeling that we were now coming to the reason for my visit.

"It's all along of the sudden death of Sir Thomas Treslyn."

My heart had begun to leap in a disconcerting manner.

"But," I said, "he is buried now. We went to his funeral."

"Yes, yes. But that need not be the end, Miss Leigh."

"I don't understand, Mrs. Polgrey."

"Well, there's been rumours . . . nasty rumours, and letters have been sent."

"To . . . to whom?"

"To her, Miss Leigh. . . to the widow. And, it seems, to others . . . and as a result they're going to dig him up. There's going to be an examination."

"You mean . . . they suspect someone poisoned him?"

"Well, there's been these letters, you see. And him dying so sudden. What I don't like is that he was here last. . . . It's not the sort of thing one likes to have connected with the house. . . ."

She was looking at me oddly. I thought I saw speculation in her eyes.

I wanted to shut from my mind all the unpleasant thoughts which kept coming to me.

I saw again Connan and Lady Treslyn in the punch room together, their backs towards me . . . laughing together. Had Connan loved me then? One would not have thought so. I thought of the words they had spoken in my hearing when the party was over. " It will not be long . . . now." She had said that . . . and to him. And then there was the conversation I had partly overheard in the woods.

What did this mean?

There was a question that hammered in my brain. But I would not let my mind dwell on it.

I dared not. I could not bear to see all my hopes of happiness shattered. I had to go on believing, so I would not ask myself questions.

I looked expressionlessly into Mrs. Polgrey's face.

" I thought you'd want to know," she said.


# VIII

I was afraid, more afraid than I had ever been since I came to this house.

The body of Sir Thomas Treslyn, who had died after supping at Mount Mellyn, was to be exhumed. People were suspicious of the manner in which he died and, as a result, there had been anonymous letters. Why should they be suspicious? Because his wife wanted him out of the way; and it was known that Connan and Linda Treslyn had been lovers. There had been two obstacles to their union—Alice and Sir Thomas. Both had died suddenly.

But Connan had no wish to marry Lady Treslyn. He was in love with me.

A terrible thought had struck me. Did Connan know that there was to be this exhumation? Had I been living in a fool's paradise? Was my wonderful dream-come-true nothing but a living nightmare?

Was I being used by a cynic? Why did I not use the harsher word? Was I being used by a *murderer*?

I would not believe it. I loved Connan. I had sworn to be faithful to him all my life. How could I make such a vow when I believed the worst of him at the first crisis?

I tried to reason with myself. You're crazy, Martha Leigh. Do you really think that a man such as Connan TreMellyn could suddenly fall in love with *you*!

Yes, I do. I do, I retorted hotly.

But I was a frightened woman.

I could see that the household was divided between two topics of conversation : the exhumation of Sir Thomas and the proposed marriage of the master and the governess.

I was afraid to meet the stern eyes of Mrs. Polgrey, the lewd ones of Tapperty and the excited ones of his daughters.

Did they, as I had begun to do, connect these two events?

I asked Connan what he thought of the Treslyn affair.

" Mischief-makers," he said. " They'll have an autopsy and find he died a natural death. Why, his doctor had been attending him for years and has always told him that he must expect to go off like that."

" It must be very worrying for Lady Treslyn."

" She will not worry unduly. Indeed, since she has been pestered by letter-writers she may well be relieved to have the matter brought to a head."

I pictured the medical experts. They would no doubt be men who knew the Treslyns and Connan. As Connan was going to marry me—and he was very eager to spread the news—was it possible that they would approach the matter in a different spirit from that in which they would if they believed Lady Treslyn was eager to marry again? Who could say?

I must drive away these terrible thoughts. I would believe in Connan, I had to; if I did not I must face the fact that I had fallen in love with a murderer.

The invitations for the ball had gone out hastily—too hastily, I thought. Lady Treslyn, being in mourning and with the autopsy pending, was of course not invited. It was to take place only four days after our return from Penlandstow.

Celestine and Peter Nansellock rode over the day before the ball.

Celestine put her arms about me and kissed me.

"My dear," she said, "how happy I am. I have watched you with Alvean and I know what this is going to mean to her." There were tears in her eyes. "Alice would be so happy."

I thanked her and said: "You have always been such a good friend to me."

"I was so grateful that at last the child had found a governess who really understood her."

I said: "I thought Miss Jansen did that."

"Miss Jansen, yes. We all thought so. It was a pity she was not honest. Perhaps though it was the temptation of a moment. I did all I could to help her."

"I'm so glad somebody did."

Peter had come up. He took my hand and kissed it lightly. Connan's look of displeasure made my heart beat fast with happiness, and I was ashamed of my suspicions.

"Fortunate Connan," cried Peter exuberantly. "No need to tell you how much I envy you, is there! I think I've made it clear. I've brought over Jacinth. I told you I'd make you a present of her, didn't I? Well, she's my wedding present. You can't object to that, can you?"

I looked at Connan. "A present for us both," I said.

"Oh no," said Peter. "She's for you. I'll think of something else for Con."

"Thank you, Peter," I said. "It's most generous of you."

He shook his head. "Couldn't bear the thought of her going to anyone else. I feel sentimental about that mare. I want a good home for her. You know I'm going at the end of next week."

"So soon?"

"Everything has been speeded up. There's no point in delaying further." He looked at me significantly; "Now," he added.

I saw that Kitty, who was serving us with wine, was listening with all attention.

Celestine was talking earnestly to Connan, and Peter went on : " So it's you and Con after all. Well, you'll keep him in order, Miss Leigh. I'm sure of that."

" I'm not going to be his governess, you know."

" I'm not sure. Once a governess, always a governess. I thought Alvean seemed not displeased by the new arrangement."

" I think she's going to accept me."

" I think you're an even greater favourite than Miss Jansen was."

" Poor Miss Jansen ! I wonder what became of her."

" Celeste did something for her. She was rather worried about the poor girl, I think."

" Oh, I'm so glad."

" Helped her to find another place . . . with some friends of ours actually. The Merrivales who have a place on the edge of Dartmoor. I wonder how our gay Miss Jansen likes Hoodfield Manor. Finds it a bit dull, I should imagine, with Tavistock, the nearest town, quite six miles away."

" It was very kind of Celestine to help her."

" Well, that's Celestine all over." He lifted his glass. " To your happiness, Miss Leigh. And whenever you ride Jacinth, think of me."

" I shall . . . and of Jacinth's namesake, Miss Jansen."

He laughed. " And if," he went on, " you should change your mind. . . ."

I raised my eyebrows.

" About marrying Connan, I mean. There'll be a little homestead for you on the other side of the world. You'll find me ever faithful, Miss Leigh."

I laughed and sipped my wine.


The next day Alvean and I went riding together, and I was mounted on Jacinth. She was a wonderful creature and I enjoyed every moment of the ride. I felt that this was another of the glorious things which were happening to me. I even had my own mount now.

H

The ball was a great success and I was surprised how ready the neighbourhood was to accept me. The fact that I had been Alvean's governess was forgotten. I felt that Connan's neighbours were reminding each other that I was an educated young woman and that my family background was passibly good. Perhaps those who were fond of him were relieved because he was engaged to be married, for they would not wish him to be involved in the Treslyn scandal.

The day after the ball Connan had to go away again on business.

" I neglected a great deal during our stay in Penlandstow," he said. " There were things I simply forgot to do. It is understandable. My mind was on other matters. I shall be away a week, I think, and when I come back it'll be but a fortnight before our wedding. You'll be getting on with your preparations, and darling, if there's anything you want to do in the house . . . if there's anything you want to change, do say so. It mightn't be a bad idea to ask Celestine's advice; she's an expert on old houses."

I said I would, because it would please her, and I wanted to please her.

" She was kind to me right from the first," I said. " I shall always have a soft feeling for her."

He said good-bye and drove off while I stood at my window, waving. I did not care to do so from the porch because I was still a little shy of the servants.

When I went out of my room I found Gilly standing outside the door. Since I had told her that I was to be Mrs. TreMellyn she had taken to following me around. I was beginning to understand the way her mind worked. She was fond of me in exactly the same way that she had been fond of Alice and, with the passing of each day, the two of us became in her mind merged into one. Alice had disappeared from her life; she was going to make sure that I did not.

" Hallo, Gilly," I said.

She dropped her head in that characteristic way of hers and laughed to herself.

Then she put her hand in mine and I led her back to my room.

" Well, Gilly," I said, " in three weeks' time I am going to be married, and I am the happiest woman in the world."

I was really trying to reassure myself, for sometimes talking to Gilly was like talking to oneself.

I thought of what Connan had said about altering anything I wished to in the house, and I remembered that there were some parts of it which I had not even seen yet.

I suddenly thought of Miss Jansen and what I had been told about her having a different room from the one I occupied. I had never seen Miss Jansen's room and I decided that I would now go along and inspect it. I need have no qualms now about going to any part of the house I wished, for in a very short time I should be mistress of it.

" Come along, Gilly," I said. " We'll go and see Miss Jansen's room."

She trotted along contentedly by my side, and I thought how much more intelligent she was than people realised, for it was she who led me to Miss Jansen's room.

There was nothing very unusual about it. It was smaller than mine. But there was a rather striking mural. I was looking at this when Gilly tugged my arm and drew me close to it. She pulled up a chair and stood on it. Then I understood. There, in this wall, was a peep like that in the solarium. I looked through it and saw the chapel. It was of course a different view from that to be seen in the solarium, as it was from the opposite side.

Gilly looked at me, delighted to have shown me the peep. We went back to my room, and clearly she did not want to leave me.

I could see that she was apprehensive. I understood of course. Her somewhat confused mind had so clearly associated me with Alice that she expected me to disappear as Alice had done.

She was determined to keep an eye on me so that this should not happen.

All through the night a south-west gale was blowing in from the sea. The rain which came with it was driven horizontally against our windows, and even the solid foundations of Mount

Mellyn seemed to shake. It was one of the wettest nights I had known since my arrival in Cornwall.

The next day the rain continued; everything in my room—mirrors, the furniture—was misty and damp. It was what happened often enough, Mrs. Polgrey told me, when the south-west wind came bringing rain with it, which it invariably did.

Alvean and I could not go out riding that day.

By the following morning the skies had cleared a little, and the heavy rain gave way to a light drizzle. Lady Treslyn called, but I did not see her. She did not ask for me; it was Mrs. Polgrey who told me she had called and that she had wished to see Connan.

" She seemed very distressed," said Mrs. Polgrey. " She'll not rest until this terrible business is over."

I felt sure that Lady Treslyn had come over to talk to Connan about his engagement to me and that she was probably distressed because he was not at home.

Celestine Nansellock also called. We had a chat about the house. She said she was so pleased because I was becoming very interested in Mount Mellyn.

" Not only as a home," she said, " but as a house." She went on : " I have some old documents about Mount Mellyn and Mount Widden. I'll show them to you one day."

" You must help me," I told her. " It'll be fun discussing things together."

" You'll make some changes?" she asked.

" If I do," I assured her, " I shall ask your advice."

She left before luncheon, and in the afternoon Alvean and I went down to the stables for the horses.

We stood by while Billy Trehay saddled them for us.

" Jacinth be frisky, to-day, Miss," he told me.

" It's because she had no exercise yesterday." I stroked her muzzle and she rubbed against my hand to show she shared my affection.

We took our usual ride down the slope, past the cove and Mount Widden; then we went along the cliff path. The view here was particularly beautiful with the jagged coast stretched

out before us and Rame Head lying in the water, hiding
Plymouth and its Sound from view.

Some of the paths were narrow, cut into the cliffs at spots
where it had been convenient to do so. Up and down we went;
sometimes we were almost down to the sea; at others we
climbed high.

It was not very easy going, for the rain had whipped up the
mud and I began to feel a little anxious about Alvean. She sat
firmly in her saddle—no novice now—but I was conscious of
Jacinth's mood and I expected Black Prince's was not much
different, although, of course, he hadn't Jacinth's fiery temperament. At times I had to rein her in firmly; a gallop would have
been more to her taste than this necessarily slow careful walk
along paths which were a good deal more dangerous than when
we had come this way on our last ride.

There was one spot on this cliff path which was particularly
narrow; above the path loomed the cliff face, dotted with
bushes of gorse and brambles; below it, the cliff fell almost
sheer to the sea. The path was safe enough ordinarily; but I
felt a little nervous about Alvean's using it on a day like this.

I noticed that some of the cliff had fallen in places. This was
continually happening. Tapperty had often said that the sea
was gradually claiming the land, and that in his grandfather's
day there had been a road which had now completely
disappeared.

I thought of turning back, but if we did I would have to
explain my fears to Alvean; I did not want to do this while
she was mounted.

No, I thought, we'll continue on this path until we can climb
to the top road. Then we'll go home a roundabout way, but on
firm land.

We had come to that danger spot and I noticed that the
ground was even more slippery here, and that there had been a
bigger fall of cliff than I had seen on other portions of the
path.

I held Jacinth in and walked her slowly in front of Alvean
and Black Prince, for we naturally had to go in single file.

I pulled up and looked over my shoulder, saying : " We're
going very slowly here. You just follow."

Then I heard it. I turned quickly as the boulder came tumbling down bringing in its wake shale, turf and vegetation. It passed within a few inches of Jacinth. I stared, in fascinated horror, as it went hurtling down to the sea.

Jacinth reared. She was terrified and ready to plunge anywhere . . . over the cliff . . . down to the sea . . . to escape what had startled her.

It was fortunate for me that I was an experienced rider, and that Jacinth and I knew each other so well. Thus it was all over in a matter of seconds. I had her under control. She grew calm as I began to talk to her in a voice which was meant to be soothing but which shook a little.

"Miss! What happened?" It was Alvean.

"It's all over," I answered, trying to speak lightly. "You managed perfectly."

"Why, Miss, I thought Black Prince was going to start a gallop."

He would, I thought, if Jacinth had.

I was terribly shaken and afraid to show it, either to Alvean or Jacinth.

I suddenly felt the need to get off that dangerous path immediately. I glanced nervously up and said: "It's not safe to be on these paths . . . after the weather we've been having."

I don't know what I expected to see up there, but I was staring at the thickest of the bushes. Did I see a movement there, or did I imagine it? It would be easy for someone to hide up there. What if a boulder had become dislodged by the recent rains. What an excellent opportunity if someone wanted to be rid of me. It merely had to be rolled down at that moment when I was on the path—a perfect target. Alvean and I had made a habit of coming along this path at a certain time.

I shivered and said: "Let's go on. We'll get on to the top road and won't go back along the cliff path."

Alvean was silent; and when in a few minutes we were on the road she looked at me oddly. I saw that she was not unaware of the danger through which we had passed.

It was not until we were back in the house that I realised how alarmed I was. I was telling myself that a terrifying pattern was being formed. Alice had died; Sir Thomas Treslyn had died; and now I, who was to be Connan's wife, might easily have met my death on the cliff path this day.

I longed to tell Connan of my fears.

But I was a sensible, practical woman. Was I going to refuse to look facts in the face because I was afraid of what I might see there if I did so?

Suppose Connan had not really gone away. Suppose he had wanted an accident to happen to me while he was believed to be away from home. I thought of Lady Treslyn at the Christmas ball. I thought of her beauty, her sensuous, voluptuous beauty. Connan had admitted that she had been his mistress. Had been? Was it possible that anyone, knowing her, could want me?

The proposal had been so sudden. It had come at a time when his mistress's husband was about to be exhumed.

It was small wonder that the practical governess had become a frightened woman.

To whom could I go for help?

There was Peter or Celestine . . . only those two, I thought. No, I could not betray these terrible suspicions of Connan to them. It was bad enough that I entertained them myself.

" Don't panic," I cautioned myself. " Be calm. Think of something you can do."

I thought of the house, vast and full of secrets, a house in which it was possible to peep from certain rooms into others. There might be peeps as yet undiscovered. Who could say? Perhaps someone was watching me now.

I thought of the peep in Miss Jansen's room and that set me thinking of her sudden dismissal. Then I was saying to myself : " Hoodfield Manor near Tavistock."

I wondered if Miss Jansen was still there. There was a good chance that she might be for she must have gone there about the same time as I came to Mount Mellyn.

Why should I not try to meet her? She might have some light to throw on the secrets of this house.

I was desperately afraid, and at such times it is always comforting to take action.

I felt better when I had written the letter.

*Dear Miss Jansen.*

I am the governess at Mount Mellyn and I have heard
of you. I should like to meet you. I wonder if that would
be possible. If so, I should like our meeting to be as soon
as you can manage it.

*Yours sincerely, Martha Leigh.*

I went out quickly to post the letter before I could change my
mind. Then I tried to forget it.

I longed for a message from Connan. There was none.
Each day I looked for his return. I thought : When he comes
home I am going to tell him of my fears, because I must do
so. I am going to tell him of what happened on the cliff path.
I am going to ask him to tell me the truth. I am going to say
to him : Connan, why did you ask me to marry you? Was it
because you love me and want me to be your wife, or was it
because you wished to divert suspicion from yourself and Lady
Treslyn?

The devilish scheme whicht I had invented seemed to gain
credibility with every passing moment.

I said to myself : Perhaps Alice died by accident, and that
gave them the idea of ridding themselves of Sir Thomas, who
was the only obstacle to their marriage. Did they slip
something into his whisky? Why not? It could not have been
merely by chance that the boulder came hurtling down at the
precise moment. Now there was to be an exhumation of Sir
Thomas and the countryside knew of the relationship between
Connan and Lady Treslyn. So Connan became engaged to the
governess in order to divert suspicion. The governess is now an
obstacle even as Alice was, even as Sir Thomas was. So the
governess could have an accident on her newly acquired mare
to which it might be said that she had not yet grown
accustomed.

The road is clear for the guilty lovers and all they need do is
wait until scandal has blown over.

How could I imagine such things of the man I loved?
Could one love a man and think such thoughts of him?

I do love him, I told myself passionately. So much that I would rather meet death at his hands than leave him and be forced to endure an empty life without him.

Three days later there was a letter from Miss Jansen, who said she was eager to meet me. She would be in Plymouth the following day and if I would meet her at the White Hart, which was not far from the Hoe, we might have luncheon together.

I told Mrs. Polgrey that I was going into Plymouth to shop. That seemed plausible enough since my wedding was due to take place in three weeks' time.

I made straight for the White Hart.

Miss Jansen was already there—an extremely pretty fair-haired girl. She greeted me with pleasure and told me that Mrs. Plint, the innkeeper's wife, had said that we might have luncheon together in a small room of our own.

We were conducted to this private room and there took stock of each other.

The innkeeper's wife talked with enthusiasm of duck and green peas and roast beef, but we were, neither of us, very interested in food.

We ordered roast beef, I think it was, and as soon as we were alone, Miss Jansen said to me : " What do you think of Mount Mellyn?"

" It's a wonderful old place."

" One of the most interesting houses I ever saw," she replied.

" I did hear, from Mrs. Polgrey I think, that old houses specially interested you."

" They do. I was brought up in one. However, the family fortunes declined. That's what happens to so many of us who become governesses. I was sorry to leave Mount Mellyn. You have heard why I went?"

" Y . . . yes," I said hesitantly.

" It was a very distressing affair. I was furiously angry to be unjustly accused."

She was so frank and sincere that I believed her, and I made that clear.

She looked pleased; and then the food was brought in.

As we sat eating it in a somewhat desultory way she told me of the affair.

" The Treslyns and the Nansellocks had been having tea at the house. You know the Treslyn's and the Nansellocks of course?"

" Oh yes."

" I mean, I expect you know quite a lot about them. They are such friends of the family, are they not?"

" Indeed yes."

" I had been treated rather specially." She flushed slightly, and I thought, Yes, you are so pretty. Connan would have thought so. I was aware of a flash not so much of jealousy as uneasiness as I wondered whether in the years to come I was going to be continually jealous of Connan's appreciation of the attractive members of my sex.

She went on : " They had called me in to tea, because Miss Nansellock wanted to ask some questions about Alvean. She did dote on that child. Does she still?"

" Indeed yes."

" She is such a kind person. I don't know what I should have done without her."

" I am so glad somebody was kind to you."

" I think that she looks upon Alvean as her child. There was a rumour that Miss Nansellock's brother was the father of Alvean, which would make her Miss Nansellock's niece. Perhaps that is why . . ."

" She certainly does feel strongly about Alvean."

" So I was called down to talk to her, and I was given tea and chatted with them—as though I were a guest as they were. I think that Treslyn woman resented it . . . she resented my presence there altogether. Perhaps they were a little too attentive to me—I mean Mr. Peter Nansellock and Mr. TreMellyn. Lady Treslyn has a hot temper, I am sure. In any case I believe she arranged the whole thing."

" She couldn't be so vile! "

" Oh, but I am sure she could, and she was. You see, she was wearing a diamond bracelet and the safety chain had broken. It had caught in the upholstery of the chair, I think.

She said, ' I won't wear it. I'll take it down to old Pastern to get it repaired as soon as we leave.' She took it off and put it on the table. I left them at tea and went to the schoolroom to do some work with Alvean. It was while we were there that the door was thrown open and they all stood there looking at me accusingly.

" Lady Treslyn said something about having a search made because her diamond bracelet was missing. She was truculent. One would have thought she was already the mistress of the house. Mr. TreMellyn said very kindly that Lady Treslyn was asking that my room be searched, and he hoped I would not object. I was very angry and I said : ' Come on, search my room. Nothing will satisfy me, but that you should.'

" So we all went into my room, and there in a drawer, hidden under some of my things was the diamond bracelet.

" Lady Treslyn said I was caught red-handed, and she was going to have me sent to prison. The others all pleaded with her not to make a scandal. Finally they agreed that if I went at once the matter would be forgotten. I was furious. I wanted an inquiry. But what could I do? They had found the thing there, and whatever I had to say after that they wouldn't believe me."

" It must have been terrible for you," I began to shiver.

She leaned across the table and smiled in a kindly way at me. " You are afraid that they may do something similar to you. Lady Treslyn is determined to marry Connan TreMellyn."

" Do you think so?"

" I do. I am sure there was something between them. He was, after all, a widower and not the sort of man, I think, to live without women. One knows his sort."

I said : " I suppose he made advances to you?"

She shrugged her shoulders. " At least Lady Treslyn imagined that I might be a menace, and I am sure she chose that way to get rid of me."

" What a foul creature she is! But Miss Nansellock was kind."

" Very kind. She was with them, of course, when they found the bracelet; and when I was packing she came to my room. She said : ' I'm very distressed, Miss Jansen, that this should have happened. I know they found the bracelet in your drawer, but you didn't put it there, did you?' I said : ' Miss Nansellock, I swear I didn't.' I can tell you, I was hysterical. It had all happened so suddenly. I didn't know what was to become of me. I had very little money and I would have to go to some hostel to look for work, and I knew I could not expect a testimonial. I shall never forget her kindness to me. She asked me where I was going and I gave her this address in Plymouth. She said : ' I know the Merrivales are going to want a governess for a month or so. I am going to see that you get that job.' She lent me some money, which I have now paid back, although she did not want me to do so; and that's how I lived until I went to the Merrivales. I have written, thanking Miss Nansellock, but how can one thank people adequately who do so much for one when one is in such dire need?"

" Thank goodness there was someone to help."

" Heaven knows what would have become of me if she had not been there. Ours is a precarious profession, Miss Leigh. We are at the mercy of our employers. No wonder so many of us become meek and down-trodden." She brightened. " I try to forget all that. I'm going to be married. He is a doctor who looks after the family. In six months' time my governessing days will be over."

" Congratulations! As a matter of fact I, too, am engaged to be married."

" How wonderful!"

" To Connan TreMellyn," I added.

She stared at me in astonishment. " Why . . ." she stammered, " I wish you the best of luck."

I could see that she was a little embarrassed and trying to remember what she had said about Connan. I felt too that she thought I should need that good luck.

I could not explain to her that I would rather have one stormy year with Connan than a lifetime of peace with anyone else.

" I wonder," she said after a pause, " why you wanted to see me."

" It is because I had heard of you. They talk of you often. Alvean was fond of you and there are things I want to know."

" But you, who are soon to be a member of the family, will know so much more than I can tell you."

" What do you think of Gilly—Gillyflower?"

" Oh, poor little Gilly. A strange, mad Ophelia-like creature. I always felt that one day we should find her floating on the stream with rosemary in her hands."

" The child had a shock."

" Yes, the first Mrs. TreMellyn's horse nearly trampled her to death."

" You must have gone there soon after the death of Mrs. TreMellyn."

" There were two others before me. I heard they left because the house was too spooky. A house couldn't be too spooky for me."

" Oh yes, you're an expert on old houses?"

" Expert! Indeed I'm not. I just love them. I've seen a great many and I've read a great deal about them."

" There was a peep in your room. Gilly showed it to me the other day."

" Do you know, I lived in that room three weeks without knowing it was there."

" I'm not surprised. The peeps are so cleverly concealed in the murals."

" That's an excellent way of doing it. Do you know those in the solarium?"

" Oh yes."

" One overlooking the hall, the other, the chapel. I think there's a reason for that. You see, the hall and the chapel would be the most important parts of the house at the time that was built."

" You know a great deal about period and so on. At what period was Mount Mellyn built?"

" Late Elizabethan. At the time when people had to keep the presence of priests in their houses secret. I think that's why they had all these peeps and things."

" How interesting."

" Miss Nansellock is an expert on houses. That was something we had in common. Does she know we're meeting?"

" No one knows."

"You mean, you came here without telling even your future husband?"

Confidences trembled on my lips. I wondered if I dared share them with this stranger. I wished it were Phillida sitting opposite me. Then I could have poured out my heart to her; I could have listened to her advice, which I was sure would be good.

But, although I had heard Miss Jansen's name mentioned so much since I had come to Mount Mellyn, she was still a stranger to me. How could I say to a stranger: I suspect the man I am engaged to marry of being involved in a plot to murder me.

No! It was impossible.

But, I reasoned, she had suffered accusation and dismissal. There was a kind of bond between us.

How far, I asked myself, are hot-blooded people prepared to go for the satisfaction of their lust?

I could not tell her.

"He is away on business," I said. "We are to be married in three weeks' time."

"I wish you the best of luck. It must have happened very suddenly."

"It was August when I went to the house."

"And you had never met before?"

"Living in the same house one quickly gets to know people."

"Yes, I suppose that is so."

"And you yourself must have become engaged in almost as short a time."

"Oh yes, but . . ."

I knew what she was thinking. Her pleasant country doctor was a very different person from the Master of Mount Mellyn.

I went on quickly: "I wanted to meet you because I believed you had been falsely accused. I am sure that many people at the house think that."

"I'm glad."

"When Mr. TreMellyn returns I shall tell him that I have seen you, and I shall ask if something can be done."

"It is of little consequence now. Dr. Luscombe knows what

happened. He is very indignant. But I have made him see that no good purpose could be served by bringing up the matter again. If Lady Treslyn ever tried to make more mischief, then something could be done. But she won't; her only desire was to get rid of me, and that she did . . . quite effectively."

"What a wicked woman she is! She did not consider the effect on you. But for the kindness of Miss Nansellock. . . ."

"I know. But don't let's talk of it. You will tell Miss Nansellock that you have seen me?"

"Yes, I will."

"Then tell her that I am engaged now to Dr. Luscombe. She will be so pleased. And there's something else I would like her to know. Perhaps you'll be interested too. It's about the house. The house will soon be your home, won't it? I envy you the house. It's one of the most interesting places I've ever seen."

"What were you going to tell me to pass on to Miss Nansellock?"

"I've been doing a little research on architecture, and so on, of the Elizabethan period, and my fiancé arranged for me to see Cotehele, the Mount Edgcumbes' place. They were delighted to let me see it because they are understandably proud of it. It's more like Mount Mellyn than any house I've ever seen. The chapel is almost identical, even to the lepers' squint. But the squint at Mount Mellyn is much bigger, and the construction of the walls is slightly different. As a matter of fact I've never seen a squint quite like that at Mount Mellyn before. Do tell Miss Nansellock. She would be most interested, I'm sure."

"I'll tell her. I expect she'll be more interested to hear that you are so happy and that you are going to marry."

"Don't forget to tell her too that I remember I owe it all to her. Give her my kindest regards and my best thanks."

"I will," I said.

We parted, and on my journey home I felt I had obtained from Miss Jansen some fresh light on my problem.

There was no doubt that Lady Treslyn arranged for Miss Jansen's dismissal. Miss Jansen was very pretty indeed. Connan admired her and Alvean was fond of her. Connan would consider marriage because he would want sons; and Lady

Treslyn, possessive as a tigress, was not going to allow him to marry anyone but herself.

I believed now that Lady Treslyn was planning to remove me as she had removed Miss Jansen; but because I was already engaged to Connan she would have to use more drastic methods in my case.

But Connan did not know of this attempt on my life.

I refused to believe that of him and, refusing, I felt a great deal happier.

Moreover, I had made up my mind. When Connan came back I was going to tell him everything—all I had discovered, all I had feared.

The decision brought me great comfort.

Two days passed, and still Connan had not returned.

Peter Nansellock came over to say good-bye. He was leaving late that night for London on his way to join the ship which would carry him to Australia.

Celestine was with him when he came to say good-bye. They thought Connan would have returned by now. As a matter of fact while they were there a letter arrived from Connan. He was coming back if possible late that night; if not, as early as possible next day.

I felt tremendously happy.

I gave them tea and, as we talked, I mentioned Miss Jansen.

I saw no reason why I should not do so in front of Peter, because it was he who had told me that Celestine had found her a job with the Merrivales.

" I met Miss Jansen the other day," I began.

They were both startled.

" But how?" asked Peter.

" I wrote and asked her to meet me."

" What made you do that?" asked Celestine.

" Well, she had lived here, and there was a mystery about her, and I thought it would be rather interesting, so, as I was going to Plymouth. . . ."

" A charming creature," mused Peter.

" Yes. You'll be pleased to hear that she's engaged to be married."

" How interesting," cried Celestine, her face growing pink. " I'm delighted."

" To the local doctor," I added.

" She'll make an excellent doctor's wife," said Celestine.

" Her husband's male patients will all be in love with her," put in Peter.

" That could be disconcerting," I replied.

" But good for business," murmured Peter. " Did she send us greetings?"

" Particularly to your sister," I smiled at Celestine. " She is so grateful to you; you were wonderful to her. She says she'll never forget."

" It was nothing. I could not let that woman do what she did and stand by doing nothing."

" You think Lady Treslyn deliberately planted that theft on her? I know Miss Jansen does."

" There is no doubt of it," said Celestine firmly.

" What an unscrupulous woman she must be!"

" I believe that to be so."

" Well, Miss Jansen is happy now, so good came out of evil. By the way, I have a special message for you. It's about the house."

" What house?" asked Celestine with great interest.

" This one. Miss Jansen has been to Cotehele and has been comparing their squint, in the chapel, with ours. She says ours is quite unique."

" Oh really! That's very interesting."

" It's bigger, she says—I mean ours is. And there's something about the construction of the walls."

" Celestine is aching to go down and have a look at it," said Peter.

She smiled at me. " We'll look at it together sometime. You're going to be the Mistress of the house, so you ought to take an interest in it."

" I'm becoming more and more interested. I'm going to ask you to teach me lots about it."

She smiled at me warmly. " I'll be glad."

I asked Peter what train he was catching, and he answered that it would be the ten o'clock from St. Germans.

" I'll ride to the station," he said, " and stable the horse there. The baggage has gone on ahead of me. I shall go alone. I don't want any fond farewells at the station. After all, I shall no doubt be home this time next year . . . with a fortune. *Au revoir,* Miss Leigh," he went on. " I'll come back one day. And if you do feel like coming with me . . . it's not too late even now."

He spoke flippantly, and his eyes were full of mischief. I wondered what he would say if I suddenly agreed to his proposal, if I suddenly told him that I was filled with terrible doubts about the man I had promised to marry.

I went down to the porch to say my last farewells. The servants were there for he was a great favourite. I guessed that he had bestowed many a sly kiss on Daisy and Kitty, and they were sad to see him go.

He looked very handsome in the saddle and beside him Celestine seemed insignificant.

We stood waving to them.

His last words were : " Don't forget, Miss Leigh . . . if you should change your mind!"

Everybody laughed and I joined in with them. I think we all felt a little sad that he was going.


As we were going back into the house, Mrs. Polgrey said to me : " Miss Leigh, could I have a word with you?"

" But certainly. Shall I come to your room?"

She led the way there.

" I've just had word," she said. " The result of the autopsy. Death through natural causes."

I felt floods of relief sweeping over me.

" Oh, I'm so pleased about that."

" So are we all. I can tell you, I didn't like the things that were being said . . . and him dying after he'd had supper here."

" It seems as though it was all a storm in a teacup," I said.

" Something like that, Miss Leigh. But there you are— people talk and something has to be done."

" Well, it must be a great relief to Lady Treslyn."

She looked a little embarrassed and I guessed she was wondering what she had said to me in the past about Connan and Lady Treslyn. It must have been disconcerting to discover that I was going to be Connan's wife. I decided to sweep aside her embarrassment for ever, and said : " I hoped you were going to offer me a cup of your special Earl Grey."

She was pleased and rang for Kitty.

We talked of household affairs while the kettle boiled, and when tea was made she tentatively brought out the whisky and when I nodded a tea-spoonful was put into each cup. I felt then that we had indeed resumed the old friendly relationship.

I was glad, because I could see this made her happy, and I wanted everyone about me to be as happy as I was.

I kept on telling myself : If Lady Treslyn really did attempt to kill me by sending that boulder crashing down in front of me when I was mounted on Jacinth, Connan knew nothing about it. Sir Thomas died a natural death, so there was nothing to hide; he had no reason to ask me to marry him except the one which he gave me; he loves me.

It was nine o'clock and the children were in bed. It had been a warm and sunny day and there were signs of spring everywhere.

Connan was coming home either to-night or to-morrow and I was happy.

I wondered what time he would arrive. Perhaps at midnight. I went to the porch to look for him because I had imagined I heard horses' hoofs in the distance.

I waited. The night was still. The house always seemed very quiet at times like this for all the servants would be in their own quarters.

I guessed that Peter would be on his way to the station by now. It was strange to think that I might never see him again. I thought of our first meeting in the train; he had begun by playing his mischievous tricks on me even then.

Then I saw someone coming towards me. It was Celestine, and she had come by way of the woods, not along the drive as usual.

She was rather breathless.

"Why, hallo," she said. "I came to see you. I felt so lonely. Peter's gone. It's rather sad to think that I shan't see him for a long time."

"It does make one sad."

"He played the fool a great deal, of course, but I am very fond of him. Now I've lost both my brothers."

"Come in," I said.

"Connan's not back, I suppose?"

"No. I don't think he can possibly be here before midnight. He wrote that he had business to attend to this morning. I expect he'll arrive to-morrow. Won't you come in?"

"Do you know, I rather hoped you'd be alone."

"Did you?"

"I wanted to have a look at the chapel . . . that squint, you know. Ever since you gave me Miss Jansen's message I've been eager to see it. I didn't say so in front of Peter. He's apt to laugh at my enthusiasm."

"Do you want to have a look at it now?"

"Yes, please. I've a theory about it. There may be a door in the panelling which leads to another part of the house. Wouldn't it be fun if we could discover it and tell Connan about it when he arrives?"

"Yes," I agreed, "it would."

"Let's go now then."

We went through the hall and, as we did so, I glanced up at the peep, because I had an uncanny feeling that we were being watched. I thought I saw a movement up there, but I was not sure, and said nothing.

We went along to the end of the hall, through the door, down the stone steps, and were in the chapel.

The place smelt damp. I said: "It smells as though it hasn't been used for years." And my voice echoed weirdly through the place.

Celestine did not answer. She had lighted one of the candles which stood on the altar. I watched the long shadow which the flickering light threw against the wall.

"Let's get into the squint," she said. "Through this door. There is another door in the squint itself which opens on to the walled garden. That was the way the lepers used to come in."

She carried the candle high and I found that we were in a small chamber.

" This is the place," I said, " which is bigger than most of its kind."

She did not answer. She was pressing different parts of the wall.

I watched her long fingers at work.

Suddenly she turned and smiled at me. " I've always had a theory that somewhere in this house there is a priest's hole . . . you know, the hidy hole of the resident priest into which he scuttled when the queen's men arrived. As a matter of fact I know that one TreMellyn did toy with the idea of becoming a Catholic. I'll swear there is a priest's hole somewhere. Connan would be delighted if we found it. He loves this place as much as I do . . . as much as you're going to. If I found it . . . it would be the best wedding present I could give him, wouldn't it? After all, what can you give people who have all they want?"

She hesitated, and her voice was high with excitement. " Just a minute. There's something here." I came close to her, and caught my breath with amazement, for the panel had moved inward and shown itself as a long narrow door.

She turned to look at me and she looked unlike herself. Her eyes were brilliant with excitement. She put her head inside the aperture and was about to go forward when she said : " No, you first. It's going to be your house. You should be the first to enter it."

I had caught her excitement. I knew how pleased Connan would be.

I stepped ahead of her and was aware of an unrecognisable pungent odour.

She said : " Have a quick look. It's probably a bit foul in there. Careful. There are probably steps." She held the candle high, and I saw there were two of them. I went down those steps and, as I did so, the door shut behind me.

" Celestine!" I cried in terror. But there was no answer.
" Open that door," I screamed. But my voice was caught and

imprisoned in the darkness, and I knew that I was a prisoner too—Celestine's prisoner.

The darkness shut me in. It was cold and eerie—foul, evil. Panic seized me. How can I explain such terror? There are no words to describe it. Only those who have suffered it could understand.

Thoughts—hideous thoughts—seemed to be battering on my brain. I had been a fool. I had been trapped. I had accepted what seemed obvious, I had walked the way she who wished to be rid of me had directed; and like a fool I had asked no questions.

My fear numbed my brain as it did my body.

I was terrified.

I mounted the two steps. I beat my fists against what now seemed to be a wall. "Let me out. Let me out . . ." I cried.

But I knew that my voice would not be heard beyond the lepers' squint. And how often did people go to the chapel?

She would slip away . . . no one would know she had even been in the house.

I was so frightened I did not know what to do. I heard my own voice sobbing out my terror, and it frightened me afresh because, for the moment, I did not recognise it as my own.

I felt exhausted and limp. I knew that one could not live for long in this dark, damp place. I pulled at the wall until I tore my nails and I felt the blood on my hands.

I began to look about me because my eyes were becoming familiar to the gloom. Then I saw that I was not alone.

Someone had come here before me. What was left of Alice lay there. At last I had found her.

"Alice," I screamed. "Alice. It is you then? So you were here in the house all the time?"

There was no answer from Alice. Her lips had been silent for more than a year.

I covered my face with my hands. I could not bear to look. There was the smell of death and decay everywhere.

I wondered: How long did Alice live after the door had closed on *her*? I wanted to know because so long I might expect to live.

I think I must have fainted for a long time and I was delirious when I came to. I heard a voice babbling; it must have been my own because it could not have belonged to Alice.

I was mercifully only half-conscious. But it was as though a part of me understood so much.

During that time I spent in the dark and gruesome place I was not sure who I was. Was I Martha? Was I Alice?

Our stories were so much alike. I believed the pattern was similar. They had said she ran away with Geoffry. They would say I had run away with Peter. Our departure had been cleverly timed. "But why . . ." I said, "but why. . . ."

I knew whose shadow I had seen on the blind. It was hers . . . that diabolical woman. She had known of the existence of that little diary which I had discovered in Alice's coat pocket and she was searching for it because she knew it could provide one of those small clues which might lead to discovery.

I knew that she did not love Alvean, that she had tricked us all with her gentle demeanour. I knew that she was incapable of loving anyone. She had used Alvean as she had used others, as she was going to use Connan.

It was the house that she loved.

I pictured her during those delirious moments looking from her window at Mount Widden across the cove—coveting a house as fiercely as man ever coveted woman or woman man.

"Alice," I said. "Alice we were her victims . . . you and I."

And I fancied Alice talked to me . . . and told me of the day Geoffry had caught the London train and how Celestine had come to the house and told her of the great discovery in the chapel.

I saw Alice . . . pale, pretty, fragile Alice crying out in pleasure at the discovery, taking those fatal steps forward to death.

But it was not Alice's voice I heard. It was my own.

Yet I thought she was with me. I thought that at last I had found her, and that we had comfort to offer each other as I waited to go with her into the shadowy world which had been hers since she was led by Celestine Nansellock into the lepers' squint.

There was a blinding light in my eyes. I was being carried.

I said: "Am I dead then, Alice?"

And a voice answered: "My darling . . . my darling . . . you are safe."

It was Connan's voice, and it was his arms which held me.

"Are there dreams in death then, Alice?" I asked.

I was conscious of a voice which whispered: "My dearest . . . oh, my dearest. . . ." And I was laid upon a bed, and many people stood about me.

Then I saw the light glinting on hair which looked almost white.

"Alice, there is an angel."

Then the angel answered and said: "It's Gilly. Gilly brought them to you. Gilly watched and Gilly saw. . . ."

And oddly enough it was Gilly who brought me back to the world of reality. I knew that I was not dead, that some miracle had happened; that it was in truth Connan's arms which I had felt about me, Connan's voice I heard.

I was in my own bedroom from the window of which I could see the lawns and the palm trees and the room which had once been Alice's, on the blind of which I had seen the shadow of Alice's murderer who had sought to kill me too.

I called out in terror. But Connan was beside me.

I heard his voice, tender, soothing, loving. "It's all right, my love . . . my only love. I'm here . . . I'm with you for evermore."

## Afterwards

This is the story I tell my great-grandchildren. They have heard it many times, but there is always a first time for some.

They ask for it again and again. They play in the park and in the woods; they bring me flowers from the south gardens, a

tribute to the old lady who can always charm them with the
story of how she married their great-grandfather.

To me it is as clear as though it happened yesterday. Vividly
I remember my arrival at the house and all that preceded those
terrifying hours I spent in the dark with dead Alice.

The years which followed with Connan have often been
stormy ones. Connan and I were both too strong-willed, I
suppose, to live in perpetual peace; but they were years in
which I felt I had lived life richly, and what more could one
ask than that?

Now he is old, as I am, and three more Connans have been
born since that day we married—our son, grandson and great-
grandson. I was glad I was able to give Connan children.
We had five sons and five daughters, and they in their turn
were fruitful.

When the children hear the story they like to check up all the
details. They want every incident explained.

Why was it believed that the woman who died in the train
was Alice? Because of the locket she wore. But it was
Celestine who identified the locket as one which, she said, she
had given Alice, but which, of course, she had never seen
before in her life.

She had been eager that I should accept Jacinth when Peter
had first offered the mare to me—I suppose because she feared
it was just possible that Connan might be interested in me and
therefore she was ready to encourage the friendship between
myself and Peter; and it was she who later, discovering the
loosened boulder on the cliff, had lain in wait for me and
attempted to kill or maim me.

She was the sender of the anonymous letters to Lady Treslyn
and the public prosecutor, commenting on the suspicious
circumstances of Sir Thomas's death. She had believed that if
there was a big enough scandal, marriage between Connan and
Lady Treslyn would have been impossible for years. She had
reckoned without Connan's feelings for me; thus when she
knew that I was engaged to marry him, she immediately
planned to remove me. She failed to do this on the cliff path;
therefore I was to join Alice; the fact that Peter was leaving
for Australia on that day must have made her decide on this

method. The whole household knew that Peter's attitude to me had been a flirtatious one, and it would appear that I had run away with him.

It was Celestine who had put the diamond bracelet in Miss Jansen's room because the governess was learning too much about the house and the knowledge would inevitably lead her to the lepers' squint and Alice. She had worked on Lady Treslyn's jealousy of the pretty young governess for she had known Lady Treslyn to be a vindictive woman who, given the opportunity, would bring all her malice to bear on Miss Jansen.

She was in love—passionately in love with Mount Mellyn and she wanted to marry Connan only because thus she would be Mistress of the house. So in the first place, discovering the secret of the squint she had kept it to herself, and had chosen her opportunity to murder Alice. She knew of the love affair between Alice and her brother Geoffry; she knew that Alvean was his child. It worked out so easily because she had waited for her opportunity. If it had not been possible to make Alice's death appear to have occurred in the train accident she would have found some other way of disposing of her as she had intended to dispose of me through Jacinth.

But she had reckoned without Gilly. Who would have thought that a poor simple child should play such a big part in this diabolical plan? But Gilly had loved Alice as later she was to love me. Gilly had known Alice was in the house for Alice had made a habit of coming to say good night to her when she did the same to Alvean; she had always done it before she went out to a dinner party. Because she had never forgotten, Gilly did not believe she had forgotten this time. Gilly therefore continued to believe that Alice had never left the house, and had gone on looking for her. It was Gilly's face which I had seen at the peep. Gilly knew all the peeps in the house and used them frequently, because she was always watching for Alice.

Thus she had seen Celestine and myself enter the hall from the solarium. I imagined her crossing the room and looking through the peep on the other side of the room so that she saw us enter the chapel. We crossed to the squint, but that side of the chapel could not easily be seen from the solarium peep, and so Gilly sped along to Miss Jansen's room, where from that peep she could have a good view of the squint. She was just in time to see us disappearing through the door, and waited for us to come out. She waited and waited, for Celestine naturally left by the door to the courtyard and slipped away so that, since she believed that no one had seen her come into the house except myself, she could let it appear that she had not been there at all.

Thus, while I lived through that period of horror in Alice's death-chamber, Gilly was standing on her stool in Miss Jansen's room, watching the door to the lepers' squint.

Connan returned at eleven and expected the household to give him a welcome.

Mrs. Polgrey received him. "Go and tell Miss Leigh that I am here," he said. He must have been a little piqued because he was—and still is—the sort of man who demands the utmost affection and attention, and the fact that I could be sleeping when he came home was inconceivable to him.

I pictured the scene : Mrs. Polgrey reporting that I was not in my room, the search for me, that terrible moment when Connan believed what Celestine had intended he should believe.

"Mr. Nansellock came over this afternoon to say good-bye. He caught the ten o'clock from St. Germans. . . ."

I have wondered often how long it would have been before they discovered that I had not run away with Peter. I could imagine what might have happened. Connan's losing that belief in life which I believed I was beginning to bring back to him, perhaps continuing his *affaire* with Linda Treslyn. But it would not have led to marriage, Celestine would have seen to that. And in time she would have found some way of making herself mistress of Mount Mellyn; insidiously she would have made herself necessary to Alvean and to him.

How strange, I thought, that all this might have come to pass and the only two who could have told the truth would have been two skeletons behind the walls of the lepers' squint. Who would have believed that even at this day the story of

Alice and Martha would never have been known, had not a simple child, born in sorrow, living in shadow, led the way to the truth.

Connan told me often of the uproar in the house when I was missing. He told me of the child, who came and stood patiently beside him, waiting to be heard; how she tugged at his coat and sought for the words to explain.

"God forgive us," he says, "it was some time before we would listen to her, and so we delayed bringing you out of that hellish place."

But she had led them there . . . through the door into the lepers' squint.

She had seen us, she said.

And for a moment Connan had thought that Peter and I had left the house together, slipping out that way so that we should not be noticed.

It was dusty in the squint—for no one had entered it since Alice had gone there with her murderer; but in the dust on the wall was the mark of a hand, and when Connan saw it he began to take Gilly seriously.

It was not easy to find the secret spring in the door even if it had been known that it was there. There was an agonising search of ten minutes while Connan was ready to tear the walls down.

But they found it and they found me. The found Alice too.

They took Celestine to Bodmin where she was eventually to be tried for the murder of Alice. But before the trial could take place she was a raving lunatic. At first I believed that this was yet another scheme of hers. It may have started that way, but she did not die until twenty years after, and all that time she spent locked away from the world.

Alice's remains were buried in the vault where those of an unknown woman lay. Connan and I were married three months after he had brought me out of the darkness. That experience had affected me even more than I realised at the time, and I suffered from nightmares for a year or more. It was a great shock to have been buried alive even though one's tomb was opened before life was extinguished.

Phillida came to my wedding with William and the children. She was delighted. So was Aunt Adelaide, who insisted that the wedding take place from her town house. Thus Connan and I had a smart London wedding. Not that we cared, but it pleased Aunt Adelaide who, for some reason, seemed to have the idea in her head that it was all her doing.

And so we honeymooned, as we had originally intended, in Italy and then we came home to Mount Mellyn.

I dream over the past when I have told the story to the children. I think of Alvean happily married to a Devonshire squire. As for Gilly, she never left me. She is with me now. At any moment she will appear on the lawn with the eleven o'clock coffee which on warm days we take in that arbour in the south gardens where I first saw Lady Treslyn and Connan together.

I must confess that Lady Treslyn continued to plague me during the first years of my married life. I discovered that I could be a jealous woman—and a passionate one. Sometimes I think Connan liked to tease me, in repayment, he said, for the jealousy he had felt of Peter Nansellock.

But she went to London after a few years, and we heard she married there.

Peter came back some fifteen years after he left. He had acquired a wife and two children but no fortune; he was, however, as gay and full of vitality as ever. In the meantime Mount Widden had been sold; and later one of my daughters married the owner, so the place has become almost as much home to me as Mount Mellyn.

Connan said he was glad when Peter came back, and I laughed at the thought of his ever feeling he needed to be jealous. When I told him this, he replied: "You're even more foolish about Linda Treslyn."

That was one of those moments when we both knew that there was no one for us but each other.

And so the years passed and now, as I sit here thinking of it all, Connan is coming down the path from the gardens. In a moment I shall hear his voice.

Because we are alone he will say: "Ah, my dear Miss Leigh . . ." as he often does in his most tender moments.

That is to remind me that he does not forget those early days; and there will be a smile on his lips which tells me that he is seeing me, not as I am now, but as I was then, the governess somewhat resentful of her fate, desperately clinging to her pride and her dignity—falling in love in spite of herself—his dear Miss Leigh.

Then we shall sit in the warm sunshine, thankful for all the good things which life has brought us.

Here he comes and Gilly is behind him . . . still a little different from other people, still speaking rarely, singing as she works, in the off-key voice that makes us think she is a little out of this world.

As I watch her I can see so clearly the child she once was, and I think of the story of Jennifer, the mother who one day walked into the sea, and how that story was part of my story, and how delicately and intricately our lives were woven together.

Nothing remains, I thought, but the earth and the sea which are here just as they were on the day Gilly was conceived, on the day Alice walked unheeding into her tomb, on the day I felt Connan's arms about me and I knew he had brought me back to life.

We are born, we suffer, we love, we die, but the waves continue to beat upon the rocks; the seed time and the harvest come and go, but the earth remains.

# Victoria Holt

The supreme writer of the 'gothic romance', a compulsive storyteller whose gripping novels of the darker face of love have thrilled millions all over the world.

**The Shadow of the Lynx** 40p

**King of the Castle** 40p

**Menfreya** 40p

**Mistress of Mellyn** 40p

**The Secret Woman** 40p

**Bride of Pendorric** 35p

**Kirkland Revels** 40p

**The Legend of the Seventh Virgin** 35p

**The Queen's Confession** 50p

**The Shivering Sands** 35p

*All available in Fontana Books*

Victoria Holt also writes as

# Jean Plaidy

'One of England's foremost historical novelists.'

*Birmingham Mail*

**The Thistle and the Rose** 40p

**Murder Most Royal** 35p

**The Sixth Wife** 30p

**The Spanish Bridegroom** 35p

**Madame Serpent** 35p

**The Italian Woman** 35p

**Queen Jezebel** 35p

**The Murder in the Tower** 35p

**A Health Unto His Majesty** 35p

**Here Lies Our Sovereign Lord** 35p

**The Wandering Prince** 35p

**The Three Crowns** 35p

**The Queen's Favourites** 40p

**Royal Road to Fotheringay** 35p

**The Captive Queen of Scots** 35p

**Madonna of the Seven Hills** 35p

**Light on Lucrezia** 35p

**The Road to Compiègne** 35p

**Louis the Well-Beloved** 30p

**Flaunting, Extravagant Queen** 35p

**Beyond the Blue Mountains** 40p

**The Goldsmith's Wife** 35p

**Evergreen Gallant** 30p

**The Daughter of Satan** 35p

**The Haunted Sisters** 40p

*All available in Pan Books*

# Fontana Books

Fontana is best known as one of the leading paperback publishers of popular fiction and non-fiction. It also includes an outstanding, and expanding, section of books on history, natural history, religion and social sciences.

Most of the fiction authors need no introduction. They include Agatha Christie, Hammond Innes, Alistair MacLean, Catherine Gaskin, Victoria Holt and Lucy Walker. Desmond Bagley and Maureen Peters are among the relative newcomers.

The non-fiction list features a superb collection of animal books by such favourites as Gerald Durrell and Joy Adamson.

All Fontana books are available at your bookshop or newsagent; or can be ordered direct. Just fill in the form below and list the titles you want.

- - - - - - - - - - - - - - - - - - - - - - - - -

FONTANA BOOKS, Cash Sales Department, P.O. Box 4, Godalming, Surrey, GU7 1JY. Please send purchase price plus 7p postage per book by cheque, postal or money order. No currency.

NAME (Block letters)

_____

ADDRESS

_____

_____

_____